The Empath

BOOK II OF THE FIRE TRILOGY

LISA VELDKAMP

DMP

The Empath

BOOK II OF THE FIRE TRILOGY

LISA VELDKAMP

"**You can choose** to handle each situation to the best of your ability, or you can let it consume you. I hope I will always choose the first. And Druidry has strengthened me in that resolve."

-Lisa Veldkamp

First of all, a big thank you to my team Pam Elise Harris, Rhianna Davies, and Lisa Gilliam. Without you wonderful ladies, *The Empath* would never be as good as it is now. I'm so glad you all hopped on the Dragon Moon Press joy train and supported me all the way. You girls are the best!

Thanks also to Gwen Gades, founder of Dragon Moon Press, for taking a chance on me after my former publisher went out of business. Can't thank you enough for believing in me!

As always, my eternal gratitude to Placebo. Your music and lyrics are the foundation of The Fire Trilogy. Tristan's struggle with love and relationships in general is based on the *Loud Like Love* era. Thank you for providing the inspiration. Keep making magic together, boys!

Last, but not least, to my partner, family, and friends. You keep me grounded when I'm floating in space. You make me fly when I'm down. A special thanks to Nico Vermaas and Olav Sanders for providing me with detailed information on all things NASA and what it takes to fly an actual Syberjet. You saved me from looking like a complete idiot. Thanks, guys!

And my home away from home, Barista Café. Thanks for the coffee, the quiet spots, saving me my favourite table, confiscating my phone when the deadline was approaching way too fast (I do understand, but really!) and letting me sample the new cakes. Couldn't have done it without your support. Save me a seat for the final installment!

PROLOGUE

It was deadly quiet in the corridors of the mental hospital. A woman walked purposefully towards her destination, room 612. Sixth floor, sixth door on her left. Two men were walking behind her, keeping a respectful distance. She knew the schematics of the building by heart. The company had been planning this to the detail, and she was ready.

"There will be trouble," her boss had said to her. "You will have to block him out immediately once he's revived." For that was her main gift. She was the company's top reviver. They rarely used her main gift, though. So when she got this assignment, she got very excited. She couldn't care less that she was going to revive a dangerous man. That was not her problem. The company would deal with him accordingly. She smiled to herself. They had not hired her for her warm and caring personality.

Hence the distance between me and my "bodyguards," she thought with a slight smirk. They feared her. And rightfully so.

She stopped in front of 612. Showtime. She turned to look at the two men behind her. They gave her an almost imperceptible nod. She was good to go. Slowly she opened the door, stepped into the room and closed the door softly behind her. Near the window a man with long white hair was lying on a typical hospital bed. He wasn't strapped down or anything, probably because he wasn't in any condition to go anywhere. His eyes were open, she noticed, but they were empty. Fascinating. Whoever did this to him must have had great power indeed. She walked over to his side and stared into his face. Nothing. No blink, no dilation of his pupils, not a single response to her presence. Hmm, this could turn out to be more difficult than she had anticipated. She felt the excitement inside her growing. She loved a good challenge. Looking at his face one more time, she leaned over and whispered in his ear, "This is going to hurt you more than me."

* * *

Tristan Visconti was not in a good mood. He had just been assigned to what he considered to be a suicide mission. He ignored the looks from the waiter in the café and drained his last sip of coffee. He had even quarrelled with his boss about it, which was a first. But apparently there was no room for argument here.

"Listen, Tristan, this comes from upstairs, way above even my clearance, and they want you, so they must really think we still have a shot," his boss had said to him. "In other words, don't even think about screwing this one up. Too much is at stake here, and we have less than a month to get you in position. Okay? So stop sulking and get your act together."

It was the first time Tristan had received a reprimand from Trevor Johnsson, his boss. And that didn't sit very well with him. So he had apologized and asked if he could at least pick his own team members.

"Sure, no problem. As long as you include Charles Murray and Roy Morgan. You're going to need a blocker and a planner to pull this off," his boss had replied. Tristan had assured him he was going to include them anyway, and they had said their goodbyes to one another.

He ordered another coffee when the waiter passed his table and sighed. Tristan might as well get started and learn all there was to know about his new client. Opening his case file, the first page showed a large photo of a woman in her mid-thirties with long, blond hair. The caption read: Client: Catherine van Dyk—Elemental.

A MONTH LATER

Tristan looked out of his window. In his late forties, his hair still dark brown with one or two stray grey hairs and dark blue eyes, which currently held a brooding look, Tristan was the embodiment of vitality. He was back in London, Shoreditch to be exact. He didn't mind. He actually liked London. It was the reason *why* he was here he didn't like. And the company had had a lot more trouble moving him into this building than they had anticipated. He took that as a bad sign. They actually had to modify the memories of the people who used to live in his apartment to make it look plausible that they suddenly wanted to sell the place. It was almost as if the entire building was protected or cloaked or something. As an empath, Tristan was very perceptible to these things, and this building oozed protective power all over the place.

Probably the elemental at work, he thought with a smirk. He sighed. That wouldn't do. He should learn to think of her as Catherine, not the elemental. It would make his task easier.

Furthermore, the company had lost one of their "key ingredients" a little over a week ago. Tristan only knew him as the white man, but he knew he was the elemental's—no Catherine's—ex. Not a pleasant fellow, and it did make Tristan wonder what she had seen in him in the first place. Tristan couldn't remember anyone escaping from the company. Ever.

"Must give him credit for that," Tristan said with a smile while he turned away from the window. He ran a hand through his hair. It was getting too long for his taste, but Catherine liked men with longer hair. Or so their research said. So he'd decided to forego his visit to the hair salon. It couldn't hurt his chances to win her over. And win her over he must…and fast. They had little over a week now. Normally, that wouldn't bother Tristan. With his powers, he could win over practically anybody within a couple of seconds. But this lady had powers of her own, and they most likely outshone his. Besides, she wasn't the only one. Catherine had lots of friends with powers. One of them, Leah Winter, or Lee, as Catherine called her, could be arriving any moment from New York. Her file had her down as a seer. If he wasn't careful, she would see him coming a mile away.

That's where Charles Murray came in. Charles was what Tristan liked to refer to as old school. They'd worked together from the beginning when Charles had saved him from what could have been quite an embarrassing beginning at the company. With Charles's blocking powers, he had warned Tristan that not all people working at the company were known for their nice characters and he should learn to shield his empathic abilities whenever he was near some of his more colourful colleagues. Eve, of course, had turned his abilities into mashed potatoes, and Charles had warned him about her. Not that he had listened. Not back then. He had been young and foolish. It was common knowledge that relationships within the company were not allowed, but, for some reason, they had never put a stop to it. Maybe even the company feared the wrath of their top reviver. And not without reason, Tristan mused. Charles had looked out for him ever since, and Tristan trusted him with his life. Even his soul, if one believed in such a thing. Just in his early sixties, Charles was still an excellent blocker and in perfect health. He could probably outrun most forty year olds.

Tristan looked out the window again to see if he could see Roy Morgan, his co-worker and best friend both inside and outside the company. He saw a tall, blond man, leaning casually against the brick wall, talking into a phone. Tristan grinned. "Hey, Roy, do you think you could pick me up that cute redhead across the street?" he said.

The man on the street looked up and smiled. Then, he looked across the street. "Not your type, old dog. Best stick to elementals," Tristan heard in his ear.

He rolled his eyes, not that Roy could see that. "Any sign of Miss Winter?" he asked.

The man below shook his head. "No, not yet. She should be here soon, though. As soon as she's gone up, you can come down again. I have another couple of boxes at the ready and a nice orchid for you to take upstairs." Roy looked up and grinned.

"An orchid? Why the hell should I take an orchid upstairs?"

"It presents a nice, homey feel. She's an elemental, right? It's likely she has a great fondness for nature. Orchids imply a great deal of care."

Tristan glared at the man below. "You've lost your marbles, you know. I think we should have you checked over back at the company. Obviously, you're going soft in your old age."

"Well, I am two months your senior, so I'm pretty sure that means you should take my advice," Roy said into his phone when a man walked by. To any innocent bystander, he appeared to be having a normal conversation. Tristan sighed in defeat, and he could see Roy smile. Suddenly, Roy's body language changed and Tristan saw his friend was on full alert.

"Here we go," he heard Roy say in his ear. "Wait for my signal to come down. We don't want you bumping into Miss Winter on her way up."

Tristan moved away from the window and walked towards the hallway. He carefully opened his front door. "Nobody on my floor," he whispered to Roy.

"Okay, she's in the lift. Take the stairs. Now!" Tristan moved fast and heard the lift pass his floor as he moved to take the staircases. He took them at double speed and was downstairs in no time. He walked outside to the side of the building where a moving van was waiting for him. Roy was already in the back, getting two small boxes ready for him. He moved to the front of the van, where Charles was sitting, with a look of deep concentration on his face.

"Hi, Charles. Am I good to go?" Tristan laid his hand on the older man's arm.

Charles turned to the side, so he could look at him. "This is as good as it gets, sir. I can't guarantee Miss Winter won't pick up anything, but as long as you stay in the hallway, my block should be able to keep her from seeing your immediate future."

Tristan nodded. "Okay then. Thanks, Charles."

Roy came over with the two boxes and gave them to Tristan. "They're not heavy. Keep them under one arm. Oh, and here's your orchid," he said with a grin.

Tristan decided not to take the bait and held the orchid in his other hand with as much dignity as he could muster. It actually was quite beautiful, and it sure smelled nice. He walked back into the building and waited for the lift doors to open.

"Could you please hold it for me?" he asked when two women got out of the lift.

Catherine, who was the last one to exit, held one leg inside the lift to keep the doors from closing. "Sure," she said with a smile. "Moving in?"

"Yes," he replied, putting down the boxes to block the doors and keep the lift from going up. He held out his hand to her. "Tristan Visconti, nice to meet you."

"Catherine van Dyk," she replied while shaking his hand.

Tristan had to exercise every bit of self-control he had the moment she touched his hand. *Bloody hell, that hurt!* It felt like his flesh was being scorched to the bone. Thankfully, she let go pretty quickly. Afraid she still might have noticed something, he tried to appear relaxed.

"Well, welcome to the building. Are you moving into apartment 3B?" she asked with a slightly confused expression.

Hmm, best to divert the attention to someone else, Tristan thought. "Yes," he said, deliberately looking at her friend. Thankfully, she took the hint.

"Oh, I'm sorry," he heard her say. "This is my very good friend Leah Winter. Leah, say hello to Tristan."

Leah seemed to try to hide a smile but shook his hand nonetheless. Thankfully, the contact didn't hurt at all. *Definitely related to Catherine, then.* He made a mental note of that. "I thought you looked familiar," he said with a smile. "You're the author of *Frozen* and *When Autumn Comes.* It's an honour meeting you, Miss Winter."

She appeared a bit embarrassed. He let go of her hand just as she replied, "Thank you."

Hmm…a seer and a celebrated author without the attitude. He might actually like this woman for real. He heard Catherine's voice behind him.

"Visconti is quite an unusual name. Are you Italian, if you don't mind me asking?"

He turned around to look at her. *So she was interested? Good.* "My family comes from Milan, yes, and I was born there, but we moved to England when I was a boy, so I consider myself an Englishman. I visit Milan on a regular basis, though. Have you ever been there?" Tristan was quite surprised to hear himself say these things. *Well, that was certainly a tad too much honest information. What the hell was wrong with him? Was it something she was doing?* He focussed and noticed she was actually starting to feel uncomfortable.

"Uhm no, but I always wanted to. From what I've seen on TV, it's a beautiful city," she said politely.

Too polite. He felt something else as well. He wasn't sure, but it might be awkwardness. He was losing her. "It is. If you ever have the chance, you should go, I have a feeling you would like it," he said while giving her his best, boyish smile. He felt her relax immediately and was overwhelmed by the feeling of suddenly finding himself in a warm bath or something. He could actually feel the water. *This must be the weirdest meeting I have ever had.* Not sticking to the plan, he decided to just end the conversation. Things might turn even more awkward if he lingered any longer. "Well, I'd better get these boxes up. It was nice meeting you, Catherine. I hope we'll become more than neighbours." He tried one last time to make eye contact but pulled back when he felt the water again.

She smiled at him though and said, "Time will tell." They started to walk towards the door when Catherine turned around. "Listen, I'm having a Halloween cocktail party this Thursday. You're welcome to join our party if you're free."

Tristan, who already had the boxes back under his arm, put one foot between the doors of the lift. "I would like that. You live in the penthouse, right?"

"Yes," she said, looking confused again.

Tristan sighed inwardly. *Suspicious much.* "Your name is on the doorbell outside," he decided to explain as a slight flush crossed her cheeks.

"The party starts at eight," she said. "You can bring someone if you like."

"Thank you. I'll be there," he said before he let the lift doors close.

Tristan watched the numbers on the panel move up to the third floor and got out of the lift. He opened and closed the door to his apartment and carelessly kicked off his shoes. *Well, that hadn't gone very well. What the hell was wrong with him?*

Roy came into the hall, carrying two boxes filled with books. "So, how did it go? Did you manage to bump into her?"

Tristan frowned. "Yes, I managed to bump into her, Roy, but either my abilities are off or she is the weirdest elemental I've ever come across."

Roy put down the boxes. "Why? I mean, did something go wrong?"

Tristan ran a hand through his hair and looked frustrated. "I don't know. The end result was pretty okay, I guess. She invited us to her cocktail party. Well, she invited me, but she said I could bring someone, so we're in."

Roy nodded. "Well, that's good, right?"

Tristan sighed. "Yes, I suppose it is, but I can't read her, Roy. It took everything I had to make her trust me. That's not exactly normal by my usual standards, you know. And I think I got burned." He rubbed the inside of his hand.

"Come again?" Roy looked at Tristan's right hand with a rather confused expression. There was an angry red blotch on its inside. "How the hell did this did happen?" Roy asked. "Charles! Charles, come take a look at Tristan's hand."

Charles came into the hallway as well. "Sir?" he asked, looking at Tristan. Charles refused to call him by his given name as he thought it was inappropriate for a blocker to take such liberties with an empath. Charles had impeccable manners and had taught Tristan quite a few new ones he had not learned from his parents. After a few months, Tristan had given up trying to turn Charles into someone he wasn't and accepted the fact that Charles would always see him as more valuable than himself. He was now gently holding Tristan's hand, making *Mmmm* sounds to himself.

"Well?" Tristan asked, a bit anxious.

Charles let go of his hand and looked at his face. "It's certainly fascinating. This happened the moment your hands touched?" he verified.

Tristan nodded. "Yes, the second she took my hand. It felt like fire, and it's a miracle I didn't let out a scream, to be frank. I don't want to sound like a baby, but it hurt. A lot," he said with a glare at Roy, who was looking at him with a smirk on his face.

Roy tried to look sympathetic but failed.

Charles went into the living room and motioned for the two men to follow him. After browsing through his suitcase, he gave Tristan a gel-like substance.

"What's this?" he asked.

"Aloe vera gel. It's for burned skin. If it doesn't go away quickly, we'll have to get you to a healer. Maybe I should inform headquarters. We could drop by this afternoon."

Tristan shook his head. "Over a little burn? Come on, I would be the laughing stock of the company. No thanks. Let's try this first." He opened it and applied a generous amount of gel on the burn. It felt cool to his skin, and he let out a thankful sigh. "It's working. What I'm more concerned about is how to avoid this next time. It's quite hard to get close to someone if I can't use physical contact. Any thoughts?"

Roy shrugged his shoulders. "Don't look at me, man. I can plan, hack and bug just about anything, and I'm good with weapons, but this is beyond my capabilities."

Tristan looked at Charles, who seemed to be lost in thought. "Charles?" he asked.

"Maybe, but it's just a theory. You said you felt this the moment she touched your hand, correct?"

Tristan nodded.

"Miss van Dyk is an elemental, but what if her powers are attached to her emotions? You said she looked interested and her star sign is connected to fire. It would make sense that would be the first element you would pick up on."

Tristan raised an eyebrow. "Her star sign? Really, Charles, her star sign? That I would live to see the day to hear you say something like this with a straight face." He shook his head, but there was a twinkle in his eyes.

"Yes, well, with all due respect, sir, I'm not the one who got burned," Charles replied.

Tristan's twinkle disappeared. "Which leads back to my original question. Any thoughts?" he asked, still looking at Charles. He didn't like the look on his face. It was rather smug. Charles was never smug, not without good reason.

Tristan wasn't going to like the answer.

"My best guess would be that you let her in, sir."

Tristan laughed. "What? That's ridiculous. Charles. I'm an empath for God's sake. I don't let anybody in if I don't want them to." He knew he shouldn't have said that the second he finished his sentence.

Charles just smiled at him. "My point exactly, sir."

Roy did his best not to laugh at his friend, who looked quite dumbstruck.

"Well, that's just lovely," he mumbled to himself. *Letting someone in. Someone with considerable power. Oh the joy.*

Tristan had learned how to block other people's emotions the hard way. Sure, it was nice to know someone cared for you, but not so much when you felt their disappointment or worse. The last person he had really let in was his ex, Eve, the company's top reviver. The fact they were both still standing after their break-up was nothing short of a miracle. Even Roy and Charles, whom he trusted with his life, didn't get to see everything, but they probably knew him just as well, if not better, as his parents. This morning had certainly been interesting. He couldn't deny that. Tristan was always intrigued by the unexpected. Not many people had the power to surprise him because of his abilities, but Catherine had certainly taken him by surprise. If they wanted to have any chance of succeeding, which still seemed like a suicide mission to him, he would have to be able to get close to her. He went over their conversation in his head and remembered his response to her inquiry about his last name. He had said way too much. No, he corrected himself, he hadn't said too much. Talking to her would generally be considered as a good thing. He had spoken the truth, which was the problem.

However, Charles had pointed out that this just might save him from getting burned again or any other funny stuff. God only knew what the woman was capable of. So maybe it

wouldn't be that difficult, letting her in. Apparently, he already
had on some level. He looked up to see Roy and Charles going
about their business and smiled. That's what he liked best
about his team. They always knew when to push him and
when to leave him to his thoughts.

"Roy, what do we know about her schedule for today?"

"Not much, actually. The only thing I've got confirmed is
a reservation at Claridges for tea at four p.m., but I've got
tabs on both their Oyster cards and I've hacked into their
computer. The business one, Elements. Miss Deborah de Vries
has her last client at four p.m., so she will definitely not be
joining them at Claridges. It'll probably be just the two of
them. The reservation confirms this. Oh, and I've got tabs on
the phone list you gave me."

Tristan nodded. "Quick work, Roy. All six of them?" Roy
gave him a thumbs up. "How far are we with the house?"

Roy frowned. "Not as far as I would like, boss. This whole
damn building seems to go completely bonkers when you
try to bug the place. I tried several methods here in our
apartment, but they all went haywire, even after Charles
tried his blocking thing."

"So, what are you saying? Give it to me straight. No bugs
in her house?"

"None that are working, not inside, sorry. I've got two
up in the hallway. One downstairs in the lobby and one on
her floor. They both seem to be holding up. I just tested the
sound, and your conversation in the hallway came through
loud and clear."

Tristan grimaced. "Well, that's something at least." He looked
at Roy, who looked frustrated. "Don't worry about it, I anticipated
as much. At least we'll know who's coming and going."

"I could try again at four, when they're at Claridges if you like."

Tristan shook his head. "Don't bother. It would be too
much of a risk anyway with Miss de Vries on the other side

of the wall. Elements and Catherine's home are connected, remember?"

"I know, over here." Roy pointed to a spot on the computer screen, which showed the schematics of Catherine's entire penthouse floor.

"Yes, that's the connecting wall," Tristan said, leaning over Roy to get a good view of the computer screen. "Any luck tracking down our white man?"

Roy turned around and gave him the eyebrow. "You're kidding, right? This guy is like a ghost. And another thing. I haven't got clearance to see his entire file. What's up with that? Neither does Charles, or you, for that matter. I called the boss. He says he's going to try and pull some strings but no promises."

Tristan ran a hand through his hair. "Hmm, maybe it would be easier to ask Catherine if I get the chance."

"I would be very careful stirring that particular topic, sir," Charles cut in. "From what I understand, it was an ugly break-up and I'm sure you remember that feeling all too well yourself."

Tristan made a face. "All too well, yes." He stretched out his hand. The aloe vera seemed to be working well. He could hardly feel the burn anymore. "Charles, I need to go into town. If the company is having trouble locating the white man, we need all the help we can get. I need to talk to Eve."

Both Charles and Roy looked unhappy. Tristan sighed. "Your concern is duly noted, but she is the last person who's actually interacted with him. I need to know if she experienced anything in particular. Anything that can be of use."

"And you don't think the company doesn't already know this?" Roy asked.

Tristan slowly shook his head. "No, not necessarily. Eve's loyalty is to the big boss, not to the company itself. Above all, Eve is loyal to Eve. It's possible there's more that she's willing to share. Whether I like it or not, we still have a connection.

She may not love me anymore, but I'm pretty sure she still trusts me. Besides, we should cover all our bases."

Charles got up from Tristan's couch and grabbed his coat. "I'll go and get the car, sir."

Tristan gave him a soft smile. "Thank you, Charles." He looked over to Roy. "We need this guy, Roy. Reach out to all our contacts, including the dodgy ones. Especially the dodgy ones. Don't forget to contact our homeless network as well. If he hasn't changed his appearance, and somehow I get a feeling he hasn't, they have a better chance of recognizing him than our other contacts. He won't be hiding from people he considers harmless."

Roy nodded. "Consider it done, boss. I probably shouldn't say this, but will you do me one favour? Be careful. That woman is one manipulative bitch, and for some reason she still has some pull over you. Just, don't forget that, okay?"

Tristan didn't even consider getting angry. He knew Roy meant well. "Don't worry, Roy. I'll be careful. Promise," he said.

Roy didn't bother looking up, already busy, working behind two computers and only raised one hand in acknowledgement. Tristan took the lift downstairs. Roy did have a point though. Eve still had some pull over him, as his friend had just described it. He owed her. His life, to be exact. And though he had gotten Eve out of a lot of trouble, in and outside the company, it still didn't settle the score. At least not in his book. He sighed. He sure wasn't looking forward to talking to Eve. For a moment, he considered his motives. Was it just to get information or did he want to see her as well? He shook his head. No, it was just for the information. He had worked very hard to cut out all unhealthy things in his life, and Eve was definitely unhealthy.

Downstairs, he got into the backseat of the car. Charles liked it that way, and it gave them a good cover. That of driver and employee.

"The company, I presume, sir?" Charles asked with a smile in the rear-view mirror.

"As always, Charles. As always."

* * *

"Clearance level six. Welcome, Agent Visconti," a computerized female voice said to him as he let his eye be scanned after entering a seven-digit code on the panel in front of him.

Battersea Power Station was the home of the company, though nobody knew its true location. Not even the prime minister. Only those at MI5 with a need-to-know clearance came here to visit and there were very few who needed to know. The access area had changed in 2013 when the first residential apartments went on sale. All set in motion by the company itself, of course. Having shops and apartments actually provided a better cover front, but it had taken their lawyers quite a few years to get exactly what they wanted, outwitting all the other interested parties and with English Heritage breathing down their necks declaring it in very bad condition. Eventually though, they got what they wanted. The company always got what they wanted.

Tristan had left Charles to find their boss to see if there was any progress on getting clearance to the white man's file while he was on his way to find Eve. As he had told Charles, he was going to start at the laboratories, the best place to find Eve. She liked their more "colourful" cases. Which is why he was glad the boss had upgraded his clearance level to six for this job. Tristan knew there were seven levels, or so he was told. He had been a level five agent before he was assigned to Miss van Dyk and had been quite surprised to hear his clearance had been upgraded to six. His boss was level six. As far as Tristan could tell, all the unit leaders were six, no agents. With the exception of Eve, of course.

As the glass doors of the laboratory wing closed behind him, he couldn't help but notice the air felt slightly different. It was a little harder to breathe, and he couldn't hear his own footsteps, which gave him a feeling of uneasiness. Mentally Tristan enhanced his empathic abilities, so he could at least feel someone—*or something*, he added to himself—coming. He looked down on the little piece of paper the receptionist gave to him. *One left, two times right, left fork, third door on the right.* At least, that was her last check-in location, according to the lady at the front desk. Silently moving through the pearly white hallways, he followed the directions on the piece of paper and finally reached the fork. He took the left and started counting the doors. When he reached the third, he took a deep breath. He mentally braced himself.

Don't let her get to you. Keep your emotions in check. Ask only what you want to know, and stay honest, he chanted in his head.

Eve was not only their top reviver. She was also a mind reader.

He swiped his card and heard a soft click. The room was large and a lot darker than the illuminating white of the hallways, and he had to squint to adjust his eyesight.

"Hello, Tristan. I was wondering when I would see you," a soft voice said to his right. As Tristan's eyes became more adjusted, he saw a tall woman with flowing black hair that reached to her lower back. Eve. Her eyes were extremely light, and he knew them to be lilac up close. He had never seen a human being with lilac eyes, but he knew they were her natural colour. Her eyes were searching his face now, probably scanning his thoughts.

She emitted a bell-like laugh. "Now, darling, that's not a nice thing to think about me. Come and sit. You're almost bursting with questions, and your timing couldn't have been better. I just sent out for tea. I got bored with staring at them, you see." She was looking towards the other side of the room.

He followed her gaze and only now noticed the rest of their surroundings. The hairs on the back of his neck prickled. There were two glass-like tubes in the room. They made him think of coffins. There were people inside. One man and one woman. The coffins made a soft humming noise. Behind them was a panel with all sorts of information.

Tristan could make out some of them. Vital signs, obviously, but also things that didn't make any sense to him at all. "Are you supposed to revive them?" he asked, knowing she already knew he would ask.

She smiled. "Not exactly. It's one of our latest projects. It's called Dreamcatcher. It's quite fascinating. Or it would be, if I had slightly more interesting subjects."

Tristan stared at her.

"No, darling, I won't tell you the rest. Don't worry your pretty little head. Ah…tea." She walked over to the door and opened it before the man on the other side had a chance to knock.

The man recovered quickly. "Your tea, miss." Before Eve could even open her mouth, the man had turned around the corner.

"So jumpy. Quite rude, when you think about it," she said, shaking her head. Her hair seemed to glow as it shook behind her. She put the tea tray down on the table on the other side of the room, where there were two comfortable-looking, squishy chairs. "You still like white tea, I presume?" she asked.

Tristan noticed there were two cups on the tray and sighed. "You knew I was coming."

Again she smiled. "Of course, I knew, Tristan. This is the company, you know. We do have more than one seer roaming around these fluffy, white halls." She poured the tea into a small cup and emptied it back into the teapot. "It needs another minute," she said and seated herself in one of the squishy chairs. "So, what do you want to know about Alan?"

Tristan took the seat next to her. "So his name is Alan? The white man?" he verified, just so there would be no mistaking his question.

She nodded her head slightly. "Yes, he brightened up my entire year. I dare say, Tristan, he's almost as interesting as you, though you know I prefer dark-haired men in general."

He decided not to take the bait and appealed to her honest streak. "Why are you so willing to tell me about him? Don't get me wrong. I'll count my lucky stars, but Charles is trying to get more information as we speak. I haven't got access to his file, so won't you be going against company policy if you tell me what you know?"

"Ah, Charles is here!" she exclaimed. "Dear, Charles, how I miss him. Is he doing well, the old dog?" Her eyes twinkled mischievously.

"He's fine, Eve, and I'm pretty sure the feeling is not so mutual, as you are well aware."

She pouted. "Oh pooh...still being a sourpuss then? I thought he would be thrilled since we broke up. No need for him to be all gloomy. I'm actually quite fond of him, you know," she said.

She felt sincere, but with Eve, Tristan was never sure. "I'll be sure to tell him that."

Her smile returned. "Please do! Now, I think the tea is ready. Be a dear and pour us a cup." She sighed contently as Tristan reached for the tea tray. "Just like old times, darling."

* * *

As he closed the door behind him, Tristan took a deep breath to fill up his lungs. The outside air felt like heaven, even if it was filled with smog, it felt like bliss to him. The meeting with Eve had drained him completely and once again he wondered how he could have fallen for her in the first place. Roy was right. She was a manipulative bitch. Then again, she had saved his life. By choice. So she couldn't be all bad. Nevertheless, he was glad to leave the company and very glad to leave the laboratory wing. Sometimes he wondered if they were the good guys or the bad guys. Or both. In his opinion, you could never have one without the other. And sometimes sacrifices had to be made for the greater good. Tristan huffed out loud. He wondered what Miss van Dyk would think of that little reasoning. Somehow he thought she wouldn't be too impressed. He kind of liked that. He looked over his shoulder as he heard someone approaching.

"All done, sir?" Charles asked, giving him a scrutinizing look.

"That's a yes if there ever was one, Charles. And I'm fine, to answer your silent question, though a little drained. She gave me a lot of useful information and was actually on her best behaviour. Well, for Eve standards, I suppose. Oh, by the way, she misses you," he finished with a wicked grin.

Charles's reaction did not disappoint. "Well, I have never! I can assure you, sir, the feeling is not mutual." And with that, Charles walked over to the car, his step a little more aggressive than usual. Tristan smiled.

Back in Shoreditch, they went over the information they had collected. Charles had had remarkably little trouble getting them clearance to see Alan's file. Tristan had smirked over that little titbit of information. He was sure Eve had something to do with that, though he kept this particular thought to himself. Charles was wound up enough over his meeting with Eve as it was. Roy had received quite a few responses from their homeless network concerning Alan sightings, as he now referred to them, but none of them had led to anything useful, so far.

Tristan, for his part, told them about his meeting with Eve. How she almost idolized the man and had successfully revived him and how fast Alan's responses to her were, even in pain. Being revived wasn't exactly painless. Tristan knew this from personal experience, as Eve saved his life once as well. All he remembered was it felt like being hit by lightning. If lightning felt like a thousand knives piercing your heart. Alan was, according to Eve, the most powerful empath she had ever come across. Charles and Roy both looked sceptical at this piece of information.

"You're sure she wasn't just saying that to spite you?" Roy asked.

He shook his head. "No, whether or not it is the truth,

she believed it to be true. Then again, he could have made her believe that, I suppose. If he doesn't have any scruples whatsoever, who's to say what he would do. She did, however, have another piece of information I thought very interesting. She could only sense life from him, not death. Isn't that a bit strange for someone who's supposed to be a master of death?"

Both men looked thoughtful. "Well, I don't know, boss. I mean, we've never come across a master of death, have we?" Roy said.

Charles put down Alan's file, which he had just read for the third time. It mentioned Alan being both an empath and a master of death, alongside the rather extensive list of his dubious activities in the past. "I can certainly understand why the company wants this man close-by and why he could be useful to our cause, but I can tell you one thing for sure. Miss Catherine is never going to work with this man, assuming we find him in the first place."

Tristan frowned. "Oh come off it, Charles. We don't know that. No offence, but you don't know any more about Catherine than I do, meaning we don't know anything about her or how she would respond."

Charles had a stubborn look on his face. "I beg to differ, sir. I've read her file very carefully, and I've seen her once. Miss Catherine is a force of light. This man is exactly the opposite. She won't join forces with him."

Behind Charles's back, Roy subtly shook his head, which Tristan translated as *Let it go man. It's not worth the fuss.* He let out a sigh. Fine, they could deal with it later. It had been a long and busy day, and they needed food.

"How about I make us some pizza?" Tristan asked, subtly changing the subject.

Roy and Charles both smiled. "That sounds lovely, sir. I do believe we could do with some food, and you make a killer pizza, if I may be so bold," Charles said to him. Roy secretly gave him a thumbs up as Tristan walked to the kitchen.

As they were just sitting down in Tristan's large kitchen, ready for some delicious-smelling pizza, Roy's phone beeped. "Ah, one of my team. Miss de Vries went to Suki on Gerrard Street. Apparently, the ladies are having dinner there. Both Miss Winter and Miss van Dyk came back here to pick her up and went with her."

"If she comes home early, sir, you could try to ask her out for drinks at The Albion. She goes there frequently, and it's just around the corner."

"I know where it is, Charles. I've read her file as well, you know," Tristan said sarcastically, but his eyes were gentle. He looked at Roy. "How come we didn't know they came back here?" Tristan looked at the alarm system they had set up when he first moved in. After all, there was a lot of equipment lying around in plain sight that non-company people were not allowed to see and they needed an early warning system.

Roy answered, a bite of pizza still in his mouth. "We did— well I did—but I silenced the sound. The alarm will go off though if someone gets out on our floor. I thought you could use a break during dinner."

Tristan had an annoyed look on his face. "Yes, thank you, Roy.

Roy laughed. He knew his friend was more annoyed about his bad manners than his turning off the sound. But he got up nonetheless and put the sound back on. As he sat down again and reached over the table for another slice of pizza, he asked, "Happy?"

As it turned out, Catherine did return home early, and more importantly, alone. They saw her entering the hall to retrieve her mail. Before Roy or Charles could make a comment, Tristan had jumped up to grab his coat and ran out of the door.

"Okay. Well, bye then," Roy said to the closed door.

Charles laughed at him. "Come on. We'll do the dishes together."

Roy got up with a grumbling sound. "We could listen in to their conversation in the hallway," he suggested.

But Charles had already stuffed a drying towel in his hand.

"Let's give them some privacy."

As Tristan got out of the lift, Catherine almost crashed into him, sending her letters flying.

"Oh, I'm sorry!" he heard her say, while he steadied her back on both feet and then let go of her arm to retrieve the letters which had fallen onto the floor. *No burning sensation, phew.*

When he handed them back to her, she mumbled a thank you. She had a lovely blush on her cheeks, he noticed.

"How clumsy of me," she continued, "I guess I was lost in thought. So sorry. Did I hurt you?"

Tristan looked into her eyes, determined to let her in. "Not at all," he said with a soft smile. "But you could make it up to me by joining me for a cup of tea. I was just going to go out to get one. There's supposed to be a really nice place nearby called Albion. I understood from their website they're open till eleven, you could fill me in on the dos and don'ts around Shoreditch?"

She seemed to be considering his request, and he let his wall down even more. He felt a slight warmth come over him, but other than that, he felt fine. More than fine actually. It was a nice feeling. She nodded her approval.

"Albion is really nice. I go there regularly, and I suppose I could give you some pointers," she said with a smile. He noticed she put her letters in her purse. "Shall we then?" Catherine asked.

Tristan, perfect gentleman that he was, held the door for her. "Lead the way, milady."

She let out a laugh. He let it wash over him. It sang. He remembered the bell-like sound Eve's laugh had made. He had always loved that sound, but sometimes it seemed too intense. Catherine's laugh was subtler, like a gentle caress. He liked it. As they walked through the streets, he noticed she was observing him, and he smiled to himself. He could pick up curiosity and a slight feeling of desire as well. *So, she wasn't averse to his physical aspects. Well, he certainly didn't object to the way she looked, either.* Catherine was a very beautiful woman, though perhaps a bit too petite. She looked fragile, probably enhanced by her lack of height, but Tristan knew looks could be deceiving. He had always been surrounded by strong women, especially since he had joined the company. His mother was probably the tiniest woman he knew, and even she was taller than Catherine. Tristan had slowed down their pace, realising she had trouble keeping up with him, and saw her relax.

After just a few blocks, she pointed to her right. "It's at the end of this street. We're almost there."

When they arrived at Albion, Tristan held the door for her again and waited until she was seated before sitting down himself and taking in his environment. He could understand why she came here. It had a cosy feeling. Tristan was no stranger to London. Shoreditch, however, was not his speciality.

"Do you like it?" she asked.

"It has a very pleasant atmosphere. You come here often, you said?"

"Yes, quite often. They're open all day, and they serve a really nice breakfast as well. So whenever I'm feeling lazy, I come here for breakfast," she said, giving him a smile. Another wave of warmth spread through him.

"Also," she continued, "they have a killer rooftop, part of The Boundary. They do wine tastings as well, and the view is really nice, especially during sunset." She stopped when one of the waiters arrived at their table.

Tristan looked at her. "What would you like, Catherine?"

"A pot of fresh mint tea for me, please."

Hmm, that sounds nice, even though he usually stuck to white tea, but his latest afternoon encounter with white tea had left a bad taste in his mouth. *Maybe it's time to try something new.*

"Same for me, please," Tristan said to the waiter, who left to get them their tea. He was about to ask if she'd had a nice day when she asked him a question.

"So have you settled in a bit? I'm sorry. You wanted to say something?"

He shook his head to reassure her. "Not at all. And thank you for asking. All the furniture is in place, so it comes down to emptying boxes now, which is not my favourite chore, but thankfully they are mostly filled with books, so it shouldn't take that long to sort them out. I still have a few more days before I have to go back to work, so I'd better make the most of it." A little white lie. Somehow it didn't sit too well with him.

"Do you mind me asking what it is you do for a living?" She looked at him with a genuinely interested expression. *Now there's an interesting question*, he thought. *How to answer?* Catherine was no mind reader, but he felt uncomfortable lying to her.

"My company helps people and organisations to improve the world. I could give you the details, but I'm afraid I'll bore you to death. It's not very interesting. I do a lot of travelling though, which makes it rather enjoyable. I always loved seeing the world, and my job allows me to see a great deal of it," he said. *Well, that wasn't a lie. He did like that part, very much.*

Catherine looked unconvinced. "That doesn't sound boring at all!" she said. "So you work for an environmental organisation or something?"

He couldn't help himself and grinned mischievously. "Or something," he replied. *Time to turn the tables.* "So what about you? I noticed your apartment is divided into two spaces, and I saw the name Elements outside."

She nodded. "Yes, that's the name of our private practice. My friend Deborah and I are the co-owners, and we have two more ladies working for us. It's a massage and coaching practice. We treat everyone who needs our help, but our main clientele are people in the music or acting industry. It didn't start out that way, but apparently our treatments have quite an impact."

Tristan noticed her face lit up when she talked about her company, and she was obviously proud of what she had achieved. *Well, good for her.*

"Elements," he said. "Elements. It has a nice ring to it. I like it. What made you choose that word?" And he did like it, but he was curious to hear what she would say. For a second, he felt like there was a waterfall between them, but just when he started to feel slightly panicked, it subsided.

"Well, I have a thing with the elements. You know, earth, air, fire and water. A theory of mine is that when body, mind and soul are in balance, the elements inside you are in balance, or in perfect harmony. Whatever you want to call it. So I thought it would be a nice name to represent what it is I do." Her tone changed to something slightly cheekier. "Also, it makes for very pretty brochures when you can work with the elements."

He smiled at her. "That's a beautiful theory, Catherine. Now I like the name even more."

She waved a hand in the air. "Oh, please...call me Kate. Everybody calls me Kate."

Tristan tilted his head a bit to the side. *Did they now? She wasn't a Kate. She looked way more sophisticated to him.* "Do they?" he said. "I like Catherine. You are a Catherine to me. Would you mind if I keep calling you Catherine?"

She had that nice blush again, and he felt a gentle sense of pleasure as well.

"No, it's fine. I'm just not used to being called Catherine anymore, except by my mother," she said, laughing. "My mother always calls me Catherine, so I guess you're in good company."

As he gave her another smile, he had a weird sensation of feeling a bit seasick. *What on earth was this woman doing to him?*

"You're an odd duck, Tristan Visconti," she said to him with a smile.

He couldn't help but let out a laugh. *Really? Now he was the weird one?* "An odd duck? Well, that's something new. What made you say that?"

She shrugged. "I'm usually pretty good at reading people, but I find it very hard to make out your character."

Now that was an interesting bit of information. How would the elements help her to define people? She wasn't an empath after all, and as far as they knew, neither were her friends. Although they suspected Miss de Vries might be one, the company could neither confirm nor deny their suspicions. So Charles's theory might prove to be true. If her powers were connected to her emotions, maybe this was how she read people.

"Then let me return the favour by stating the exact same thing about you," he said to her.

She looked at him with an incredulous expression on her face. Obviously, his remark surprised her.

"Really? People are always telling me I'm an open book." She suddenly seemed sad and lost in her own thoughts, fiddling with her necklace. Tristan felt the water coming back, now like a drowning feeling. He needed to snap her out of her thoughts.

"You're not an open book to me," he said. Thankfully, she looked up at him and the feeling of water surrounding him disappeared. She was still playing with her necklace. "That's a beautiful ruby. It goes well with your ring. Anniversary present?" he asked with a hint of cheek in his voice.

It worked. Catherine snapped out of it and laughed.

"Good God, no. I'm not married or anything. They're family heirlooms. The ring was my grandmother's, and my father got me the necklace." Suddenly, her expression changed and her eyes twinkled at him. "What about you? How many little Tristans are roaming the Earth?"

Cheeky little thing, he thought. As he raised an eyebrow, he said, "None that I know of, at least. Over the years, it has come to my attention that my line of profession doesn't really go well with a long-lasting relationship. Women tend to want more than a monthly visit, and I can't say I blame them. I would want more myself."

He thought it only fair to give her a warning. Yes, he needed to win her trust, and he was starting to like her more by the minute, but it was completely pointless to get involved. Let alone what the company would have to say about that.

Catherine stirred her tea. "Sounds kind of lonely, Mr. Visconti."

"It does, doesn't it." He smiled. No need to push her away completely. He just needed her to be on her guard. He wouldn't be any good for her. So he added, "Maybe I'm just trying to win your sympathy so you'll feel sorry for me."

She leaned back and tossed her hair over her shoulder. It was even longer than Eve's, he noticed. "Well, then it's working. I'm a sucker for people who are lonely. Everybody deserves some company in life. I think it's what keeps us sane. Though in all fairness, you don't really strike me as the type people feel sorry for, in general I mean. You seem very umm… self-sufficient is the word, I believe?"

Tristan laughed out loud, producing a deep rumbling sound. "Do I now? That was exactly the compliment I was looking for. Self-sufficient." He rolled his eyes at her, which made her laugh.

"Well, you are rather pleasing to look at as well," she said to him.

Oh my! She was flirting with him! It made him feel boyish. "Thank heavens, I still have my looks!" he said with a grin. He was thinking of returning home, but he was honestly having a good time and he decided to see if Catherine would care for a glass of wine. He could certainly do with one.

"Do you want another pot of tea or would you care for a glass of wine? I'm thinking of having one myself." He picked up the menu to see if they had anything he liked.

"They have a nice Chardonnay," she said to him with a smile on her face. "I think I could do with one glass of wine."

"Excellent!" Tristan signalled to one of the waiters, and he came over to their table at once. "Two Chardonnays, please," he ordered. He looked at Catherine. "Would you care for some olives as well?"

"Sure."

"And some olives, please." The waiter nodded and left their table. Relaxing into his chair, Tristan asked, "So Catherine, pray tell, what should I expect from this Halloween cocktail party?"

Catherine grinned. "Good you asked. I almost forgot. It's a theme party, so I hope you have a creative streak inside you."

A theme party, the joy. Roy would love that, and Tristan already dreaded what his friend and colleague would come up with for them to wear. He pretended—well not completely— to look horrified. "Oh dear, well, that would depend on the theme, I suppose."

"The theme is movies, but a TV character is also okay. Perhaps you could go as Shrek," she suggested to him. Her eyes had that twinkle again.

Oh really? He just stared at her.

She grinned and the twinkle brightened even further. She obviously wasn't intimidated by him.

"I'm going to ignore that last remark, I think. So, which character are you going to be?" he asked.

She shook her head. "Nuhuh, not tellin'. You'll have to wait and see, but I'm quite pleased with it."

He sighed in defeat. Obviously, she wasn't going to share and tell. "Are you expecting a lot of people?" He moved his body a little to the side so the waiter could put down their glasses and their olives.

"Give or take a hundred. Not everybody's coming, but this is an annual thing for us and our clientele and friends, so it's become rather popular over the years. Usually it's no more than a hundred people, though. Fortunately, I have a very large rooftop, which can be closed depending on the weather, so I never have any trouble with a large crowd. And I can always throw some people off the roof when it becomes too crowded."

She sounded dead serious, but the twinkle was still there, he noticed. *Weird sense of humour, but I kind of like it.*

"And you're calling me an odd duck," he said, trying to suppress a grin.

Catherine raised her glass. "A toast, Mr. Visconti. May you approve of Shoreditch and may Shoreditch approve of you."

Tristan looked into her eyes as he raised his glass to touch hers. "Cin cin," he said. When he'd taken another sip, he asked, "So are there going to be a lot of famous people in our building this Thursday?"

She nodded. "Give or take a hundred."

He looked surprised. He knew she had quite a few clients who could be considered famous, but he hadn't expected such a high number and that certainly didn't include himself.

"I would hardly consider myself a famous person, Catherine," he replied without thinking.

She smiled mischievously. "No, but you'll be dressed as one."

He put his head on the table. *Wow, I can't believe I didn't see that one coming. My brain must need rest.* "Wow, I fell right into that one, didn't I?" he said after he looked up again.

She looked rather smug and happy. "Yep, you did," she said. "But to give you a sincerer answer, I'm sure you'll see one or two familiar faces in the crowd, depending on your movie, reading or music knowledge. Deborah knows way more people than I do, though. I always have to ask her what he or she is famous for so as not to offend anyone because half the time I don't recognize them. Not even if I like their music. It's easier with actors and actresses, because you see them a lot on TV or on the big screen, but with writers and musicians it's much harder to connect a face to a book or band. Well, for me it is anyway. She's always drilling me a week before the cocktail party so I won't mix up names and bands. She actually has a book this year," she finished with a laugh.

"I'm very good with faces," Tristan said while he noticed she shifted and focussed her full attention on him, "but terrible with names." He had a rather eclectic interest in movies, books and music, but it would be a lot harder to recognize actors, musicians and authors when they were dressed up as someone else. "I think I could do with one of Deborah's books. You think she would make one for me?" he asked with a grin.

Catherine smiled back at him. It was a sunny feeling. "I'll ask her, but be careful what you wish for. She's a real drill master when it comes to these things. If you get one question wrong, you won't get a cupcake and trust me, you don't want to miss out on her cupcakes."

"I'll be sure to remember that," he replied.

"So are you settling down here in London?" she asked. "You said your work has you moving around a lot. That must be hard. Never to call a place home."

Tristan stabbed an olive and held it out to her to buy himself some time. Her fingers brushed his when she took it from him. No burning sensation, but he did feel a rush of desire. Whether it came from him or her, he couldn't tell. He took another olive himself and sipped his wine.

"Sometimes it is, but I've gotten used to it, I suppose. I'm not sure how long I'll be staying here, though. I would like to stay for a longer period of time. I would like that very much indeed." He made sure to make eye contact while he said this and noticed her cheeks turned a lovely shade of pink.

He continued, "It all depends on how fast I'll be able to get through to my client. The people I work with have such great influences on our world that often they don't realize how much power they hold. That's where I come in. I have to make them see what they can do or sometimes can't do. Sometimes this means people have to let go of their power, and most people don't even like the thought of that, let alone act on it.

Then I have to, let's say, persuade them, to come to my way of thinking and that's not always a lot of fun."

Christ, what was he thinking! Way too honest, way too honest, his mind screamed. Any moment now, she would get up and run away, screaming. She didn't, though she did look uncomfortable. *Time for some damage control.*

"Fortunately for me, it's the other way around this time. My client needs encouraging, and I really love that part of my job. It's very rewarding. I'm sure you have that as well when you see one of your clients back in perfect balance out there facing the world again." He gave her a warm smile.

She nodded understandingly and he felt her relax again.

"That is very fulfilling indeed. Although I do not dare to presume I have that much impact on my clients' lives. Your clientele sounds a lot more, I don't know, heavyweight? Suddenly I have visions of Shell's top dog and such," she said.

Tristan laughed. "I can well imagine. And you wouldn't be far off either. Some of our clientele are businessmen, but like you we get all kinds of flavour." He winked at her.

The waiter came to their table to ask if they wanted anything more from the bar before closing time. Tristan looked at Catherine, who shook her head. "No, just the bill. Thank you," he said.

"Very well, sir. I'll be with you in a moment," the waiter replied.

Tristan looked at Catherine. "Now I still don't know anything about the dos and don'ts around Shoreditch. I'm afraid this will lead to more tea on another day."

He felt a nice warm glow and she certainly looked pleased.

"I'd be happy to. Well, at least you know Albion now, but Shoreditch has many gems."

The waiter returned with their bill. When he noticed that Catherine tried to look at the amount, he put the bill in his pocket. He had her picked as an independent woman. By her look, she just proved him right, but this had nothing to do with independence. When he noticed she was about to object, he simply remarked, "I asked you to accompany me, remember?"

She shrugged and excused herself to leave for the ladies' room. When she returned, he helped her into her coat. Without her noticing, Tristan placed a little bugging device on the inside of it. It probably wouldn't work in the building as they'd been having a lot of trouble setting up any kind of surveillance, but it was worth a try.

"Thank you," she said, turning around to face him. Tristan let her pass him through the door and breathed in the fresh air. They walked side by side in silence. It wasn't an uncomfortable silence, but he did sense some mixed feelings from her. Did she want him to take her hand? Surely not. He had had a really good time. Actually, he couldn't remember when he had felt so relaxed. It was very easy to just be with Catherine if he let her in and put his guard down.

"It's very quiet here for a Saturday night," he remarked.

He could see her nod. "This part is quiet, but when you walk towards Great Eastern Street, it becomes more crowded and noisy. A lot of clubs are located there."

"Are you a club kind of person?" he asked. Somehow he could not picture her in a noisy club.

She made that gentle, laughing sound again, and he had to pull himself together not to gravitate towards her. "No, not really. I used to be, but I'm more of a restaurant or café kind of girl nowadays. Getting older, you know."

"And how old is old these days? Though I realize you should never ask this of a lady."

"Then how dare you ask!" She laughed again. "I'm thirty-five, if you must know."

"A spring chicken, then. I'm forty-seven myself."

He could feel her surprise immediately and was secretly pleased.

"Really? You don't look it." Her voice sounded sincere.

"Why thank you. You're being too kind, milady."

They had reached their apartment building and Tristan got his keys out of his coat to open the door for them. He also widened his reach of his emphatic abilities and automatically sensed both Charles and Roy as he knew they would be staying in the building till tomorrow morning. Their emotions were blurry. They had obviously not waited up for him. Good. Catherine went inside first and pushed the button for the lift.

"I had a really nice evening," she said to him. Suddenly, he was hit by a weird warm feeling. Looking at her more closely, he realised she was embarrassed. He was starting to recognize her emotions little by little.

So he gave her his most genuine smile. "Me too. You still owe me another date though. You promised me the inside scoop on Shoreditch. I cannot be trusted out there on the streets on my own, you know." He gave her a pleading look.

Catherine grabbed her iPhone, flipping through it, checking her schedule, and he happily went along with her little game of pretending.

Finally, with a big sigh she said, "I might be able to squeeze you in on Monday. How about lunch?"

Lunch? I think not. "Make it dinner and I'll agree," he replied with an arrogant smile.

She gave in. "Dinner it is then."

Tristan felt pretty satisfied.

"I'll even let you choose the place," she added rather wickedly. "See how you're getting on in Shoreditch and judge if you're able to pick a nice place."

Bugger! Charles or Roy would have to find him someplace nice. He was dreadful in choosing restaurants. "I'll do my best," he humbly replied. "Shall I pick you up at six thirty?"

They had reached the third floor and the doors opened. He held the door from closing and turned towards her.

"That sounds good. Six thirty it is," she replied.

"Goodnight, Catherine. I'm very glad to have moved to Shoreditch. I had a lovely evening." He took her left hand and bowed over it. Softly his lips touched her skin, and he could feel her tremble.

"You, too, Tristan," he heard her say as the doors of the lift closed and he went inside his apartment. This could turn into an even more interesting week than he had anticipated. A very interesting week indeed.

SUNDAY

Tristan woke up with a start. After a few seconds of disorientation, he remembered where he was when he heard sounds coming from the kitchen and the smell of eggs and bacon. He'd had a weird dream about the people in the coffin-like tubes at the company. Eve had been standing over them, a misty substance coming from her forehead, like she was sucking the life out of them. It had scared the hell out of him. He shook his head and stretched to shake the feeling the dream had given him.

Starting his morning routine of doing his daily push-ups, he heard Roy's voice on the other side of the door.

"Are you up? Breakfast in ten!"

Tristan raised his voice between two push-ups to acknowledge his friend's question. After reaching one hundred, he lay down on the floor. For a moment, he wondered if Catherine would be awake already. Her file didn't state anything about her sleeping habits, which meant she probably had a regular pattern, otherwise it would have been mentioned in the report. Last night had been nice. More than nice actually. He liked her. Getting up from the floor, he let out a big sigh. *Just perfect. The world is about to end and you choose this moment to finally like another woman. Excellent timing, Tristan, you sure know how to pick them.* Shaking his head to lose that thought, Tristan headed for his bathroom to take a quick shower.

"So, what's on the agenda today, boss?" Roy asked while tossing another fried egg onto his plate. Tristan frowned at his friend and colleague. He'd never understand how Roy managed to maintain his weight with the amount of food he generally shovelled into his mouth.

"I think Alan should be our number one priority for today. I have a dinner date with Catherine tomorrow and I don't want to scare her off by going into stalker mode, so we'll leave her to her own devices for the day."

Roy gave him a lopsided grin.

Tristan rolled his eyes. "Well, you know what I mean. No actual interaction. Of the verbal kind, I might add, before you start to get any ideas."

"I'm not saying anything," Roy replied. "But that dinner date is nice work. Where are you two going?"

Tristan sighed. "Yes, about that. Do you know of a suitable place here in Shoreditch? This part of town isn't exactly my expertise. And you're usually pretty good at this stuff."

"Where did you go last night?" Roy asked.

"The Albion. It was actually my kind of place, just not for a first dinner date, I think."

Roy was already googling the place. "Ah yes, The Albion. Oh, look here, it's part of The Boundary. That could work, looks rather fancy and they even have a rooftop terrace."

"I think she mentioned something about that. The rooftop terrace, I mean," Tristan said while looking over Roy's shoulder to get a better view of the pictures he was sliding through.

"Certainly looks nice. Well, that's one option, then."

"They went to Suki's last night, so she's obviously into Asian food. Hakkasan would be perfect to impress her, but it's not located in Shoreditch. Charles can tell you all about it. I think it's one of his favourite restaurants. It's rather pricy, though. Do you think that would intimidate her?"

Tristan shook his head. "No, I think there's very little that would intimidate Miss van Dyk. Certainly not a restaurant. She'll fuss about the bill, though. She almost did last night."

"You didn't let her pay, did you, sir?" Charles said, wrapping a towel around his head.

"I do have some manners, Charles. Did you sleep well?"

Charles nodded. "Quite well, sir, thank you. And I know you're a good lad. She's lucky to have you looking out for her. Which restaurant were you referring to?"

"Hakkasan. It's not in Shoreditch, though," Tristan said to Charles. "Roy said you know it well?"

Charles nodded fervently. "Yes, it's perfect for Miss Catherine. I just know she would really appreciate the ambiance. You can blame the not-in-Shoreditch part on me, saying I suggested it to you. Which, in any case, is true most of the time, n'est-ce pas?"

Tristan rolled his eyes, as did Roy. "Roy, would you be so kind to make the reservations?" Tristan asked. "I also need to check at least three locations this morning with regard to our missing white man. Eve mentioned that Alan showed a particular interest in a special collection of paintings the National Gallery is now featuring. I also want a permanent surveillance at Meg's store. She works at Elements part time, and we're pretty sure she's part of Catherine's inner circle. It is probable Alan has intimate knowledge of Catherine's best friends and he will either try to contact her or at least check on her. Last, but definitely not least, I want extra protective detail on Catherine's friend Sue. We have her on file as a very strong healer. Eve might have successfully revived Alan. She implied that his escape may have left him injured. How she came by this knowledge I do not know, nor did I ask. Point is, he might turn to Sue for help, whether she's willing to give it to him or not."

Roy was already on the phone talking to one of his team leaders, quietly giving instructions for both Meg and Sue's locations. Tristan and Charles were going over their connections at the gallery when Roy joined them.

"Reservation is made. Surveillance is being set up as we speak. Now I was thinking of contacting Mr. Black at the National. He's quick and discreet."

Charles nodded. "Mr. Visconti and I just came to the same conclusion. Do you want Roy to set it up, sir?" Charles asked. He looked at Tristan for confirmation.

Tristan bobbed his head. "Yes, not in the gallery, though. Perhaps the café?" Charles smiled to indicate his approval while Roy walked away again.

"Good choice, sir. And I think I have just the thing to get Mr. Black in a sharing, generous mood."

Tristan raised one eyebrow, but Charles just shook his head.

"Just leave that to me. I'll have it ready before you set out. Nothing illegal, I promise." He laughed, obviously pleased with his own little joke. Tristan had to bite his lip in spite of his more serious mood. Charles often made him smile.

"Pfff, okay, you're all set," Roy huffed, re-entering the room while putting his phone back in his pocket. "He could squeeze you in at eleven-thirty and not a minute later. He wasn't too happy, but he agreed in the end. He definitely knows something. He sounded way too nervous, so be sure to have your abilities on full force."

Tristan put a hand through his hair.

"I don't like being in the dark. I'm not used to having this little information. It leaves too much room for error."

"Sir, I'd never let anything happen to you...," Charles began but fell silent when Tristan raised his hand.

"I know that, Charles. That is not my concern. I guess this case is getting to me. There are too many liabilities. Catherine herself, for example. We have no idea how she'll react to our news."

"Which is why we agreed to tell her at the last possible moment," Roy cut in.

"Yes, but that's just the tip of the iceberg, Roy," said Tristan, his voice raising a little, and started to pace the room. "Alan is missing. We have no clue how he got out of his cell, let alone the entire building. Eve is behaving out of character. Our clearance level has been upgraded, no questions asked. Now Mr. Black appears to know something we do not, and we cannot afford room for failure. None. Because—tiny detail—an asteroid is about to end the world as we know it. That, gentlemen, is my point."

Both Roy and Charles just stared at Tristan, who sighed.

"I'm sorry. This is not helping. I don't know what the hell is wrong with me. Ever since we entered this building, my emotions seem to be in turmoil."

"There's no need to apologize, sir. Like you pointed out—perhaps a little less delicately—a lot is riding on this. The world to be exact, so emotional outbursts are only to be expected. From each and every one of us," Charles said, throwing an evil glance at Roy, probably to stop him from arguing.

Tristan smiled at Charles and looked over to Roy who raised his chin to meet his eyes.

"We're good, boss. Besides, best to get it all out here, right? Won't do any good to bottle it all up and risk explosion in front of the elemental. Or Eve, for that matter. You know I don't trust that snake any further than I can throw her." Roy smiled, but Tristan noticed his eyes were dead serious.

"Your input, as always, is invaluable," Tristan said to both of them and he meant it. He could already feel himself calming down and regaining his usual standards of control. He felt a wave of concern emanating from Charles.

"Really, Charles, I'm fine. Don't worry."

Charles shook his head. "It's not that, sir. It's just your remark about this building and your emotions. What if there is some weird mumbo jumbo going on? Roy's had a hard time getting any decent camera surveillance up in the building. Your emotions are running high and my blocking abilities feel slightly off as well here. Do you think it's just Miss Catherine or could it be something, more?"

"God, let's hope not. We have enough to deal with as it is. That being said, I'm not ruling anything out." Tristan sighed. "Any thoughts?"

Roy looked like he wanted to say something but thought better of it. Tristan immediately picked up on his hesitation.

"Now's not the time to be holding back, Roy. Out with it. We can't afford to miss something."

Roy shrugged. "It's silly. I just thought it's like the building thinks we're working against it."

"That's not that silly, Roy. I think you might be on to something," Charles chipped in. "No, just hear me out," he said when Roy started to interrupt him. "What if the building actually *is* protecting Miss Catherine? Maybe even all the occupants? Then we just burst in with our surveillance equipment. Maybe we should make our intentions clear?"

Roy let out a snort.

"Oh, come off it, Charles. What would you have us do? Stroke the walls and say we're here to save the bloody planet? Would it please be so kind to aid us in our quest? What exactly?"

"There's no need for sarcasm, Roy. And I'll be accepting your apologies when you see I'm right about this," Charles said, an undercurrent of irritation in his voice. Tristan held up a hand, and both men fell silent.

"Like I just said, we can't afford to miss something. What if Charles is right? Then we'd be wasting valuable time. If not, we look silly for a few minutes and we never speak of it again. So, are we all on board?"

Roy looked like he thought Tristan had just lost his marbles but nodded. Charles beamed at him.

"Leaves the question, how do we go about this?" Tristan asked. Charles just smiled.

"I thought Roy made an excellent suggestion, why don't we try that? These things are all about intent though. We have to mean it. It can't be a joke. And I think it's important we all say it. Perhaps we should each touch a wall?"

Even Tristan felt a bit doubtful about all of this, but seeing the look on Roy's face, he tried to hide that emotion immediately. It couldn't hurt to try, and they could not afford the building to be working against them. So he put on a serious face and reached out to the nearest wall.

"Roy, why don't you take the other side, and Charles, you can touch the wall in the hall near the front door." He watched the two men take their position. "Okay, so are we all ready?"

"Can I just mumble? Would that be okay? I'm really not that comfortable with speaking out loud to a wall." Roy looked rather unhappy.

Charles's voice came from the hallway.

"I think that won't be a problem, Roy. Just make sure your intentions are good and you convey those intentions. I really believe it's more about that than the actual words."

Tristan saw the instant relief spreading across Roy's face.

"Okay, then I'm all set. Ready when you guys are."

Tristan pushed the palm of his hand to the wall. "Okay. On three. One...two...three..."

Tristan softly whispered to the wall, imagining he was speaking to the entire building.

We're not here to cause any harm, you know. It might feel like that, but we need to keep an eye on her. We can't do that the same way you do. We need equipment for that. It's really important you let us do that. The fate of our planet depends on it. I promise I will do everything in my power to protect her.

As he whispered to the wall, Tristan realized with a shock he actually meant it. He would do anything in his power to protect her. This was getting weirder by the minute. He felt a slight tingle running through the palm of his hand. It felt good. When he let go, the room felt slightly warmer, peaceful. He smiled when he noticed Roy was still mumbling to his wall, both his hand and his cheek touching the surface. Roy was just finished when Charles came back into the room.

"Well, that was certainly a new experience. I think it worked. Well, something worked. I definitely felt a shift. Did you feel anything?" he asked.

"As much as I would like to deny it—in your words—I definitely felt something shift," Roy said. "You?" He looked at Tristan.

"Me too. It feels more peaceful in here. How do we know for sure?"

Roy walked over to his laptop and let out a roar. "It did work! All the cameras are up. In her apartment, in Elements, they all work. Hey, you got a bug on her coat as well. Good for you. What the hell?"

Charles looked rather smug. Tristan laughed when he saw the look on Roy's face.

"Better get it over with, mate," he said grinning.

Roy took a deep breath. "Sorry, Charles. You were absolutely right. However, you do understand that from this moment on, you're now marked as my new guru?"

Charles let out a deep rumbling laugh. "I can live with that, Roy. Apology accepted."

"Well, I must say, this is a vast improvement. At least, if Alan tries anything here, we'll know. I'll add his features to the program right now so the system will give us a warning if he comes anywhere near the building."

Tristan hesitated but then continued, "Maybe you should add Eve to the system as well, Roy. Just in case."

Roy snorted again. "Way ahead of you, boss. She's already in the system. Don't give me that look. You know I don't trust her one bit, and frankly Charles agrees with me on this point."

Tristan turned to Charles, who suddenly pretended to be busy fetching his coat and keys.

"Fine. Whatever. Anyway, I asked. I'm over it."

Charles came back into the room. "Good, then we can go. You don't want to be late for your appointment with Mr. Black and we have to make a quick stop on the way there," Charles said, putting on his coat.

Tristan waited to see whether Charles would elaborate, but after a few seconds he grabbed his coat as well and decided it was better to just go with it.

* * *

Charles softly closed the door of the car. "Got it, sir." He handed Tristan a small jewellery box. Tristan opened it to find a coin inside.

"It's special, I presume?" Charles nodded.

"To him, it is. It's the one he's missing from his collection. I came by it several weeks ago, and I was waiting for the right opportunity to make use of it. Now seems like a pretty good moment." Tristan closed the box and put it in his left jetted pocket.

"Thank you, Charles. This will go a long way, I think. Well, let's get this show on the road."

* * *

Tristan entered the café of the National Gallery at precisely eleven fifteen and took a quick look around. Mr. Black wasn't there yet. Good. Tristan liked to be able to choose his own spot. Also, arriving first made him appear serious about this meeting in the eyes of Mr. Black and gave him ample opportunity to take a look around. After a few seconds, Tristan chose a table next to a young man and woman. Obviously tourists who'd just ordered an early lunch, which meant they would be staying here for at least half an hour. They were going over a map of London, discussing where they would go next. They would not be interested in his conversation with Mr. Black, unlike the two old ladies on the other side of the room, who looked like they'd be interested in anything that would spice up their lives. Just like the three twenty-something girls who were already gossiping away about the sexual preference of the waiter who had just left their table. Tristan sat down and ordered a double espresso and scanned the two businessmen three tables across from him, just out of habit. He felt nothing to worry him, just business. It felt good to check, though. Ever since meeting Catherine, he'd felt a bit off. Like his abilities weren't working properly. It was good to notice there was nothing wrong with him after all. *Must be related to her, then. Or the combination of the two of us together*, he added as an afterthought.

At precisely eleven thirty, Mr. Black entered the café. He was dressed in a dark-grey suit, tailored, of course. His black hair lay flat against his head. He stopped to clean his glasses and to look around. Tristan gave him a slight nod, which he immediately picked up on. Putting his glasses back on, he walked over to Tristan's table. As he came into his proximity, Tristan could feel his thoughts were in turmoil. He was nervous all right!

"Mr. Black, always a pleasure. I hope I'm not interfering with your schedule?" Tristan asked.

Mr. Black shook his head and sat down across the table. "Not at all, Mr. Visconti. Although I do hope you'll forgive me for having limited time. We're very busy at the moment. However, if the company asks, one makes time." He took a nervous glance at his watch.

"I understand you might have some information for me?" Tristan asked. Sometimes it was best to just dive in. Mr. Black was nervous enough already. No need to add to those feelings. Tristan let a wave of calm wash over the man and visibly noticed him relax.

"Yes, yes. I'm not sure if it's of any interest to you, Mr. Visconti. Your company did say to always mention anything out of the ordinary though, so when your man called, I was sure he was referring to our new exhibit. How you people always find out so soon, I'll never understand."

Though Tristan had no idea what the man was on about, he made sure Mr. Black didn't pick up on it. He just nodded and said, "Obviously. And that's none of your concern Mr.

Black. We're in the business of knowing things." He let just a touch of frost shine through in his voice. The man before him bowed his head.

"But of course. Forgive me, I forgot to whom I was speaking. I did not mean to be rude," Mr. Black mumbled. Tristan nodded his head in acknowledgment and motioned for him to continue.

"It's to do with our Peru collection. Most of it is quite old and therefore extremely valuable. We keep very strict records of every item that is in our care, whether temporary or on a more permanent basis."

"Of course," Tristan replied in an encouraging voice. Mr. Black looked satisfied by Tristan's tone and continued.

"There should have been fifty-four items." His voice dropped to a whisper. "Instead there were fifty-five. I counted them myself. Three times."

Okay, so there was an extra item delivered to the gallery. Could be an honest mistake. Could be an attempt to steal something, trying to hide it through legal channels. Could be anything. Tristan was starting to get impatient.

"I assume you checked your supplier and your records?" He almost felt silly for asking and hoped he would not insult Mr. Black, but he had to know more. This wasn't enough to go on.

"Naturally, sir. Like I said, we take things very seriously here at the Gallery."

Tristan wasn't sure he could make use of this information, but Mr. Black had agreed to see him at his earliest convenience. He might as well give him the coin. It would put him in a good light for future references. He reached inside his left pocket and discretely pushed the little box across the table.

"For your troubles, Mr. Black. I very much appreciate you seeing me on such short notice." Mr. Black looked taken aback for a moment and took a peek inside the box. He could barely contain a soft gasp as he saw the contents inside.

"How did you come by this? I cannot possibly accept," he muttered in awe.

"Of course, you can." Tristan's voice was final. In a flash, the little box disappeared inside Mr. Black's jacket. Tristan was about to get up and take care of their bill when Mr. Black stopped him by grabbing hold of his wrist.

"It's still here, you know," he whispered. Tristan stared at him. "The painting. Item fifty-five, Urubamba Valley."

Tristan didn't know what to think of this. "Why on earth didn't you sent it back?"

Mr. Black quickly looked around with a nervous look in his eyes. "That's the weird part. The curator wouldn't let us. Got really angry when we wanted to return it. Said it was part of the collection and if we valued our jobs, we should go about our business. I've never seen him behave like that. Ever. It was like somebody brainwashed him."

And that's when it hit Tristan. Alan. Somebody did brainwash the curator. Hadn't Eve said that Alan was the strongest empath she ever had ever come across? He could've easily convinced the curator to include a painting in the Peru collection. The question was why. A trip to the Gallery itself seemed in order.

"Again, Mr. Black, you've been most helpful. If you'll excuse me, I'd like to take a look at this painting myself. And I'm sure I've taken up too much of your time as it is." This time Tristan did get up from the table, leaving Mr. Black no choice but to follow suit.

"Would you like me to acco…," Mr. Black began when Tristan shook his head.

"No, thank you, Mr. Black. You've done quite enough. I'm sure I can find my way to the Gallery." He held out his hand. Mr. Black shook it and then took off in a hurry, obviously glad to be rid of him. Tristan paid for their coffee and texted Charles that he would quickly swing by the Gallery. He added,

Coin worked like a charm!

He had just reached the right wing when he received a text from Charles.

Of course, it did!

Tristan smiled and put his phone back in his pocket. He scanned the paintings on the wall, bypassing the sculptures and other items in the middle. Mr. Black mentioned a painting, not a sculpture. There it was, item fifty-five. Tristan squinted to read the card next to it. *Sacred Valley of the Incas, also known as Urubamba Valley, located in the Andes of Peru, by Carlos Vargas.*

It was a dark painting of a corn field. Tristan didn't like the feel of it. He looked around to see if there was any chance he could get away with putting a bug on the painting. None. Not only were there cameras, there was also a guard on duty.

"Bugger," he said softly. He tried to get a feel for the painting. Other than a slight creepy sense he didn't get anything, though. After another glance Tristan left the building and made straight for the car. No sense in wasting time. Charles looked in his rear-view mirror.

"And?"

"I think it's safe to assume dear Alan put his lovely powers to work on the curator to include a certain painting in the Peru collection. How he got it there and why is for us to find out."

"Is it, sir? Or could this be a wild goose chase? Have us focus on this painting while he makes his move towards Miss Catherine?"

Tristan looked at Charles. "You make a valid point, Charles, but we can't afford to let this go either way. Roy can get someone of his team on it. Just one. We can afford one, right?" Tristan's voice sounded insecure even to himself.

"I think Roy can spare someone for a couple of hours, sir. If not, he'll say so. You have to trust his opinion." Tristan nodded and then realized Charles didn't see his response as his eyes were focussed on the road again.

"You're right, Charles. Thank you. By the way, how did you come by that coin? I struck pure gold the moment I gave it to him." He saw Charles smile.

"Ask me no questions and I'll tell you no lies, sir," he said with a wink.

Tristan let out a laugh. "Fair enough, Charles. Fair enough. For now, I think it's best to head back to Shoreditch. I have some connections in the art world I'd like to check up on and perhaps you could trace that painting for me as well? At least as far as possible."

"Certainly, sir. Will you be needing the car?"

"No, I'll take my bike. It's quicker and easier to manoeuvre in central London." While Charles drove them back to Shoreditch, Tristan turned on the computer screen in the car to check Catherine's whereabouts. If she was wearing the coat he bugged, at least. The screen indicated she was and was just travelling back from Greenford.

"Catherine's mother lives in Greenford, right?" he asked just to be sure.

"Yes, sir. Is she there?"

"Not anymore. Her dot is moving pretty fast in a straight line, so she's probably in the tube heading back home. I'd like to be gone before she arrives back there."

"Not going to be a problem. Greenford is almost an hour by tube and we're almost there."

Tristan leaned back and went over the places he needed to visit. There were a couple of places near the river which would be good places to start. He texted a contact with his inquiry for any information on the latest shipment for the National Gallery and added—*Need intel asap. Double the usual fee.*

That should get his lazy ass into action, Tristan thought. Not a minute had passed when he received a reply.

On it! Give me 15. Meet me at usual place. Bring money.

When they arrived at the building, Tristan got out of the car to get his bike while Charles waited for him so he could park the car. Putting on his leather jacket and helmet, Tristan got on his Suzuki Hayabusa, gave Charles a wave and sped off.

Tristan manoeuvred through the streets of London like a snake. He loved the feel of the motorcycle beneath him. Though he could really appreciate a fast or beautiful old car, he always had a soft spot for motorcycles. Whenever he had the chance, he was on one. Being able to handle all sorts of vehicles was also kind of mandatory at the company. Besides cars and motorcycles, Tristan was also capable of flying a plane and made good use of his speedboat during summer. He even had been known to ride the occasional horse, though it had been a while and he wasn't sure if he could jump right back on. Raw power fascinated him. How it worked and what could be done with it. Tristan had pushed his own power to its limit for this very reason. He wanted to know why he could do the things he did. That was also how he found the company. Or perhaps he should be fair and admit it had been the other way around. They'd been tracking him for years, seeing how he would develop. Tristan did find their headquarters, however, and made first contact, so to speak, and that was unheard of within the company. People did not find the company. They found people. So when Tristan had calmly walked into the hall of headquarters, this had triggered more than one alarm. Of course, he'd had to go through the motions of regular training, but after that, Tristan had risen quickly through the ranks of the company. Very quickly. He could pick his own team members, which nearly always included Charles and Roy, and most of the time he had his pick of cases as well. Except for now. He hadn't had a choice in this. Though one could argue the entire company was on this particular case. What else was there to do if there wouldn't be a planet left to run? Still, it was his team that had been assigned to Catherine and her friends.

And yes, she was special. He'd figured out that much after two encounters, but was she special enough to stop an asteroid? Tristan still thought that was asking a lot from one human being. Even if she did have gifted friends.

Arriving at the river with several minutes to spare, he drove straight past some containers to the back and came to a screeching halt. He left the motor running and kept his helmet on. Seconds ticked by when suddenly Tristan felt the emotions of a man turning up out of nowhere on his left before he actually saw him. It was a nice little warning system which left almost no room for sudden surprises. He turned his head to the left and held out his hand. The man gave him an envelope, which Tristan pocketed, giving the man an envelope in return. After a short nod, Tristan did a one-eighty and sped off again. Tristan was always very careful with his more colourful contacts. He never allowed them to see his face or hear his voice. When he was near the Tate, he slowed down. No time like the present to see if his contact came through. Tristan came to a full stop and reached for the envelope in his inner pocket. The moment he held it in his hand, something brushed his arm and the envelope was gone.

For a split second, Tristan was completely stunned. He looked up to a see another motorcycle speeding away with his envelope. Pulling himself together, Tristan kicked his bike into gear and sped off in pursuit. A second later, he was yelling into his helmet.

"Roy! Get me some backup. Now! Someone took the envelope. I'm on his tail, but I don't know how long before I lose him out of my sight. Roy! Where the hell are you?"

"Sorry, boss. Right here. I've got you. Satellite is coming online any second now. Come on, come on...here it is. Red bike. Ducati by the looks of it?"

"Yes! Stay with it, for the love of God. Whatever's in that envelope must be important. We need it back. I can't believe I let this happen. I didn't even feel him coming. Goddammit!"

"Language, sir." Tristan heard Charles's voice inside his helmet.

"Charles…not now. Bugger, this guy can ride."

"Or woman," Charles replied.

"Yes, by all means, Charles, let's discuss the importance of equality. Seems like the perfect moment for it."

"Hate to break up the sarcasm, lads, but you're falling behind, boss. Hard right, hard right!"

Tristan hit the brakes, missed a truck by an inch, turned around the corner and sped forward.

"I see him! He's turning back. Where the hell is he going?" Tristan tried to get close enough to get some sort of reading on the person on the bike in front of him. Mind control wasn't really his style, but desperate times called for desperate measures. If he could stop him and retrieve the envelope, it might be worth it. There was the Tate again. The bike took another turn.

"No, you wouldn't. You're kidding me, right?" Tristan cried out, and he said something in Italian that wasn't in any dictionary, his voice slightly higher than usual.

"Umm, boss, why are you on the Millennium Bridge?" he heard Roy say in his ear.

"Because this idiot in front of me is on the Millennium Bridge, Roy! Move people, move!" Tristan waved with one arm to get people out of the way. The Ducati rider almost hit a young boy, and Tristan curved around him just in time. He heard Charles mumbling something about damage control while Roy was shouting instructions left and right in his ear.

Tristan saw a young woman run towards the child and felt a wave of fear and anger as he sped by her, the feelings blending with his own guilt. He had to stay focussed though. The end of the bridge was in his line of sight and the Ducati was accelerating, putting more distance between them. Thankfully people were now standing on the edge of the bridge, giving them space. Though Tristan was well aware most people also had their smartphones out. Damage control, indeed.

In the distance, he could make out the pearly white dome of St Paul's Cathedral and it was Sunday. At least that meant there were no schoolchildren on the street as he passed the City of London School. But there were a lot of tourists out and about. This could turn very ugly.

"What time does Sung Eucharist end at St Paul's?" Tristan yelled. He heard Roy hitting the keys like crazy.

"Shit, now! It just ended, boss."

The cathedral was getting closer and closer. The Ducati took a left and Tristan realized he was heading for the entrance. As he followed suit, he saw a stream of people exiting the cathedral. His focus swayed from the bike in front of him to the people standing closest and spread a wave of fear to get them moving. Not two seconds had passed. When he turned his head, the bike was gone.

"Where the hell is he?" Tristan yelled. "Find him, Roy, find him."

"It must be somewhere near the end on the left side. Look near the trees! The satellite has difficulty tracking movement near or under trees."

Tristan slowed his speed not to attract any further attention and drove over to the trees. Yes, there the motorcycle was.

"Bugger. Yes, it's there, but it's lying on the ground abandoned. Anything in the crowd, Roy?"

"Already scanning, boss, but they're spreading out. Too many people leaving church. I'm assuming we're looking for Alan, but we have no clue if he's working alone or if he has any associates. I have to say, this was excellent timing."

Tristan switched their connection to his phone as he took off his helmet.

"It most certainly was. Makes you wonder, doesn't it? How is it possible this guy is one step ahead of us? We're flying blind,

Roy. And what are his motives? What does he have to gain?"

"Does he know we're facing impending doom?" Roy asked.

"Yes, he does. Eve told him. Don't ask. That makes it even stranger, though. If he knows the world is about to come to an end, why would he get in our way? I mean, who wants the world to end? Let's say you're a terrorist or an extreme religious nutcase—and he is neither as far as we know. Even most people in said categories don't want the world to end," Tristan said, still looking left and right, trying to pick up on Alan's emotions. Nothing. He made his way to the other side of the cathedral.

"Okay," he heard Charles's voice in his ear, "then let's assume he is working towards the same goal we are. Then maybe we got in his way with the painting. Perhaps it's essential in some way?"

"Go on, Charles. How could it be essential?" Tristan heard a sigh and could practically see Charles's expression. His right brow would go slightly up and his left a bit down and he was probably pinching the bridge of his nose. A black van drove towards the location of the bike, and he was just about to ask when Roy confirmed his thoughts in his ear.

"Our guys are here to pick up the Ducati, boss. We'll see if we can get any leads from that."

"Good," he said and watched as two company men loaded the Ducati into the van. "Charles? Any more thoughts on that painting?"

"Well, I looked it up on the Internet, and it is a peculiar painting to have in such a collection. The painter is known to have dabbled in the occult. Maybe it's special?" Charles's voice sounded dubious, probably even to himself.

"You mean like hidden powers? Like a portal or a doorway or something? Guys, come on, we are not the Avengers."

"Okay, okay. I was just spit balling here. How about if it's special to Miss Catherine?" Charles said, obviously a bit irritated.

Tristan had come full circle and reached the main entrance again. "Mm, you could be onto something there. It might be special to her. Is there anything in her file on paintings or art in general? Nothing comes to mind."

"That's because there's nothing special in her file, except for some guy who makes vases. He also paints. She has one of each. A vase and a painting. Magne Furuholmen."

"Sounds familiar," Tristan said. "The name, I mean. Not from the art world, though. Strange."

"Not that strange, boss. He's also a musician. He was one of the a-ha trio. You know? 'Take on Me,' 'The Living Daylights'? That stuff." Tristan heard the grin in Roy's voice.

"Of course, Norwegian blokes. Yes, that's it. No link between Peru and him, I suppose?"

"Nope, none. And Catherine likes to visit ballet, opera and exhibitions, but she has no interest in painting or sculpting herself."

He sighed. "Okay, this is getting us nowhere. Not now, anyway. I'm coming in. Roy, I need at least three analysers for the rest of the afternoon and, Charles, get us a seer. We need one desperately. How are we on damage control from my little stunt on the bridge?"

"Already on it, sir. Tomorrow's paper will feature a hit and run article involving a child and a man on a motorcycle. The latter was successfully chased by a police officer alongside the river. Unfortunately, the man took the Millennium Bridge. Thankfully, they got the scoundrel and nobody got hurt. At least that is what it will read. And I'll go and see if they can spare us a seer. Shall I also pick up some lunch for us all?"

Charles, always the practical one.

Tristan smiled. "That would be great, Charles, thanks. See you in a bit. Tristan out."

He walked towards where he had left his bike, lost in thought. *Could Alan be trying to help them? Was that possible?*

Maybe even the reason he escaped? Or had been let free? Tristan grimaced. He didn't, for one second, believe Alan would have been able to escape on his own. He must have had inside help. And he was pretty sure he knew at least one person who had seemed only too happy about their new "prisoner."

* * *

Tristan parked his bike and took the stairs to his apartment. No need to take risks, and he knew from her file Catherine almost never did. When he walked through the door, he could see his team had been busy. Two women and two men were busy behind laptops, all of them wearing in-ear pieces. He knew three of them and gave them a nod.

"Boss, meet Gilly. Gilly, Tristan," Roy yelled from the kitchen.

Tristan went over to shake her hand, and she gave him a shy smile. He felt a wave of respect wash over him.

"Pleased to meet you, sir. It's an honour to be working on your team."

"Thank you, Gilly. I wish it could have been under better circumstances." He gave her a smile in return.

"Not at all, sir. I'm very confident we will still be here at the end of this week. Like I said, it's an honour."

He gave her a nod and walked over to Roy, who was currently standing in front of the fridge stuffing everything Charles was handing to him inside.

"Hello, boss. Like I said, that's Gilly Meyers. Short for Gillian. Twenty-seven years old, three years with the company. Was selected by MI5, but we got to her first. Besides being a great analytic, she also has an uncanny way of seeing patterns. Best thing we could come up with after the negative on the seer." That last part he ended in a near whisper.

"What?" Tristan also lowered his voice and looked to Charles who shrugged.

"Sorry, sir. It was a definite no on the request for a seer. Apparently, they're all otherwise engaged. Besides, and I quote,

'We cannot risk assigning you a seer and change short-term events because of the things he or she might see. It will affect the long-term events, and we cannot have that. That is final.'"

Tristan sighed. *Great, just peachy.* "Trace on the Ducati?"

Roy nodded. "Sure thing, but it's a rental and it was all paid for in cash. The ID he left is a fake, of course. I had expected as much. It might even have been his real ID come to think of it. He could have used his powers on them."

Tristan nodded. "That could very well be true. Even if he's not working against us—which I'm by no means sure of—he's no saint, that's for sure."

He walked back into the living room.

"Okay people, listen up. We need intel, and we need it bad. Alan is a priority as is his whereabouts. Catherine, what can she really do, what will she need, how can we assist without her knowing. At least as long as possible. The painting, we need a tracer on it asap, and access to the cameras in that wing." He looked at Gilly. "Gilly. Patterns. Anything that connects the three of them? Get me a theory."

They all nodded. "Yes, boss."

"And don't forget to make sure you stuff your gobs with a couple of sandwiches. I'm pretty sure Roy will eat yours otherwise," he finished with a grin. They all laughed.

Tristan turned back to the kitchen. "Roy, get me Eve on the phone. I need to talk to her."

Roy sighed but handed him an earpiece nonetheless. "Calling, boss."

Tristan sighed as well. This was going to be a long day.

MONDAY

Tristan took the stairs to Catherine's penthouse and arrived at her door with precisely two minutes to spare. He always made a point of being punctual. It had taken him ages to decide what to wear. In the end, he went with dark blue. He liked the colour, and he had a feeling Catherine might like it, too. His hair was down, of course. It gave him a more boyish appearance, or so Charles had told him. Tristan smiled at the recent memory.

Well, here goes. Showtime, he thought and rang the bell.

Catherine opened the door in an astonishing dark blue dress that clung to her body at just the right places. He thought it was very sophisticated, yet sexy as hell. He felt a warm wave wash over him. *Fire again, so she's probably pleased by the way I look as well. Good.* He tried to keep a straight face and focus on what she was saying to him. *Was it warmer up here or had it become a little bit harder to breathe?*

"Do you want to leave straightaway or would you like to come in?" she asked.

"I'd love to come in, but the car is waiting for us downstairs, so perhaps some other time? You look truly beautiful, by the way, Catherine. Blue becomes you." He meant it. Blue did become her, and he gave her one of his warmest smiles. She blushed. *How sweet!*

"Thank you, Tristan. You look very handsome as well. And we match, it seems."

"I was rather hoping we would," he heard himself say before he stopped himself. *You idiot! Way too flirty.* He tried to sense her feelings and could tell by her body language she was slightly uncomfortable. She was fidgeting with her keys as well. He felt the heat intensify. *Mm, maybe not too bad then. Perhaps the idea of them matching wasn't such an unwelcome thought and she was just being shy.* Thankfully, the lift arrived, and he stepped aside to hold it for her.

"After you, milady," he said.

"Thank you," Catherine replied.

Once they arrived downstairs, Tristan led her to a silver Mercedes. Charles already had the motor running. She looked at him, her eyes obviously held a question, but he went ahead and opened the door for her. She stepped in, and he got in beside her in the backseat.

"Evening, Mr. Visconti," Charles said. "Where to this evening?"

Of course, Charles knew very well where they would be going, but Charles had impeccable manners and always left the final decision to Tristan.

"Hakkasan at Hanway Place, if you'd be so kind, Charles. And may I introduce you to Miss Catherine van Dyk. Catherine, this is Charles Hayley. He's been my personal driver for quite some time now."

Charles looked in his rear-view mirror and smiled. "Nice meeting you, miss."

"Nice to meet you too, Charles," she replied and tried to inconspicuously pull out her smartphone. As the car was pretty dark and Tristan had perfect eyesight, he could see she was texting. Not that she noticed he was looking at her.

Hakkasan at Hanway. Now sod off ;-). Tristan smiled. The text was probably to Leah or Deborah, her two closest friends. Well, good for her. At least she was being careful and responsible. He would have expected nothing less. After all, they'd just met. For all she knew he could be a mass murderer. As a matter of fact, some people would consider him a mass murderer. And rightly so.

"I hope you'll forgive me for not picking a restaurant in Shoreditch, but I took a chance and thought you might like Asian food and this place excels in it, or so Charles has promised me. So if you hate it, you have to blame him, you see, not me."

Catherine rolled her eyes. "Well, as long as Charles promises to show me your bat cave, I think you'll both be safe since I'm quite fond of Asian food."

Good God, does she think I'm Batman? Tristan bit his lip.

He saw Charles trying to hide a snigger when he said, "I think I like her already, sir," before driving off into town.

It took a while to get through traffic, but since it wasn't the weekend, it wasn't too bad. Tristan hoped she would like the place. He'd only seen some pictures of the restaurant online, but Charles was confident Catherine would like the atmosphere and Tristan trusted Charles's opinion.

When they arrived at the restaurant, Tristan was out of the car in no time to open the door for her.

"Just let me know when you want to leave, sir. I'll be here. Enjoy your evening, miss," Charles said.

"Thank you, Charles," she replied.

They walked to the restaurant and then headed down the dimly lit staircase, surrounded by cooling slate walls filled with tiny crimson lights. Tristan gave them his name at the desk, and a waitress came to lead them to a table in the back. She pulled Catherine's chair for her to take a seat. She asked if they'd like anything to drink. Tristan looked at Catherine.

"A Chardonnay for me please and some water, perhaps?"

Tristan nodded. "Make that a bottle of water and two Chardonnays. Do you prefer still or sparkling, Catherine?"

"Still, if you don't mind," she said. The waitress handed them their menus and then left to get their drinks. Catherine looked around and Tristan took the opportunity to take a good look at her. She seemed at ease, definitely interested in her surroundings. He liked it, too. Charles had chosen well. The restaurant was bathed in a mysterious icy-blue light. Carefully placed screens provided an air of intimacy and subterfuge, further enhanced by the shadows created by the many candles. He could see why she would feel at ease here. The lighting resembled that of her own home. Thanks to the working cameras, he knew quite a bit about Catherine's place. Both her private home and company. His eyes focussed on her. Yes, she definitely liked it. He was starting to recognise the warm waves radiating off her. If it was a sort of gentle, rolling sort of wave, she was pleased or at ease at least. Water was obviously tied to her feelings of anxiety and fear. He would try to avoid those at all costs. It felt like drowning or choking on water. Zero fun.

"Do you like it?" he asked.

"Very much. If the food is as good as the atmosphere, this is going in my top ten list, I think," she said.

That pleased him. Probably more than it should have, but her answer was so open and honest that he felt compelled to return the gesture. "I'm glad you like it. I wasn't sure what kind of cuisine you liked. I completely forgot to ask. Nerves, I suppose. I'm pleased I did something right, at least."

"Well, if you must know, I stood for half an hour in front of my wardrobe, realising it wasn't very smart of me to have zero idea where we were going. I was worried I'd be over or underdressed," Catherine said.

Tristan gave a soft laugh. "I changed three times," he said.

"Oh good. Then I'm not the only loser here," Catherine said, grinning. "Did you have a nice Sunday?"

He looked up from the menu. "Rather dull, really. Well, besides stressing over finding the perfect restaurant, of course. I played some cello, though. That was nice. It's been a while since I've been able to play." *Not one lie in there,* he thought, pretty proud of himself.

It had been a rather dull day. Well, dull for him. Tristan hated research, and he'd had a full day of it. Sunday night had been dreadful trying to get information from Eve. And when

Eve didn't want to give any, it was like pulling teeth. That had left him in a bad mood. Today had been no different. The entire team was in full research mode, and it had gotten them nowhere. He needed Catherine to open up to him and fast. She was their best bet now to get more information on the elusive Alan. He'd have to build up to it though.

"You play the cello? I love the cello," he heard her say and snapped out of it. "It's such a beautiful instrument. I play the harp. Lever harp, not pedal harp. Goes really well with the cello, by the way."

"Does it now?" he asked with a laugh. "Then we must perform as a duet someday. I didn't know you were musical." *How the hell could that not be in her file!* He went over her file in his head but came up blank. He was sure there was nothing in there about her playing music. Only that Deborah had a background in the music business. He was not very familiar with the lever harp. As his own studies had been classical, he only knew the sound of the pedal harp, which was used as part of the orchestra. He'd never heard a lever harp except on YouTube. He would love to hear her play.

"How could you?" she replied.

Good question, he thought but said nothing, hoping she'd continue. Fortunately, she did.

"The harp is a fairly soft instrument. You wouldn't hear me even with the windows open, and I don't play as much as I used to. Busy, busy, busy. You know how it is. Do you play other instruments as well?"

He nodded. "Piano, but when I started travelling so much, I moved it to my parents' house. They moved back to Italy when they both retired. My father plays as well, so it's put to good use."

Talking to her came easy, he noticed, and he liked the way she had her full focus on him.

"Do you visit them often?" she asked.

"Not as often as I'd like, but every chance I get, yes. My

family is important to me. What about you?"

"I'm very close to my mother, and I have an uncle I'm very fond of. My father died several years ago, and I'm an only child, so it was just me and my mom. She moved back here to live closer to her brother, and I decided to move closer to her within the year."

He smiled. "I thought I heard the tiniest accent. Dutch?" *Ha! As if he needed to ask.* He was getting better at this, though. He noticed it didn't bother him as much as long as he wasn't actually downright lying to her.

"Good guess. Yes, I'm half Dutch on my father's side. Sometimes I still miss Amsterdam, but I visit friends over there quite often, so I'm quite reconciled with living here now. Leah's of Dutch origin as well. We've been friends for as long as I can remember. Though we always speak English to one another, we still swear in Dutch," she finished with a grin.

He laughed. "I can relate. Swearing is apparently a primal force. I often swear in Italian."

"You speak Italian fluently?" she asked.

"Yes. We moved to England when I was young, but we always went back to visit family and friends several times a year. And my parents thought it'd benefit me to speak both languages, so I was raised bilingual," he finished with a smile.

"What are you going to have?" Catherine asked, looking at the menu.

He looked at the menu as well. "Do you like dim sum? We could order a dim sum platter for two to start."

She nodded. "I love dim sum. I'm okay with that. I think I'll go for the fish then, as a main course. This sha cha seafood toban sounds rather good."

He leaned over the table to read what she showed him. "Hmm, scallops, prawns, squid. It does sound good, but I think I'll go for something that used to be a cow." He gave her his most boyish grin and felt a flash of warmth spread over him. He could get used to this. Well, for the few days they had left anyway. The waiter came straight to their table as soon as they put their menus down. He placed their orders with the waiter and asked Catherine if she'd like another Chardonnay.

She looked at her almost empty glass. "Yes, please."

The waiter looked at Tristan. "Another one for you as well, sir?" Tristan nodded. The waiter took their menus and left.

"I always wanted to learn a foreign language like French or Spanish or Italian," she said. "I just never found the time. A shame, really, but you can't have it all I suppose."

"Oh, I don't know. I consider Dutch to be a very foreign language. It's a very difficult language to learn, you know. I tried once, but gave up after a couple of months. I think the only thing I remember is *dank u wel* and *goedendag*. Oh, and something I learned off the streets. *Goedkoper dan bij de Hema*, but I never really understood what that meant." Obviously, he had said something terribly funny because she was trying desperately not to laugh in his face. He felt the heat rise in his own cheeks. "Did I say something offensive?"

"Oh, God, no. It's just a very touristy remark," she replied, still laughing. "In England, it'd be the same as saying something like 'Cheaper than at Boots.' Your 'thank you' and 'good day' were correct, by the way. People almost never get the 'g' right, though."

He frowned. "Well, that explains why I heard it on the streets so much when someone tried to sell me something. They always said it at the end, so I thought it must be a kind of parting remark. Shows what I know." He rolled his eyes. He didn't like being made a fool of, but she didn't ridicule him. So she probably just thought it was funny. He noticed she was trying to hide the start of a giggle.

"It's not so bad. It could have been much worse. We're not exactly known for our subtle nature, you know."

He smiled. "Now that I know."

The waiter came back with their Chardonnays and their dim sum platter. He explained the different dim sums and then left again after saying, "Enjoy your dinner."

Catherine raised her glass. "Cheers, Tristan. Even though it's not in Shoreditch, I dare say you picked a very nice place."

He grinned. "Good. Cheers, Catherine. I'm very glad you're willing to take a chance on your new neighbour."

She smiled mischievously. "Well, it's only the neighbourly thing to do, you know," she said. "No, but really, I'm glad you asked me out. You seem like a really nice guy. We're neighbours now, and frankly, it's been a while since I went out with, well, you know, a man."

He saw the colour rise in her cheeks and found it endearing. She was really being honest with him, and he was interested to know the reason behind her not dating. "Too busy with work?" he asked seriously.

She shrugged. "That's part of it, yes. Or that used to be part of it. Now I'm just using that as an excuse, to be honest."

She looked annoyed after that last statement, and he guessed she regretted that remark. It was a rather bold remark for a first date, after all. He felt a wave of heat. This one was short and intense though, not like he experienced before. *Anger*, he thought. Yes, he was starting to get the hang of this. He liked that she was being open with him, though, and decided to put her mind at ease. "I already told you that most women don't fancy a man who drops by only once a month, so you don't have to justify your choices to me, Catherine. I understand. You sound sad about it, though. Do you miss being in a relationship?" He held out a dim sum for her, and she lifted her plate so he could put the dim sum on it.

"Sometimes, yes. Don't you? I mean, getting together with your friends isn't the same. You share something special with your partner. Not that my friends aren't special. They are. Very special indeed," she said.

He immediately heard the sarcasm in her voice and had to hide a smirk. So instead he lowered his eyes and nodded. He knew exactly just how special her friends were. "I do know what you mean. A partner is the first person you see when you wake up and when you return home. You can share daily life with your partner like no other, not even your parents. Being in a relationship is a magical thing I think, but it's also something I'm not really good at." He felt her retreat a little. Though he wanted to give her fair warning, he didn't want to alienate her from him, so he added; "With all the moving around, I mean."

She seemed to ponder her answer. "You're here now, right?" she asked, picking up her dim sum with her chopsticks.

He smiled. "Yes, I'm here now, and I hope for quite some time. I like it here."

"London is a beautiful city," she agreed.

"London is nice as well, yes," he replied with a crooked grin.

"Are you flirting with me, Mr. Visconti?" she asked, fake shock written all over her face.

He smiled at her, but he made sure his eyes were serious. "That depends."

"On what?"

"On whether or not you'd like me to flirt with you."

"Oh. Um. I'm not quite sure how to respond to that." She let out a laugh which sounded nervous. "You can be very direct, you know." She stared at him accusingly.

He shrugged. "I guess I don't see the point in beating around the bush. Don't get me wrong, I like a good chase as much as the next man, but I'm not blind. When I meet a beautiful and intelligent woman, why hide my interest? You could be running off with another neighbour, for all I know. I'm not about to let that happen if I can help it." He gave her his most intense look. Eve had once called it the look that will raise anybody's blood pressure.

"I don't think you have a lot of competition at the moment, Tristan," she said rather shyly.

He raised an eyebrow. Was she that oblivious to her surroundings? "Really? Hmm, follow me around the room, then. Two tables across from us there are two businessmen. The one in the dark suit wants you desperately. I'm absolutely sure. Then there's the group three tables on your left. The girl with the brown hair just had an argument with that young man sitting opposite her. He checked you out several times before she said something out it. He's been sulking ever since. Should I continue?" he asked with a smile. She was blushing deep red.

"Please don't. And I'm sure you're wrong. You can't possibly know that businessman is interested in me."

"Not quite how I put it, Catherine, but believe me, I know. I'm a pretty good judge of character, and I've learned to trust my instincts." Wow, he was getting dangerously close to telling her the truth about his empathic abilities. He wasn't sure whether that was a good thing or not.

"Sounds as if you have a pretty handy skill there."

"It does, doesn't it?" he said. "I'll tell you mine, if you tell me yours." He grinned. He meant it as well. He would tell her. After all, everything depended or her trusting him, so he should help her any way he could, right? Why not tell her? She could handle it. She was an elemental for crying out loud. And he noticed she liked the playful banter. Catherine was quick-witted. Something he thought was very sexy in any woman.

"So you think I have a handy skill as well, huh?" she said with a smile.

"No, I know you have a handy skill. There's a difference. I'm just not sure what it is, and that, I have to admit, puzzles me. No pressure. I have a feeling you'll either tell me yourself or I'll find out soon enough."

"Is that so?" she asked. "You sound pretty sure of yourself. My 'skill' might not be something you like, you know."

There was a small rush of the drowning sense. *Fear.* He recognised it now, and while acknowledging her feeling of fear, it went away. She was afraid he'd run a mile if he knew she was an elemental. Of course, he already knew, but she didn't know that. Time to take away that fear. "Impossible," he said with absolute certainty in his voice. "I may not know what it is you're gifted with, dear Catherine, but I am, however, sure you're a force of good. So whatever skill hides within you, it won't scare me away." She seemed to consider that. He had never wanted to be a mind reader. He knew all too well how bad a burden it could be from his years with Eve. But at moments like these, it would come in handy to know what Catherine was thinking. He didn't fully trust his empathic abilities with her.

"And what makes you a good judge of character, pray tell?" she asked, a smile in her voice. "If you believe me to be a force of good, then you must have no reservations sharing your particular gift with me."

Clever girl, he thought and couldn't help a grin. She wanted to know the truth? Fine. He was sure Roy would not approve, so it was a good thing Roy was not in charge.

"Ah, clever," he said. "And you're convinced I'm going to explain why I can't tell you. Not at this point, at least, but someday soon. I'll look mysterious while saying this, of course, and you'll feel disappointed but accept my explanation. Only I'm not one for playing games, remember? If you're asking, I'm telling. I'm an empath, which basically means I can read and feel other peoples' emotions. It's a curse, really. Ever since I was a young boy, I never knew if children wanted to play with me because they liked me or because I'd somehow made them like me. I learned to block my gift during my teens, but I guess that wasn't really a smart thing to do because I had terrible headaches and worse. Go figure. So after a while, I accepted I was a little freak and let the emotions back in. I'm able to filter them now, though, so I don't have to feel everyone around me." It had been murder growing up. Tristan was the first of his family to have been "gifted." Even thinking the word left a bad taste in his mouth. He'd always known how people felt about him. In school, he'd been an outsider, having no friends to play with because they either thought he was a freak or just very scary. Over the years, he'd gotten better at hiding his abilities. There had been many slip-ups during his childhood years, when he would react to someone's thoughts as opposed to what they were actually saying. Enough to start avoiding him altogether. He'd adjusted that part for Catherine's sake, he didn't want her to feel sorry for him over something that was trivial to him now. Later in life, he came to see the advantages of his gift and started to use them for his own benefit. He had been known to help others during his teens, but not many. That had started when the company recruited him.

He lifted his head to look at her face. She looked pained. *Why did she look pained? Obviously, his news hadn't scared her. He hadn't expected her to be scared, but he'd hurt her. How? Dammit!*

"You're not a freak," she said softly. "Don't ever say that."

Oh bollocks! You inconsiderate arse. "I didn't mean to imply that you're any kind of freak, Catherine. Please forgive me if you thought so. I only referred to myself." The wave of heat again. Anger. She was angry with him. Why?

"I know that, but I still don't like it." Her voice was sharp. "Being an empath can be something wonderful. Yes, it can be terribly dangerous and manipulative as well. Believe me, I know. And it must be hard to always doubt people's motives to want to be around you. Did you try to make me like you?" she asked with a frown.

No anger wave of heat this time. So she didn't really think he'd done that. She just wanted to know. "Of course, I did, but not in the way you think. I turned on the charm because I wanted to get to know you better. I never interfered with your free will. You were a bit nervous around me when we first met. Sometimes you still are, like now." He smiled at her. "I can help you relax without losing your focus. It's supposed to even help you think clearer. Watch." He let a wave of calm embrace her like a warm safety blanket, and he even felt her relax. It was quite an intimate feeling. He never experienced it like this before.

"See. How could you possibly be a freak if you can help people in such a way?" she asked, smiling.

He returned her smile, feeling a bit emotional himself. "Thank you, Catherine. That means a lot coming from you. I don't know why exactly, but it does. It's strange, you know. I usually get all sorts of emotions from people when I put in an effort, but every time I focus on your emotions, I either almost get burned or I feel as if someone dropped a bucket of water over my head or something." He laughed. She was staring at him, though, so he stopped laughing immediately. "What?" he asked. "Did I say something wrong?"

"No, you said something right, I think. The reason you probably felt elements is because I'm an elemental," she said with an expression that said, "Brace for impact."

Calm, remain calm. No sign of shock. Certainly no fear. Not that he felt any of those things. He was just pleased as punch she actually told him herself and relatively soon. Well, it was still the longest it had ever taken him for someone to tell him the truth, but still. Pretty pleased, yes. "I figured as much. So, you can control fire and water? Two elements. That's rather special, you know." He'd never heard of elementals who could control more than one element. That's what made them elementals in the first place. He almost didn't catch what she said next.

"No, that's apparently just what you felt up until now, Tristan. I can control all four of them, of course."

She could what? Impossible. There was no such thing. "You can control all the elements?" he asked in a whisper. "How is that even possible?"

"You don't seem to be very surprised by my being an elemental. Why would you be surprised that I can control the elements? Isn't that what being one is all about?"

He shook his head. "I'm sorry. I should explain. Over the years, I've met quite a few people with gifts and sort of researched what kind of abilities there were, so to speak. I've come across elementals before but never one who could control all of them."

She looked at him. "But one element is not the same. Take pyrokinesis, for instance. That is control over fire…"

He shook his head to interrupt her. "No, you misunderstand me. Pyrokinesis is not the same as being an elemental. You. You are fire. Fire manipulators can only control fire. There's a difference. And you're the other elements as well, as it turns out. Sorry, I'm still a bit shell-shocked by that little fact. No wonder you're so careful around people. You should be. I know people who'd like to dissect you like a frog." He smiled, but he also had a serious undertone in his voice.

"You seem to know more about my gift than I do," she replied softly.

That seemed to make her sad. He could understand that feeling. He hated not knowing as well. "In theory, yes, but again, I've never met someone who could control all four. You have no idea how good that makes me feel. I think there might actually be some hope, after all, for this planet," he said before he could stop himself. He was on a high. Even now, he could feel the adrenaline pumping through his veins. She could control all four! They really did have a chance. Would it kill her? He didn't know. He worried about that. *For the greater good*, said a voice inside his head, but he pushed it away. Not if he could help it. She was talking again, he had to stay focussed.

"You speak in riddles, Tristan Visconti," she said while staring at him. The waiter arrived with their main courses, and they fell silent until he left again.

"I know I am. Did you forget? I like to be mysterious, remember?" He winked. Yep, definitely still on a high. He knew he was confusing the hell out of her, but he didn't care. He was just too happy.

She rolled her eyes but had apparently decided to accept the situation for now. "How could I forget? Well, *bon appétit*, mystery man."

She held out her glass to him. Tristan raised his to toast with her.

"*Bon appétit*, indeed!"

* * *

Tristan softly closed the door to his apartment behind him. He wanted a moment to himself before he walked into the room. That had been some goodnight kiss. And it had been one hell of a night. She'd asked if he would play his cello for her, and he'd agreed under the condition that she'd bring lunch. They had settled for Wednesday because he'd probably be busy like crazy tomorrow. She'd seemed pleased that he'd agreed to play for her. He had desperately wanted to come inside but knew it would have been too soon. *Nice phrasing there, Tristan.* He smiled to himself. Besides, she'd been hesitant, and he hadn't wanted to push her, so he'd kept his powers to himself like a good little boy. Not that he would have. Well… no, he wouldn't have. Probably.

The kiss had been intense. He could control someone's mind, if he wanted to, but he'd never shared a mind with someone else. It was a little scary but also the most magical experience of his life so far, and he'd experienced his share of magical moments. Unfortunately, it had taken every bit of his self-control to break it off. Much more than he anticipated, which left him confused with a lot to think about. For the first time since he'd been assigned to this dreadful mission, he felt hope. She could actually pull this off. Maybe not alone, but if she really had all the elements running through her veins, she could connect to the asteroid. He was sure she could. Which left the question on how to destroy it. Maybe the fire part in her? Make it explode? The asteroid would have to be quite close by though, for her to do that. No, probably not an option then, still too much damage. Maybe as a contingency plan.

Tristan sighed and leaned his head against the door. He thought this had been it. His life was over. Basically he had shut down since he heard the news from his boss. He tried to hide it best he could from his team, including Charles and Roy, but he knew they weren't fooled. They probably thought they were on a suicide mission as well. They were there because that's where he was. They would always follow him, even into death. Tristan would never slack off on the job, but his heart hadn't been in it. He had put a big lock on his own emotions, leaving him to act purely on his intellect and a bit of sarcasm. It had kept him sane. Now he'd unlocked his own emotions again. Which left him with a feeling of hope, but also with a feeling of dread. Catherine was really something special. He'd pretty much known that from the first moment their hands met. He still had the mark to prove it, as the burn still hadn't faded away entirely. She could do this. She could really do this. He didn't know why or how to explain it, but he really believed she could save the planet. When he'd looked into her eyes and realized she was an elemental, he'd felt her power and it was nothing like he'd ever seen before. It had one big downside, though. For the first time, he was afraid to die. He felt that this could be it. Not for death itself. He imagined it would be relatively quick, hardly noticeable. And there were worse ways to go. At least he wouldn't go alone. There were people he cared about, however, and their lives. The possibility they could still have a life after Saturday. It filled him with fear. Because now he really, truly believed he could do something about it. The company must have known they really had a chance. They said as much. He just hadn't believed it. He did now. And that was scary. He felt the responsibility crashing down on him. *Okay, breathe. You're not alone in this. Imagine how she would feel if she knew what she's going to have to pull off. You have an entire team at your beck and call. You're not alone in this. You just have to make the right decisions and not fuck it up.* He straightened his back. Right, he could do this. They would save this planet. Together.

* * *

"She's a what?" Roy was staring at Tristan, a gobsmacked expression on his face.

"A true elemental, like I just explained…again," he said with as much patience in his voice as he could muster. "All four run through her. She has total control over them." Tristan knew it would be hard to convince them that there was hope. Acknowledging hope meant letting in the fear as well. He understood only too well what it was Charles and Roy were struggling with. They were sitting in Tristan's bedroom, away from the rest of the team. He wanted to run this by his two best friends first.

"Will it kill her?"

Charles. Always thinking of other people. Tristan gave him a soft smile. "I don't know, my friend. I'm not going to lie to you. It's a possibility, yes. Her powers are very strong. The strongest I think our world has ever seen. That's still an asteroid out there, though."

"I know the safety of the many outweighs that of one person, but we have to give it our all to prevent that from happening, sir."

Tristan looked at him with a sad smile. "If you could save our planet by giving your life, would you?"

"Of course, I would. You know I would!" Charles said with a hint of outrage in his voice.

Tristan nodded. "I know, Charles. I just said it because I think if Catherine knows what's at stake, she will say the same thing."

Charles immediately backed down. "Oh, I see. Yes, you're right, of course. She would. Well, I'm a blocker. That might help protect her."

Roy gave him an incredulous look. "Seriously, Charles? An asteroid? What, you're going to stand next to her when it hits the earth and give it all you got?"

"And why the bloody hell not? It's the least I can do to give Miss Catherine a fighting chance. In case you hadn't noticed, we'll all be dead anyway!" Charles said, his voice agitated.

Tristan raised his hands. "Guys, come on. It'll do us no good if we turn on each other. We have to work this out before we tell the rest of the team. Look, I understand it's scary as hell. I'm painfully aware you're both here because I am here. I'm not a fool. I know you think we're on a suicide mission. I know because I feel the same way. Or I felt the same way. I really believe she can do this. Perhaps with the aid of us and her 'special' friends. I haven't worked out the details, obviously. This has thrown me as well. I never thought we had an actual chance. I was just going through the motions and doing my best not to fall apart." He ran a hand through his hair and continued. "I really believe we have a chance, though. And yes, I know that's a scary thought because with it comes hope. But we must draw strength from that feeling, not fear or dread. We need to inform the team and get as much solid information on this particular asteroid. What does it consist of? What are the percentages? Everything that might help Catherine to actually destroy it. We have a lot already, but we've been focussing on when and where it hits. We know it's no use to nuke the thing. We already tried that. It didn't even steer off course. We have to let it come close, I think. We'll have to drag NASA back for another meeting."

Roy looked at him with a deadly serious expression. "You really think she can do this, boss?"

Tristan nodded. "Yes. Yes, I really do."

Roy nodded as well. That apparently was good enough for him. He'd finally accepted that they really had a chance. Tristan knew he would do anything in his power to help. Not that he hadn't already. Their mission had just taken a different turn, though. It wasn't a suicide mission anymore. It was now a rescue mission.

"Okay then," Roy said. "Let's do this thing. I think you're on to something about the asteroid being close. I don't think she'll be able to 'connect' to it if she can't see it. Or she would have to be able to 'feel' it or something?" He was thinking out loud now. "No, that probably wouldn't work. Still, it won't hurt to ask her. Shit, that leaves us with a disastrous timeframe."

"How disastrous?" Charles asked before Tristan could voice the same question.

"Well, you can't actually see it until it hits the atmosphere. So that gives us, like what, ten seconds? Maybe even less. You're right. We'll have to check with NASA. I'll set it up," Roy said.

"Lovely, just lovely," Tristan said, his voice dripping with sarcasm.

Roy grimaced. "Yeah, like I said, disastrous. It's all we have, though. Unless she can somehow sense it before it hits the atmosphere. Are you going to tell her?" he asked.

Charles looked at him as well. Tristan shook his head. "No, not right now anyway. We've been over this before, Roy. I think the three of us all agree that Catherine should be in on the plan as soon as possible, but the boss said no. Apparently, her ignorance is pivotal to the success of this whole idiotic plan." He ran a hand through his hair. "Besides it would only increase her fear and I still think we should keep her sane as long as possible. How would you feel if you knew the future of the earth depended on you?"

Charles and Roy both smiled. Tristan smiled, too. Stupid question. They already were responsible. Maybe not for the actual destroying, but they had this hanging over their heads for over a month now. And they had tried to destroy it. Several times. "Yes, well, still stands to argue we should keep her sane and focussed for as long as possible."

"She's going to explode the moment you do tell her. You realise that, don't you? She'll see it as betrayal, a lack of trust," Charles said to him.

"I know. That's a risk I'm willing to take, though. And please give me some credit. I still have my powers, Charles. If she thinks I'm a male chauvinistic pig trying to protect her, then so be it. I am a male chauvinistic pig," he said with a shrug. "She'd never run away from her responsibility. I'm sure of that."

Roy laughed. "I'll leave that to your good judgement, boss. When you do decide to tell her, though, it might be wise to have Charles around. Just in case you need him."

"Har har, very funny, Roy." His friend had found his sense of humour again. Tristan was thankful for that, even though most of his remarks were at his expense. He looked at the watch on his wrist. One thirty a.m. They'd been talking for over two hours now. No wonder he felt exhausted. It had taken a long time to convince his two best friends they really had a chance to survive. Now that he finally had them on board, there was still the task of convincing the rest of the team.

"Well, I suppose I'd better go in there and fill in the others," Roy said, getting up from the bed.

"You don't have to do that, Roy," Tristan said when Roy interrupted him.

"Yes, I do. I mean, you're the boss and all, but most of these guys take direct orders from me. I know them like the back of my hand. Trust me. I don't need your empathic abilities to gauge their reaction. And I can handle it. Really. Besides, Charles has to catch you up on another development." He looked at Charles who nodded. Quite gravely, Tristan noticed.

"Okay. If you need any help, though…"

"I'll holler, I promise," Roy said with a grin, leaving the room.

Tristan looked at Charles. "So, what news? It can't get any worse, right?"

Charles smiled. "No, sir, it can't. However, you're not going to like it. The police found a body floating in the river tonight while you were out with Miss Catherine. Our guys identified him as your contact. The one who gave you the info on the painting."

Tristan just looked at him. He held no particular fondness for most of his contacts, but he was pretty sure this death was on his shoulders. It wasn't a pleasant feeling. It never was.

"When?" he asked.

"Roy and I deduced it must have been pretty quick after he spoke with you. An hour, two at most, we think."

"Jesus. Alan?" Tristan ran a hand through his hair. Charles looked at him.

"Perhaps. Or one of his associates. We don't know if he's working alone or not."

"Were there any indications...," Tristan began when Charles shook his head.

"Of mind control or a sudden heart attack? No, sir. His neck was broken. Someone snapped it. Quick and fast. People can do a lot of things, but breaking your own neck can be a bit tricky, I think. Besides, there would have been easier ways if it really was Alan who killed your contact, sir. Why not make him eat a bullet or, indeed, make his heart stop? He is a master of death, after all."

Tristan nodded. "No, you're right. Then again, he might have realized this himself and chosen a clean kill instead. Something that wouldn't lead back to him." He let out a deep sigh. "Well, one thing's for sure. That painting must be pretty goddamn important."

Charles frowned. "Language, sir."

Tristan rolled his eyes. Just because he used to swear a lot when he first started at the company, Charles was always on his back to improve his gentlemanly behaviour. Keeping your cool under all circumstances and having impeccable manners was kind of like the company's trademark. If someone failed at either one, that person would never reach the top. So it was Charles's personal mission to turn him into some sort of Mr. Darcy. "You have to admit this is one of the weirdest things we've come across so far."

"Oh, I don't know, sir. We've had some pretty bizarre situations in the past. And I find an asteroid nothing to sneeze at," Charles said with a laugh in his voice.

Tristan smiled. "I said bizarre, Charles. That asteroid is, I grant you, a real party pooper, but it's not a bizarre concept. They exist. Sometimes they hit things. End of story. This, it reeks of the supernatural. You and I, we've seen a lot of things. We know what people are capable of, the hidden powers they can hold. I mean, look at Catherine. Before today, I had no idea one person could hold that much power. So why? Why would someone go through all this trouble for one lousy painting? What secrets does it hold? I've seen it up close. I saw nothing special. I sensed nothing special."

"Maybe it's attuned to a single person?" Charles suggested.

"Like Alan, you mean?"

"I don't know, sir. I'm just as in the dark as you are."

Tristan noticed Charles hesitated. "What is it, Charles? Out with it. We've discussed this before. There can't be any holding back. We can't afford to miss the tiniest thing."

Charles sighed. "I was just thinking it might be worth a try to see what Eve thinks of that painting. She is a mind reader, after all. She might pick up on something. Lingering thoughts? It's a stretch, I know."

"No. No, it's a good idea. I'll ask her. Don't worry, Charles. I can handle myself around Eve. She's not interested in me anymore. Not in that way. You have nothing to fear."

Charles looked very sceptical.

"Okay, nothing to fear is a bit of a bold statement, but I

assure you, even though some part of her still loves me, she doesn't *want* me. I would pick up on that. Give me some credit." He sensed Charles relax. At least a little.

"Fair enough, sir. And you know I always trust your judgement. With Eve, it's just…difficult. You have a history together. She hurt you. You hurt her. I don't trust her. I don't know if I ever will again."

"To use your words, fair enough," Tristan said with a smile. He stretched his arms above his head and tried to stifle a yawn. "I think I don't hear anyone in the room anymore. Which means Roy has finished explaining and hopefully sent everybody home. God, I'm exhausted."

"We should all try to get some sleep. I'll see if we can wrap up for the night." Charles opened and closed the door.

Tristan could hear him talking to Roy but didn't bother to focus on the conversation outside his bedroom. He sat down on the bed and turned on the telly. Reaching for the remote, he switched it to the cameras in Catherine's apartment. One showed her living room, one her bedroom, one faced her hallway, and another the reception of her private practice. That one was dark except for the emergency exit light. He clicked the bedroom frame to full screen. She was asleep, but her nightstand lamp was still on. She looked so peaceful. He wished he could feel that peaceful. No, he wouldn't tell her until it was absolutely necessary. He would try to keep her peaceful as long as possible. He just kept staring at the screen. Somewhere in the back of his head he felt like a peeping tom, but the rest of him was so blissfully at ease, he pushed that part away. It'd been a long time since he felt this relaxed. He felt his eyes getting heavier. The last thing he registered was someone coming into his room and pulling off his shoes.

TUESDAY

And why is it you think I look different, Tristan?"

Tristan carefully weighed his answer. Not that it would help. Eve could listen to his every thought. Still, he did think she looked different. Why was that? Though he was no mind reader, Eve had always been easy to read. To him, anyway. She'd never hid her emotions from him. So that had to be it. She was hiding something. Of course, she was always hiding something. They all were. Not from him, though. He saw the corners of her mouth twitch, trying to hide a smile. She pushed back her hair. It shined like black silk. She was wearing black leather trousers and a lilac top, highlighting the colour of her eyes even more than usual. Eve knew how to turn heads. Men and women alike. And heads had been turned when they'd entered the Espresso Bar.

"Perhaps I should rephrase my thoughts. It's not that you look different. We both know you're still gorgeous. So I guess you *feel* different. I don't suppose you'd care to elaborate?"

Eve looked at him through her lashes. "Thank you, darling. You flatter me. How do I feel different then? I'd really like to know. I must say, I was pleasantly surprised by your invitation. We haven't had coffee together in such a long time."

"We had tea this week, Eve," he reminded her.

"Oh pooh. Hardly the same and you know it," she said. "We rarely go out anymore. I miss it, you know."

"No, you don't."

Eve stared at him. He felt her annoyance rise to the surface. About what, though? Annoyance that he didn't believe her or that he saw through her? He couldn't tell. That was what was different. He could always tell. It made him feel off balance.

He didn't like it.

"What if I did? Miss it? Would you oblige me, Tristan, or would you turn me down?"

Tristan sighed. "Do you really want to have this conversation, Eve? Here?" He lowered his voice. "Let's be honest with each other. You don't want me back, nor I you. Do I feel attracted to you? Yes, I probably always will. Unfortunately, we don't bring out the best in each other. You know that even better than I do. So why play this game? Do you really want to go down that road again?" He watched her face carefully. She still felt slightly annoyed, but there was something else as well. Sadness, mixed with, what exactly? Jealousy? He looked around in the National Gallery's Espresso Bar. Nobody was paying them any attention.

"No, you're right. I do not. Want to go down that road, I mean. Besides, I guess you're into blondes now, aren't you, Tristan?"

Catherine. She was jealous of Catherine. Well, he hadn't seen that one coming. In hindsight, he probably should have. Eve didn't like to share. Anything. And he hadn't felt anything real for a woman since their time together. So she knew. She'd picked up on something in his thoughts. He really should be more careful. Then again, what was the point if she would put her full focus on him? His thoughts weren't safe around her. Okay, maybe that was an exaggeration, but at least they weren't private. "Jealousy doesn't become you, Eve. Besides, what's it to you?"

She shrugged. "Nothing, I suppose. And I know very well I don't have any rights, thank you very much. I guess I'm just not used to coming second. I don't plan on getting used to it, either."

Tristan twitched when she continued.

"Oh please, stop worrying, Tristan. I'm not going to hurt the girl. Don't insult me. The world doesn't revolve around you, anyway. Who knows, I might be more into blondes now as well."

She grinned like the proverbial cat that ate the canary. It made him uncomfortable, but he decided to let it go, for now. They had more important things to worry about and he needed her cooperation. And her skills. He was running out of options and Eve was basically his last resort to discover anything useful about that blasted painting. He knew he couldn't really trust her, but he also knew she'd been quite pleased when he'd asked for her help and insight. Eve liked to be of importance. Why, he would never understand. They didn't come more important with what she could do, in his opinion. Eve could hardly be described as insecure. Not by anyone who knew her professionally. There was something underneath that cold, witty facade of hers, though. He'd felt it plenty of times when they were still together. Not that he ever really got through to her. Not all the way. Still, he'd probably got closest to actually knowing the real Eve.

"Yes, I dare say you did, love," she said with a sad smile, stirring him out of his thoughts. "Now can we stop with the psychoanalysis? I believe you were in need of my assistance."

"I'm sorry, Eve," Tristan said, and he meant it. "And yes, I do need your help. There is a painting in the gallery I need you to see. People are going through a lot of trouble to keep us from finding any solid information. Whether they are connected to Alan or not has yet to be decided, but at least one person was murdered over this painting. It's Peruvian and shows a corn field in Urubamba Valley. The painting's known as *Sacred Valley of the Incas*. I don't suppose Alan might have mentioned something about Peru or the Incas?"

She looked at him with thoughtful eyes. "No, he has not. I do know, however, that Alan has a great interest in the occult. He dabbled himself, you know. He was quite vocal on the matter. Proud even, I believe. The Incas were known for their, let us say, special abilities? The painting might be special. Obviously, you're not thinking of its financial value."

It wasn't a question and Tristan nodded to confirm her train of thought. She leaned forward across the table.

"Hmm...so something else then. Something worth killing for. Well, my dear, I must say, you have my undivided attention. I do like an intriguing puzzle. Why don't we go and pay this fascinating painting of yours a visit?"

"My thoughts exactly," Tristan said. He stood up to help Eve into a little black leather jacket and then walked over to the counter to take care of their bill.

* * *

Tristan sighed. Again. He was starting to lose his patience. Fast. He looked at his Apple Watch. More than twenty minutes. Eve was still staring at the painting. Tristan made a tutting noise at the back of his throat. She made no response that she'd even heard him. When they'd first arrived, she'd approached the painting from different angles, making a humming sound every now and again. At one point, she'd even said "fascinating" without any further explanation. He tried to give her as much working space as he could without raising any eyebrows from the guards, who showed little interest in them fortunately, but he could feel his own patience slipping. *How long can you stare at one bloody painting?* Just when he thought he would burst out of his skin, Eve turned around. Her eyes looked glazed over. She shook her head, apparently to snap out of whatever it was she needed snapping out of.

She walked towards him and gracefully sank down on the bench. "Well, my dear, you do know how to pick them. That painting is definitely special. I've never seen anything so full of life."

He shifted slightly so he could see her face, meanwhile keeping his body relaxed, like they were having a normal conversation about a painting. "Interesting. Full of life, how? In a 'the artist really made the painting come to life' kind of way or in a 'the entire Trojan army is about to burst out' kind of way?" He could feel her smile before he actually saw it.

"I wouldn't go that far, but yes, the latter. There's something in there. It's whispering, but I can't understand what they're saying. It's distorted. I think…I think it might function as a portal, Tristan." She took one look at him and then refocussed her eyes on the painting in front of them.

"I don't like the sound of that, Eve. I don't like it one bit. Does it feel dangerous to you?"

She tilted her head. "I'm not sure. It could be. I think it might depend on the person. I find it very interesting that someone like you can't sense anything." She lowered her voice even more. "That alone tells me it's not attracted to special powers, so it must be attracted to something else."

"It might depend on the powers, though," he muttered to her. "Maybe there's nothing to feel, just to hear?"

She shook her head. "No, that's not it. Well, that's not entirely it, at least. It might respond to certain powers, I'll grant you that, but I still think it's more attuned to certain people. Or maybe not even plural. Maybe it's attuned to just one person?"

"Alan, you mean?"

She smiled. "I was actually thinking of Catherine."

Tristan sat up straight. "What do you mean, Catherine? What made you say that?"

"Like I said, I can't actually understand what it is I'm hearing. It's feels primal and even, dare I say it, elemental?"

His eyebrows furrowed. "Oh!" He didn't quite know what to say. "How do we find out?"

"I'd suggest you try the easy way and propose a trip to the museum. I'm sure she would love to go with you." Her voice sounded just a tad sarcastic.

He shook his head. "Too dangerous. We don't know what it will do or trigger. If it is, indeed, attuned to her, which I'm not quite convinced of." Before Eve could respond with a biting remark, he continued. "I don't doubt what you're sensing,

Eve. I'm just saying we can't afford to take any chances. We have no room for error." He stopped talking. His phone was buzzing in his pocket. As he took it out, he read Roy's message with Eve looking over his shoulder.

SHE'S AT THE PORTICO ENTRANCE OF THE FREAKIN'GALLERY. GET THE FUCK OUT! R

They both stood up at once. Eve linked their arms together. "Come, darling. Let's go over to the next wing, shall we?"

Tristan smiled at her, seemingly completely at ease. The security guard nodded to them. Tristan nodded back and saw Eve give the guard one of her dazzling smiles. Once they were out of his sight, they moved to another level. Tristan was attaching his in-ear piece. "Where is she, Roy?"

"Her coat is moving towards the Sunley Room you just left where the Peruvian collection is exhibited."

Eve halted beside him. Tristan looked at her with a bewildered expression. "What are you doing, Eve? Could we please keep moving?"

She shook her head. "Don't be stupid. This could be our chance. She's here. She's going to see that painting. She has no clue who I am, and I intend to keep it that way. Let me go back. Who knows what we'll find out."

"Absolutely not! Out of the question, Eve."

"Be reasonable, Tristan. I won't have to be anywhere near her. I could just be in the same room. That's plenty of space to pick up on her thoughts, and my hearing is also pretty good."

He still didn't like it, but curiosity gave way. "If anything happens to her, Eve…"

"I promise to protect her if necessary. Okay? Can we get a move on now?" She tapped her foot impatiently.

"Fine. Hang on." He fished another in-ear piece out of his jacket and gave it to her. "Hook her up, Roy."

Two seconds later he heard Roy's voice reply. "Done, boss."

Eve rolled her eyes. "So much for the trusting me part. Oh,

don't trouble yourself, Tristan. I'm a big girl. Well, ta-ta, love. See you in a bit." He watched her till she turned left around the corner.

Tristan decided to walk through the seventeenth-century paintings wing and move towards the learning gallery. There he could take the lift down to level zero. He could not risk bumping into Catherine. Then again, it would take him several seconds to get back here if something did go wrong. *Stop it, for God's sake. There's a reviver with her in the room. How much more protection do you want for her?* He pulled himself together.

"She's here," he heard Eve's voice whisper in his ear.

He knew that was probably all she'd be able to say. As Eve obviously appeared to be alone to anyone else, it would seem pretty strange to have her talking out loud. He sighed. Giving up any amount of control was not his strong suit, so he tried to appeal to his patience and common sense. He pretended to be interested in one particular painting. He didn't even know what wing he was currently visiting. Not five minutes had passed, however, when he heard Roy's voice again.

"Okay, she's moving, boss. So is Eve, by the way," Roy said in Tristan's ear.

"What? Eve, no. You get back here this instant." Tristan was fuming. She could blow their whole operation.

"Oh, don't have a heart attack. They're going for coffee in the Espresso Bar. I'm simply following to see if I can find out anything useful. You're welcome to join me for another cup, of course, but somehow I don't think you'll do that."

Tristan could hear Eve's heels clacking on the floor and could practically feel her sardonic smile. "If you screw this up for me, Eve, I swear to the gods…"

"Yes, yes, yes, you'll hunt me down and unleash all your empathic abilities on me. Oh wait, you already did that once. Stop being such a baby and just trust me. You remember trust, don't you, Tristan?"

"Fine," he growled, making a woman with her daughter look at him suspiciously. He took out his phone and held it to his ear not to raise any more suspicion. Not that the woman showed him any particular interest. She probably just thought he was some kind of freak. He felt the whole weirdo vibe rolling of her. He tried to give her a reassuring smile but was pretty sure he failed. He was too tense.

He decided to go for a cup of coffee himself but gave the Espresso Bar a wide berth and went straight for the National Café on the other side of the building. Phone still to his ear, he said, "Be sure to give me a heads up if Catherine decides to move this way, Roy."

"Acknowledged, boss. She's still in the Espresso Bar. I think Eve is sitting two tables behind her, judging from the distance between them. She should be fine."

Tristan heard an approving hum from Eve in his ear. He huffed. *Yes, but who would be fine? Catherine or Eve?*

"Would you like to look at the menu, sir?" the waiter asked.

"No, just coffee, please."

Two coffees later and repeated affirmations from Roy that they were still at the Espresso Bar, he received word that Eve was on the move again. A second later, he listened to her voice.

"I assume you want to leave immediately? Where should I wait for you?"

Tristan had made sure his bill was already taken care of. He stood up and took out his phone again. "Hello, dear. Just get to the car. I'll be there in five minutes." He could hear her smirk as he left the café.

"Okay, darling. I'll wait for you there. Don't be late. Kiss, kiss."

When Tristan got to the car, Eve was leaning against it, perfectly at ease. Tristan unlocked the car and opened the door for her. His manners compelled him to ask if she'd been waiting long.

She smiled at him. "I arrived maybe a minute before you,

so no. Thank you," she said as he held the door for her and got inside the car. "The company?" she asked. "My office, perhaps? I think it's best if you ask Charles and Roy to come along. If you tell them what I tell you, there will be too much room for interpretation."

Tristan couldn't fault her logic. Even though he knew Charles wouldn't like it to be in the same room with her, he was also sure he wouldn't make a scene. "Sounds like a plan. Roy? Can you and Charles come over to the company? Eve's office."

It was quiet for a few moments when Roy answered. "Sure thing, boss. We'll be there in fifteen, twenty minutes tops."

Tristan parked the car when they arrived at Battersea Park, home of the company. Eve entered her six-digit code and after they both passed the iris scan, they went up to level four. Unlike her working space, Eve's office was above ground and full of light. Tristan's own office was on the other side of the building with the other mental powers. Mind reading was also a mental power, obviously, but her ability to revive people back from the dead took precedence and so Eve had an office in the same wing as their employees with physical abilities. Tristan knew she sometimes invited people to her office instead of her working space to lure them into a false sense of security. As he entered her office, he remembered why. It was a very pleasant space to be in. Fluffy sofas and an ottoman, off-white bookcases filled with books, both fiction and non-fiction and windows from top to bottom, providing a stunning view over London. One felt at ease here. Even Tristan could almost forget she could read his every thought.

"Mm, yes, it does help," she replied. "Only when they're not aware of my powers, though."

"Do you think it works like Legilimency?" he asked.

She looked at him with a confused expression. "Legilimency? Oh, from the Harry Potter books, you mean. Well, yes and no. What I remember from the books is that a Legilimens has to focus on the person. Eye contact helps, for instance. I can hear people's thoughts from across the room. I do not have to focus at all." She looked thoughtful. "Then again, there are some similarities. For instance, our kind always knows when I'm reading their thoughts. So, that's the same. I suppose you could say that normal people, Muggles, don't." She smiled. "Funny, Tristan. I'd never given it much thought."

"How do you know people don't know what you're doing?"

She shrugged. "Same way you do, I suppose. Do people know you're reading their emotions? No, they don't. It's the same with me. They just don't feel it or sense it. Unless I screw up. Then they get suspicious."

Tristan smiled. "I can't remember you ever screwing up. Not on this account."

She returned his smile. "I was speaking hypothetically, love. Ah, Roy and Charles are in the hallway. Charles is practically leaping with joy to see me."

He had to admire the way she handled all this. She knew both Charles and Roy weren't exactly fans, but so far she hadn't made one rude or negative remark.

"Hello, boys," she said as she opened the door for them. "Do come in."

Roy gave Eve a tentative smile and Charles gave her a very curt nod before walking straight over to Tristan. He saw Eve discreetly hiding a grin. So far she was behaving awfully grown-up about this whole situation. Tristan had to give her that.

"Shall we sit down, gentlemen? No need to be uncomfortable. I'll order some tea, and we can get started. I suggested to Tristan you should be here as well. If I tell him my story and he tells you his, there will be a lot more room for interpretation and we wouldn't want that now the stakes are so high, would we?"

They could hardly disagree with that statement and Tristan nodded his approval for her to continue.

"Right. So after Roy kindly warned us—in his own sophisticated manner—to get out of there, we decided to make use of the moment and see if I could learn anything from Catherine. So, I went back to the Sunley Room and kept my mind and ears open." She walked over to the phone on her partner desk and picked it up. "Could I get tea for four in the Oak Room, please? Yes, thank you." Eve put down the receiver and joined them, taking a seat next to Roy, across from Tristan and Charles. "First thing you should all know is that Catherine had a nightmare about this very painting." She paused, looking at Tristan, giving him time to respond to that.

"What are the odds?" he said.

Roy shifted in his seat. "Slim to none, I'd say."

Eve nodded. "I agree with Roy. Chances that this is just a coincidence are practically non-existent, in my humble opinion. To be more exact, she had a nightmare about Alan and the painting featured in her dream. As far as I understood it, he was standing in the middle of the cornfield and he pulled her inside the painting. It scared the living hell out of her friend, though she did her best to make light of it and comfort her."

Tristan could feel she was adding that last part for his benefit. She looked at him with an intense expression. "She has feelings for you. I think you should know. Apparently, in her dream, Alan was very angry with her for giving up on him. She suspected he somehow knew of her feelings for you and wouldn't be too happy about that fact. Miss Winter agreed that he probably wouldn't be too happy about her having feelings for anyone else. By the way, she moved them several paces back from the painting the moment Catherine told her about the dream. I could hear in her mind that she was really worried something would happen. Later in the conversation, Miss Winter checked out the painting herself and made a joke to reassure her. Something about him being hard to miss. She never let her near the painting again, though. She's quite protective of your client."

"Our client," Tristan corrected her. "You're a part of this team now, Eve, whether you like it or not. Besides, we could really use your powers full time on this." He felt a wave of uneasiness coming from Charles sitting next to him and resisted the urge to sigh in frustration. He loved Charles very much, but his overprotectiveness could become a bit annoying at times.

She gave a stiff nod. "If you like. I'm not sure your friends agree with you, though."

Obviously, she'd be listening to Charles's every thought, and Tristan could only imagine what those thoughts would be. They would not be very flattering, in any case. "I'm sure every single member of my team understands the importance of what we're trying to do here, Eve. And your help would be greatly appreciated." Tristan felt resignation from Roy and the same from Charles, though the latter was mixed with a touch of shame and his heart went out to his oldest friend. After all, Charles was just looking out for his well-being. A grim smile from Eve told him that she'd picked up on those last thoughts, and mentally he apologized to her. A knock on the door announced the arrival of the tea. Charles, obviously trying to set a good example, stood up to get the door. The caterer looked relieved that Eve had not answered and gladly left the cart in Charles's capable hands.

Roy took one look at the cart at said, "Ah, excellent, macaroons!"
Tristan shook his head. He heard Eve laugh.

"Well, you certainly haven't changed one bit, Roy."

Roy had already stuffed one macaroon in his mouth and was in the process of taking a bite out of his second one. "Nope," he said with his mouth full, which led to Charles making a loud groaning noise.

"Could you at least pretend to have some manners when ladies are present?" he said. Tristan felt he was determined to make up for his untrusting attitude towards Eve.

Roy shrugged, slouching on the sofa with yet another macaroon. "What's the point? It would be a total charade for her benefit. Besides, Eve knows I'm a pig. Isn't that right, Eve? Be a dear and pour me some tea?"

Eve rolled her eyes but got up anyway. "Yes, my dear, I know. I'm so glad to learn you feel completely at ease in my presence." Her voice dripped with gentle sarcasm.

Roy grinned. "Knew you'd appreciate that."

Eve handed Roy his tea and proceeded to Charles. "You still take two lumps of sugar, Charles?"

Charles nodded and accepted the cup she handed to him. "Yes, miss, thank you."

Tristan accepted his cup of mint tea from her. *So she'd picked up on that as well.* He sighed, but he saw no mockery in her eyes. After she sat down, he continued, "So I assume that wasn't all?"

"Hardly. That was only the beginning. She knows he was, or is, interested in the Incas, but no more than that. To her knowledge, he never went there, but she wasn't hundred percent sure on that. She said Alan visited a lot of sacred places during his life, so she could be wrong about this or just uninformed. It matches with my own findings of him. Alan shows a lot of interest in the occult. More than your average wannabe Wiccan or pagan or whatever it is they call themselves nowadays."

"Jeez, Eve, don't be sure a pure-blood. Some of those pagans have some kick-ass powers," Roy said in a teasing voice.

"Yes, well, then they aren't exactly pagans, are they, Roy? Only they probably don't have a clue. We recruit young pagans all the time. Some turn out to be the real deal."

"The real deal for us," Tristan gently corrected her. "Being a pagan is more a way of life to most of them. I don't think it actually relates to having powers or not." He thought of Catherine and her friends. Maybe they'd consider themselves pagans. He wasn't sure.

"True." She nodded curtly. "But there are those who claim to have them. You have to admit some of them are quite silly, calling themselves high druid or what not. It's nothing more than a status symbol."

Tristan sighed. They would never agree on this. "Let's agree to disagree then. Back to the subject at hand. I think we can safely say that Alan is most certainly no wannabe."

There were varying agreeing sounds. "What else?" Tristan asked.

"Well, that was almost everything in the Sunley Room. There was one more interesting detail. She said she still wasn't seeing the big picture. It was something Alan said to her in the dream. Any thoughts on that?"

There was a moment of silence.

"He knows, right? That the world is about to end, I mean," Roy asked.

Eve nodded. "Yes, he does. I was instructed to tell him as soon as I revived him. He took it pretty well." She hesitated. "I knew he would try to escape. I heard it in his mind."

"What?" Three voices cried out.

Eve held up her hands. "You already know this, remember? For your information, I did inform the company of this fact. I was told not to worry about it. I'm pretty sure they let him escape. It's the only explanation I can come up with to him making it out of the building alive. I was supposed to revive him and I did revive him, but believe me, that was no picnic. He must have been in pain. Terrible pain. My best guess is he has a part to play, just like the rest of us. I'm sure of it."

Tristan remembered the terrible pain part all too well. Eve had saved his life once, after all. He hoped he would never need her services again. "Question remains, which part?" Tristan muttered.

"What you're really asking is, is he on our side or not?" Eve said to him.

"I can't imagine anyone not being on our side if they know what's coming," Charles said quietly.

"Well, unless he's one of those people who wants the world to end. You know, move on to the next stage and all that crap," Roy chipped in.

Eve shook her head. "Alan didn't strike me as the destructive kind. Well, not to himself, in any case. Power won't do you any good if there's nothing there to have power over."

"Good point," Tristan said to her. "So for now let's assume he's not on a path to help destroy us all, but as Charles phrased it, on our side. Still begs the question, where is he and what is he up to?"

"But if he really is on our side, shouldn't our focus lie with Catherine? I'm just saying you're spending an awful lot of time trying to track him down instead of finding out if Catherine even has a chance of defeating this thing."

Her voice held no accusation, but there was something underneath her tone as well. Was she questioning his motives? "She's a true elemental. She can command all of the elements at will. There's no one in this world who'll stand a better chance than her." His voice sounded slightly irritated.

"My point, dear Tristan, is that we know that, but does she?"

He noticed both Roy and Charles were looking slightly uncomfortable. Were they also questioning his motives? Better to explain. "You have your orders, Eve. I have mine. One of them is to keep Catherine in the dark as long as possible. I have to trust the company knows what it's doing. It's the only thing we have."

He saw Roy relax immediately. To his friend, orders were orders and he considered the company all-knowing. Charles, however, was obviously still having doubts. Though he probably wouldn't voice them. Experience had taught him the company wasn't always right. Tristan knew he'd learned that the hard way. "I may not like it either, and yes, I do share your concerns, Eve. Every night I wonder if we shouldn't be out there, practicing with Catherine to see if she's really up for this, but I can't afford to have this whole operation backfire. So, it all comes down to this. Do we trust the company's orders, yes or no?"

Eve pressed her lips together but nodded. "In the end, I would have to say yes."

"Same goes for me, boss." Roy said.

Charles looked at him. "I may not always trust the company implicitly, but I trust you, sir. So that's a yes from me as well."

"What about you, my dear?" Eve asked.

Tristan heard the teasing tone in her voice, but her eyes were deadly serious. "To quote you, in the end yes."

"Do we know anything more about their relationship? Why and how did it end, for example?" Roy asked.

"I don't exactly know why it ended, but I'm pretty sure how," Eve said to them. "She and Miss Winter were talking about her final confrontation with Alan. I think she's responsible for his vegetative state. From what I heard and picked up in her mind, it was self-defence, though. They had a fight in front of some construction building. Which Miss Winter saw, by the way. She blames herself for not being there. She was in New York. She's a seer, right?"

Charles looked at her. "Yes, she is."

"Apparently so is a woman named Meg," Eve continued. "She saw Catherine's death."

Tristan mulled over that bit of information. "She doesn't have the seer vibe, but it's hard to tell just from a picture."

"Maybe she just sees death then?" Charles put in.

"Or something more macabre?" Roy added.

A chill ran down Tristan's spine. "You mean like Alan, a master of death? Wouldn't that be nice? Two walking time bombs. I certainly hope not. Before Alan, I'd never even heard of a master of death and I would dearly love to believe there isn't more than one."

"Well, that makes two of us, darling. I can live with one counterpart, I guess. More than one would leave me quite put out." Eve smiled at him. "I think it's also important to mention that she said he was a great and wonderful man for many years, before he went—her phrasing—bonkers." She took a pause. "Catherine feels she doesn't have the best track record when it comes to men. Her father died due to unforeseen circumstances, and she couldn't save him. Obviously, this left her devastated. Then she met Alan and he went—again, her phrasing—Lord Voldemort on her. So even though it was implied they had quite a few good years together, something must have changed along the way. Miss Winter was convinced he would have killed her. I think deep down Catherine believes that as well, though her mind told me she desperately wants to believe something else. Anyway, she acted and defended herself. I think it's fair to assume that's how he ended up in the mental hospital."

Tristan gave her a warm smile. "That's valuable information, Eve. It was a good decision to follow her, I shouldn't have doubted you. Thank you."

Eve nodded coolly, but he could feel she was pleased.

"So what have we learned?" Roy said. "Catherine had a nightmare about the mysterious painting that has kept us all busy. The nightmare was about Alan dragging her inside the painting. To what purpose, we know not. He was displeased with her, whether or not this relates to her feelings for you, boss, is also unclear. He mentioned she still wasn't seeing the big picture." He looked at Eve for confirmation, who nodded. Roy took a breath and continued.

"Leah, Miss Winter, is very protective of Catherine. She wouldn't allow her near the painting again and checked for signs of Alan herself. This could possibly stem from her feeling guilty for not being there the last time Catherine faced Alan.

It stands to reason she will do anything to save Catherine. This could work to our benefit. Miss Winter saw Catherine's death. So did Meg, another one of Catherine's illustrious friends, which makes her a seer, someone who can see death or could possibly be another master of death."

Tristan smiled. This was why Roy was on his team. Besides being the best shot at the company and an excellent planner, he had an almost photographic memory. As long as Tristan had Roy around, he was always sure he wouldn't miss anything.

"Alan had or has a great interest in the occult, including the Incas," Roy went on, "but we have no confirmation of him actually having visited Peru where said painting comes from. Catherine is vulnerable when it comes to dealing with men she cares about. This is essential, boss, particularly for you. We already noticed you have to give it your best to get her to like you. All her defences will be up." Roy stood up to serve them all another cup of tea and stuffed the last macaroon in his mouth.

"Last, but not least, Alan knows about the asteroid. Eve picked up on his plans to escape, notified the company, and was ordered to do nothing about it. We discussed this and are, at least for now, inclined to believe our people know what they're doing. Was there anything else we need to know, Eve?" he finished.

"Just trivial stuff, but I'll mention it just in case. Catherine is busy with preparations for a cocktail party. They're going to a tasting at a caterer. They're also going to visit Holywell. She mentioned something about her spare harp strings running low, so I assume it's a harp shop."

Roy was already googling it. "Yep, it is," he confirmed.

"Her favourite band is Placebo, just in case you didn't know this and want to start a conversation about music," she said to Tristan. "She performs for her family and friends. I saw a memory of her playing for her family with her mother singing along. She's shy about performing in public, though.

Apparently, she composes as well because Leah," she nodded her thanks to Roy, "asked her if she would be willing to write something for Placebo. Which was a definite no, by the way. Hence the shyness. I think that's about it."

Roy nodded. "I'll add that to her file, boss. Perhaps you should brush up on your Placebo. They're not really your thing, but it's always good to appear to have something in common. You both play, so make use of that as well. She's coming over to hear him play tomorrow," he added for Eve's benefit.

"I'm sure she'll love that," Eve said without any malice. "I know I did. You play beautifully."

"Thank you," he said, "but I'm grossly out of practice. So besides brushing up on the nasal sounds of Placebo—if I remember correctly—I'd better brush up on my cello as well. Wouldn't want to make a complete fool of myself, now would I?"

They laughed in unison.

"Eve, thank you for your input and your hospitality. Do you mind if I leave a tracker and an in-ear piece here? That way I know where you are and you can contact us at any given moment," Roy said, looking at her.

She nodded her approval. "That's fine, Roy. Leave the tracker on my black leather jacket. I'll make sure to wear it when I go outside."

He made short work of that while Charles stood up to help Eve put everything back on the tea tray.

"Thank you, Charles," she said to him with a soft smile.

He nodded. "Miss."

Roy walked over to Tristan. "Are you staying here? Your meeting with the people from NASA is in one hour. Do you want me to tag along?"

Tristan checked his watch. "The boss will be there as well, but you're good at interpreting things, so yes, I think that might be best."

Charles, who heard their conversation, came over. "Then

could you drive Roy home, sir? At least, I assume you don't want us and all our lovely gadgets there tomorrow when Miss Catherine arrives." He was smiling.

Tristan returned his smile. "Seeing computer screens showing her own apartment would raise a certain amount of suspicion, yes."

"I'll return to the apartment with Tristan, clean up any suspicious stuff, and then I'll grab a tube. It'll be fine," Roy said.

Tristan shook his head. "I can drop you off afterwards, Roy, no problem. Okay, that's settled then. Eve, would you like to join the meeting?"

She shook her head. "Very gallant of you to ask, my dear, but no, thank you. You know I hold no interest in that overgrown piece of rock. I just need it to go away, and there's very little I can do about that, even with my so-called infamous powers, so I'll leave the boring stuff to you lovely fellows."

"If there's anything you do need to know about it, I'll make sure somebody fills you in," he promised.

Eve nodded her approval. "Works for me. Well, it was good seeing you boys. It has been too long. Let us hope it's not the last time."

"I'm a firm believer in second chances, miss," Charles said to her.

Eve let out a bell-like laugh. "Oh, dear Charles. I'm not, actually. I'll take what I can get, though, so I'm glad you're such a forgiving person. One of us has to have all the goodness and let's face it, that has always been you, Charles." She gave him a genuine smile.

Charles mumbled something incoherent with a faint blush on his cheeks. Tristan gave Eve a soft hug before leaving the office and saw Roy give her a quick wave. Tristan thought that there might be hope for them, yet.

Back in the hallway, they were careful to discuss their meeting. Not everyone in the company knew what they knew.

Level six and up had full access, of course, but other than that, only Tristan's team contained members below level six who knew what was really going on. After all, he'd been a level five himself until this mission. They accompanied Charles back to the lobby. Charles was going to visit Catherine's friends, mother and uncle to see if there was anything out of the ordinary.

"I'll keep my in-ear piece active, Charles. If there's really something of importance, I'll walk out of the meeting," Roy said to him. Charles nodded.

"We'll catch up later, Charles. I know I don't have to tell you to be careful, but please do. Remember, there is a killer out there. We don't know his or her motives."

"Always, sir. I'm more worried about you and Miss Catherine. So please be sure to heed your own advice. And on the topic of killing, please be careful what you say to these NASA people. Remember one of their board members went missing. He was found dead last week. Rumour has it he went blabby and the Pentagon was involved."

"Yikes!" Roy said. "Lovely organisation. Thanks for the heads-up, Charles."

Tristan nodded to him before Charles left the building after saying goodbye to the receptionist.

"Want to grab a sandwich in the cafeteria before we have to pretend we're very knowledgeable on this whole asteroid thing?" Roy asked.

"Sounds like a plan. Just say very little and nod intelligently as often as you can. That's what I'll be doing," he said with an evil grin. "Let's hope they brought their 'asteroids for dummies' version. I hope they realize were not exactly astronomers."

"I think the boss will go for either an MI5 or a military approach. Do they even know why they're here again?" Roy asked.

"I'm sure they haven't got a clue. They know more about this thing than we do, Roy, but as far as they're concerned, nothing can be done about it. Not in the military or scientific sense of the word. I'm pretty sure they would have a hissy fit if they knew what it is we do."

"Better keep them in the dark, then," Roy said with a grin and held open the door of the cafeteria. "Come on, boss. My treat."

* * *

"Tristan, I'd like to introduce you to Dr. Robert McMillan. Doctor, Tristan Visconti. He leads our special forces team," Tristan's boss said to him. *Thanks for the heads up, boss. Special forces team it is.* A bearded man wearing glasses shook Tristan's hand. He had a friendly face. Tristan estimated his age somewhere in his late sixties or early seventies; it was hard to tell. "Dr. McMillan runs the Spacewatch Project in Arizona," Tristan's boss continued.

"Thank you for coming over on such short notice, Dr. McMillan. I'm sure you're a busy man," Tristan said to him, letting go of his hand.

"Yes, well, your MI5 can be quite persuasive, Mr. Visconti. If you don't mind me saying, I can think of few things that would be more important than this. If I can give you any information that would benefit your team, I'd be a fool not to, wouldn't I?"

Tristan was spared having to answer as his boss introduced him to someone else.

"And I'm sure you remember Dr. Michael Watkins from NASA's Jet Propulsion Laboratory, JPL for short."

"Of course," Tristan replied, holding out his hand. "I wish we didn't have to meet under such unpleasant circumstances, Dr. Watkins."

Dr. Watkins shook his hand. "Mr. Visconti. I'm not sure I can tell you anything you don't already know, but I thought it might be helpful to have a fresh pair of eyes and ears present. Which is why I recommended the presence of Dr. McMillan's team. They couldn't be here last time as their attendance was required at the Pentagon. I'm sure you understand."

"Of course." Tristan looked around the room. "Ladies and gentlemen, if you'd be so kind as to take your seats. I'd like to get started." He quickly introduced Roy as his second in command, felt the approval of his boss and continued.

"I'm sure you're all wondering why you're here, and I'm afraid I can't give you any details. I'd like to start, however, with expressing my gratitude you took the trouble to fly out to London once more. This meeting, I'm sorry to be blunt, is on a need-to-know basis. Which means, were going to pick your brain and explain very little in return. If anyone has any problems with this, ethical or otherwise, you should speak up now." He looked around. "Yes, Dr. McMillan?"

"I don't have any objections giving you information. I wouldn't have come here if I did. And I understand you can't tell us everything. It would, however, help me to get a clearer sense of what it is you do. Your boss said you lead a special forces team? Are you military?"

Tristan shook his head. "No, we are not, though I understand why you would reach that conclusion."

"But you do have a licence to kill?"

Tristan hesitated. He didn't sense any anger coming from Dr. McMillan, only curiosity. And he could certainly understand where that curiosity came from, in light of recent events. McMillan was of a certain age and would have been there back in the day when NASA had employed a lot of pilots from either the air force or navy. Today's employees weren't that keen on military involvement, some might even be pacifists. He couldn't tell into which category the doctor fell. He could tell, however, the good doctor hadn't been too happy about his meeting with the Pentagon. Dr. McMillan might not be NASA, but he'd probably known the man who had turned up dead. He focussed on his boss's emotions for a second and felt nothing but approval. "We do, Doctor, but in the sense one of your police officers has a licence to kill. We, too, are here to protect and to serve. We do not interfere in warfare." Which was true. They would go after certain individuals involved in warfare, but the company was not political in the general sense of the word.

Dr. McMillan nodded. "Good enough for me. What do you want to know?"

Tristan looked at Roy, who understood this to be his cue.

"Well, we know the path of the asteroid…," Roy started.

"Predicted path," Dr. Watkins interrupted. "Even if there is a hundred percent certainty it will hit the earth, there is always room for things we cannot think of."

"Predicted path it is, Doctor," Roy continued. "Now, I'm certainly no astronomer, so you'll have to forgive me if I get things wrong. Last time we spoke extensively about the Palermo Scale. I understand there's also a Torino Scale. Before we continue, I'd like to know if there's any difference?"

"We don't really use the Torino Scale," Dr. Watkins answered. "It's more for the public, as it is more basic in its use. However, the Torino Scale categorizes the impact of NEOs."

Tristan looked at Roy. "Near Earth objects," Roy whispered to him. *Right.*

Dr. Watkins smirked. "Yes, near Earth objects. I'm sorry. Occupational hazard."

"And in what category would this asteroid fall into, according to the Torino Scale?" Tristan asked.

He saw Dr. Watkins exchange a glance with Dr. McMillan. It was the latter who replied.

"Somewhere between a nine and ten." He took off his glasses and pinched the bridge of his nose. "What you have to understand is that this wasn't supposed to happen in our lifetime, if ever. The last time we had an impact like this is when the dinosaurs roamed the earth. That impact was estimated at one hundred million megatons. In other words, a ten on the Torino scale."

"Okay, that sounds very threatening, but can you put that into perspective, Doctor?" Roy asked.

"Well, the biggest hydrogen bomb ever exploded, the Tsar Bomba, was around fifty megatons. The 1883 eruption of Krakatoa was the equivalent of roughly two hundred megatons. Does that give you any perspective?" he answered.

There was silence in the room for a few seconds.

"Umm, yes, I suppose it does," Roy answered quietly.

"What we really need to know is the essence of this particular asteroid," Tristan cut in. "How many elements does it contain? And how would that relate to percentages if you would divide them into earth, air, fire, and water?" Tristan asked. He felt his boss's tension but decided to ignore it. They really needed to know this. Catherine would have to know how to direct her elements.

"I'm not sure how that would be relevant, Mr. Visconti," Dr. Watkins replied. "We already gave all our information about this particular asteroid to the Pentagon. As we all know, it all came to nothing. I doubt there's anything you can do the Pentagon cannot. The asteroid is still on course. We're monitoring it twenty-four-seven. When we're not able to see it, our colleagues from the other side of the world take over the wheel."

"You'll have to trust that it is relevant to us, Doctor." Tristan fixed him with his most serious stare and also reached for his empathic abilities to add a wave of importance towards the man.

Dr. Watkins turned to one of his team members. "Could you display the asteroid, Janis?"

A blond woman Tristan remembered meeting before stood up, bringing along her laptop to the podium. Roy immediately offered his assistance and hooked her up. Tristan took advantage by discreetly checking his phone. *There. Janis Chodas, Director for Office of Safety and Mission Success. Check.*

"Thank you," she said to Roy. After a few clicks, the asteroid appeared on the big screen. It was a black and white image with craters splattered across the surface of the asteroid. It could have been the moon if not for the more oval shape, Tristan thought, but what did he know about astronomy? Next to nothing. He'd learned more these last few weeks than in his entire life.

"Shall I start by just adding one hundred percent of earth?" she asked with a smile.

Both McMillan and Watkins nodded. "Yes, we'll take it from there," Dr. McMillan said.

"So it's basically just made out of earth elements?" Tristan's boss asked.

"Almost entirely, yes. We wouldn't call it earth though, as we work with the periodic table to define elements. Currently, we have defined one hundred and eighteen elements." Janis looked at Dr. Watkins, who appeared to try to convey something to her. She cleared her throat. "However, I understand you just want to divide them into what most people would consider the four basic elements?"

Dr. Watkins nodded his approval to her and she continued. "This particular one could contain small traces of water due to collisions with comets. Same goes for oxygen, which would be air, obviously."

"Any thoughts on percentages?" Tristan asked her.

Janis looked over at Dr. Watkins.

"No more than two or three percent would be my guess. Bob?" he said and looked at Dr. McMillian to confirm his estimate.

"I agree. No more than a few percentages."

Janis filled in three percent for each element, leaving ninety-four percent for earth.

"Just to be sure," Roy asked, "no fire at all?"

"Not in the asteroid itself. Once it hits our atmosphere, though, there will be plenty of plasma. Out of the four elements, fire would come closest to plasma. Although it will be more like a magnetic, ionized kind of fire," Dr. McMillan replied.

"Yes, about that, is there any way a person could see it before it hits the atmosphere?" Roy asked.

"Of course, there is but not to the naked eye. I would be more than happy to help out with equipment, and I'm sure Dr. Watkins would as well." He looked over to Dr. Watkins, who nodded his approval.

"That's very kind of you, but it won't do us any good, I'm afraid." Tristan immediately felt a wave of intrigue coming from several sides. *Yes, I'll bet that little detail will leave them with questions.* Not that he was at liberty to explain. Catherine couldn't afford to divide her attention between some instrument and the actual asteroid. She would need all her focus on the real deal. When the time came, he would just have to give it to her straight. He was dreading that particular conversation already. "Back to the earth part, what are we talking about specifically?" Tristan asked.

"It has the most similarities with Vesta, one of the more famous asteroids. Well, among astronomers, at least," Janis said. "Like Vesta, it has a nickel-iron core, an olivine mantle, and a basaltic crust."

Janis went on to explain in detail. After two hours, they put an end to the meeting, which was just as well, as Tristan thought his head would explode.

His boss thanked them all for coming and had arranged taxis to drive them to a five-star hotel near Heathrow. Tristan was shaking hands. When he said goodbye to Dr. McMillan, the doctor pulled him aside.

"I'm not sure what it is you think you can do, Mr. Visconti, but I can see you really think we still have a chance. If there's anything I can do, you let me know, okay? I don't need to know what it's for or why you'd need me or any of my equipment. Just ask."

"Thank you, Doctor," he said.

"Please, call me Bob."

Tristan smiled. "Only if you'll call me Tristan." He decided to take a chance. "Do you believe in a higher power, Bob?"

Dr. McMillan frowned. "You mean like God? I'm not sure how to answer that, Tristan. As a scientist, I was taught to question everything. Having said that, I also learned it's often not about what we can think of, but the things we cannot. So, I would have to conclude I would be open to possibilities."

"Then I suggest you hold on to those possibilities, Bob," Tristan said with a smile before turning his head to shake the hands of Dr. Watkins and his team.

* * *

"That's about it, boss. Anything else you want out of sight?" Roy asked. Tristan thought he looked like he felt. Drained.

"No, Roy, thanks. You and your team take the night off, okay? I know I am going to."

Roy simply nodded, gathering his own stuff. "Sure thing, boss. I'll keep an eye on her, of course."

Tristan smiled. "Knew you would. See you tomorrow, Roy."

Tristan decided to go over his files again and started with the one they had on Alan. They had gathered a lot of extra information since they had acquired his full name. Compliments of Eve, of course. Tristan had to acknowledge she'd been quite helpful so far. He skipped over Alan's more colourful actions and focussed on the personal stuff instead. Born an only child. Belgian father, Dutch mother. Moved to the Netherlands permanently when he was five years old. He went to primary school skipping two years. Same with secondary school. Had started college at the age of fifteen and graduated magna cum laude at the age of nineteen. Double major in psychology and sociology. Lectured at the University of Leiden and Amsterdam, which is where Catherine must have met him, as her file stated the same university.

They must have had at least a couple of good years together. The darker side of Alan didn't start until seven years after

Catherine's graduation. Some burglars had broken into his parents' house and badly hurt his mother. Tristan could easily draw his own conclusions from that. Someone with Alan's powers and a situation like that were ingredients to a very dangerous recipe. And Tristan was no stranger to the taste of power.

Alan had also published quite a few articles and even a book during his years at the Amsterdam university. *Mind Control—Fact or Fiction?* Tristan snorted. Wouldn't that make for an interesting read. He browsed through the box they had on Alan and smiled when there was a copy of the book at the bottom. *Cheers, Roy!* He'd been reading for about an hour when he felt his phone vibrate.

Something's up. They're all gathering at Meg's place. They know about Alan's escape. You want me to come over? R

"Bugger!" Tristan said out loud. He scrolled down to Roy's number and hit the connect button.

"Hi, it's me. How is she? Anything else we know?"

"Not much. I intercepted Leah's call to Deborah, Sue, Romy and a few others. Something happened which led Catherine to call the hospital. I don't know what triggered that decision. Anyway, they know he's awake and left the proverbial and even literal building. Taking what Eve said this afternoon about Miss Winter into account, I think it's safe to say she was angry as a nest of Blast-Ended Skrewts."

"I bet she was." Tristan sighed. "There's no point in coming over, Roy, unless they're going out to try and track him down. As long as she stays put, I'm sure she'll be fine. Keep track of their phones and let me know when she's back home, though."

"Will do. Try and get some sleep, boss. You sound like you need it."

Tristan smiled. "I'll try, Roy. Thanks for letting me know."

"Always, boss." And they disconnected.

Tristan connected his phone to the charger, went to the kitchen to put a pizza in the oven, and sat down on the couch to continue his reading. It was after midnight when Tristan finished his book and he still hadn't heard anything from Roy. Knowing he would text him if anything happened, Tristan took his phone with him to the bedroom and turned on the sound as loud as it would go.

He fell into a state of slumber and almost hit the ceiling when his phone went off. A little after three his phone showed him as he looked to see what Roy had texted.

She's back at the apartment. All the others back home as well. I'm sure she's fine. Go back to sleep. R

Tristan smiled. Roy knew he would be worried about her state of mind. It would be a bit weird for him to go up and knock on her door in the middle of the night, though. That would certainly put him in her "weird and possibly dangerous" book. He sighed. Ugh. He hated things out of his control. He punched his pillow and tried to get some sleep. Tomorrow he would try to weasel it out of her.

WEDNESDAY

Tristan had woken up way too late, feeling a bit grouchy. He seldom had such a restless night, and it had left him in a bad mood. He knew why. He was starting to develop *feelings* for Catherine. He never got involved with his clients. Oh sure, sometimes he would pretend, to get them to do what he wanted, but he never actually cared. He couldn't afford to care. And what was so special about her, anyway? Yes, she was very powerful, and he wasn't blind. She was extremely beautiful. Somehow, though, he felt the need to protect her. To watch over her. Last night was a perfect example why this was a very slippery road. He'd been unable to sleep because he wasn't sure she was safe. Naturally the welfare of his clients was important to him. And with it, their state of mind—to a certain extent—but he never got involved. Not personally. Not emotionally. It was dangerous. It left room for error, way too much room. And they couldn't afford error. Not with this case. All their lives depended on her being able to do this. On his team enabling her to do this. Tristan had also had a nightmare about Alan, which he blamed the book for. If Tristan was fair, it had been quite an interesting read, but it had also left him with an uneasy feeling. He knew why, of course. It hit too close to home. And the dream had ended with him switching faces with Alan. He hated symbolism.

He went through his morning routine on autopilot. Thankfully, the shower helped clear his head. So he had feelings for Catherine. Big deal. He could handle that, right? She was supposed to trust him. Having feelings for her would only add to his credibility. Besides, it'd been a long time since he'd felt anything like this. Wasn't he allowed a few moments of happiness himself? Not that he was unhappy, but lately he couldn't help but feeling he was missing out on something. He'd noticed the same vibe from Eve. She was lonely. And so was he. He made a grumbling sound. *Oh, get over yourself, you whining little sod.* He would never want Eve back, but he'd meant what he said about her looks. Eve was in her early forties and very beautiful. He understood how she felt, though. Always a part of something big, but never of something small, something intimate. At least, they'd shared that. He would treasure it.

Turning the shower as cold as it would go, he felt his body respond. After a few seconds, he'd had enough and turned it off. Reaching for a towel, he rubbed himself dry and twisted it around his waist. He decided to set the dinner table instead of using the living room. The kitchen gave him a homely feel and he guessed Catherine would like it as well. One look at the clock told him it was little after twelve. Having the apartment to himself made him a lot quicker than usual. Catherine would arrive in an hour. Plenty of time to tune his cello. He hadn't played it in weeks, not since his last assignment in Prague. He lovingly stroked the instrument, a gift from his parents, before tuning it. After it was tuned, Tristan spent more than half an hour playing it, completely forgetting the time, wearing nothing but a towel, lost in his music. He'd missed playing. His head snapped up when he heard a buzzing sound.

Hope you're ready, boss. She's on her way. R, his phone read.

"Fuck!" Tristan ran to his bedroom, threw the towel in the hamper and put on some jeans and a T-shirt. He didn't have time for anything else. So much for being prepared. Thankfully his hair was almost dry and he quickly pulled his fingers through to smoothen it when the bell rang.

"Someone ordered lunch?" Catherine said with a smile as he opened the door for her.

Oh, thank God. She was dressed casually as well. Actually, she looked quite girly with her two braided pigtails. He took the picnic basket from her and gave her a quick kiss on the cheek. Friendly neighbours could do that, right? "Come in, Catherine. Perfect timing, I just finished setting up the dinner table." He walked towards the kitchen to empty the basket. *She'd even thought to bring chilled wine. How sweet!* "You didn't have to bring the wine, silly."

"Hey, when I provide lunch, I provide it well, "she said, looking around.

He caught her staring at the two black and white pictures hanging on the living room wall. She was pleased with what she saw. He could feel it. He would have given anything to have Eve's powers right now, though. It would be so helpful to actually be able to read her mind. Scary as well, probably, but helpful. He wanted her to feel at home and at ease. "Go ahead, look around," he said with a smile. "I don't mind. I'll get these on a plate and then pour us some wine while you have a peek." He was rewarded with a bright smile. He was pleased to see she took him up on his advice.

Catherine's home was more in tune with all the elements, though he'd only seen it on camera, while his home was probably more rural or outdoors. He'd always liked the colours of the earth, it reminded him of home. Home being Italy. He still had a soft spot for his homeland and his parents' place especially. He put the plates on the teak dinner table and waited for her.

"Lunch is ready," he said. She came over and he pulled her chair back before taking a seat himself. "Well? Do you like it? Does it resemble my soul?" he asked with a slight smirk.

She laughed. "Your soul, no less? I don't know about that, but it does suit you. In a way. I'll admit, I didn't expect such a country vibe, but I really like it."

He smiled. "Ah, you forget my Italian roots. My parents live in the country, and I guess I'm always trying to recreate a bit of home. I'm glad you like it, though. Lunch looks delicious, by the way, Catherine. Thank you."

"Do you want me to explain what's what? The quiche has a salmon and prawn filling with little capers and olives as well. The salad is smoked salmon with homemade croutons, anchovies, cherry tomatoes, some baby leaf spinach and some rocket. I added a bit of freshly made horseradish mayonnaise as a dressing. I hope you like it."

He was sure he would. It smelled amazing. Raising his glass, he simply said, "I love fish. *Bon appétit*, Catherine. May this be the first of many homemade lunches."

She laughed. "I'll bet, but you'll be doing as much cooking as me, mister. It's your turn next time." Their glasses touched in toast, and then Tristan sliced up the quiche.

"Did you have a busy day yesterday?" he asked. He was dying to know what had happened last night and was curious to find out how far her trust would go. Would she tell him anything? He felt her hesitation, but there was something else as well. Eagerness? Perhaps he wasn't the only one who needed information.

"Not busy really. It was a rather interesting day, though. I said I knew quite a lot about empaths, right?"

Tristan nodded at her questioning look. "Yes, you did."

"Well, that's mainly because my ex was an empath as well. I met Alan at college. He was one of my professors. Yes, how cliché, I know. We didn't start dating or anything, however, until way after my graduation. Um…look, this isn't going to be a light story. Are you sure you wanna hear this?" she asked, playing with her glass of wine.

She felt embarrassed and troubled. How terrible. He wished he could take away her pain, so he leaned over to take hold of her hand. "I have a feeling I should feel honoured you trust me enough to tell me this, Catherine. So yes, I'd like to hear the story and what happened yesterday because obviously it has something to do with Alan." He felt a rush of gratitude coming towards him and was secretly pleased she'd decided he could be trusted with the insights to her personal life.

"Thank you, Tristan, just for being you." She gave his hand a slight squeeze before she let go and then took a sip of wine. "Alan, being older than me—he's about your age, in fact— knew what I was or what I could do from the beginning. He's not only an empath, you see. He can also control death, and he recognises other people's gifts."

Tristan filed that last bit of information. They hadn't known about that.

"A dangerous combination," she continued, "but I thought he was the world. He taught psychology, which must have been a walk in the park for him, as he could tap into anybody's mind to see what their current problems were and deal with them accordingly. I was very interested in how the human mind worked, and so was he, although perhaps for different reasons. Those first years, though, Alan was a really nice guy. Yes, he did use his powers a lot, but always for the benefit of others. That changed after people hurt his family. He wasn't there, and I think he never forgave himself for that. Anyway, he became very bitter after that. As much as I tried to be there for him, he wouldn't let me in anymore. He started drinking and blocked my powers, so I couldn't heal or ground him, and we grew further and further apart. He just wouldn't listen and accused me of being too soft. Alan did a lot of things under the guise of 'for the greater good.' I let it go on for far too long, may the gods forgive me. I wasn't ready to give up on him. It would be my failure, you see. At least that was how I saw it back then."

She gave him a small smile. Tristan's heart went out to her. That must have been terrible. He understood the feeling of being responsible all too well. "Did he take people's lives?" he asked softly, not to scare her off.

She took a deep breath. "Yes. Yes, he did, though how

many I don't know. Let's just say I didn't stick around to find out. I know about one, at least. That's when we had our first big fallout. The man was a child molester, and he'd murdered a little girl in our block. Alan knew her and went completely mad. Don't get me wrong. I understand the impulse. I do. A part of me wanted that guy dead as well. The Netherlands isn't exactly known for its severe punishments, so he probably would have been out again after ten years or so. That was what Alan screamed at me, you see. 'Do you want such a man back on the streets in ten years?' Of course, I didn't. But taking a man's life...just like that? It felt so wrong. I never went to the police, though. He told me it was clean and quick. Being a master of death, Alan can just stop your heart. He never had a sadistic streak as far as I could tell. I moved out of our apartment that night. He was out with some of his friends, and I stuffed all my clothes in a suitcase, grabbed some personal items, and moved out. I stayed at Lee's for a few weeks until I got my own apartment. We did keep in touch, but he didn't trust me anymore, not completely, anyway. He knew I didn't approve of his way of life, even if I didn't turn him in. One day, though, I learned of his plan to kill another human being. Some kind of industrial hotshot. I'm sure he'd done a lot of bad things, but I couldn't let this one go. Not in advance. With the child molester, I only found out afterward, but I couldn't claim plausible deniability with this one."

She gave him a weak smile. He felt very uneasy. How much blood was on his hands? He didn't consider himself a violent person, but in his years with the company, he'd been responsible for more than one death. God, how could Catherine ever approve of him? "You stopped him, didn't you?" he said, making sure his face showed a lot of sympathy. She let out a small cry that upset him even more.

"Stopped him? Yes, I guess you could say that. Actually, until yesterday I thought I'd destroyed him. I set to prevent him from killing that man, and we ended up facing each other. I felt death coming toward me, and I was sure I was going to die. In a moment of total panic and pure will to survive, I let go of all the elements. They manifested all at once and smashed into him. He immediately fell to the ground. I rushed over. He was still alive but didn't recognise me, or himself for that matter. I anonymously called an ambulance and told them I was just passing by. They took him away. I later learned they'd transferred him to a mental hospital. He's been there ever since. Until a month ago, that is, because I called them yesterday. Apparently, Alan is fully recovered and left their institution a month ago. Where he is now they could not, or would not, tell me. Well, that's pretty much it. Some story, huh?"

She leaned back, obviously waiting for some judgement on his part. She wouldn't get any from him. He'd never felt so sorry for anyone in his life. And she still blamed herself; he could feel it. Silly girl. Tristan would have kicked Alan's ass ages ago. Probably not the best thing to tell her, though. "Again, thank you for your confidence, Catherine. It must be difficult to share this with me, though I'm glad you did. I won't say I understand Alan's choices because I really don't." *Well, part of him did, but that wouldn't do at all.* "It does, however, give me a better understanding of your reluctance towards empaths." He raised his hands in defence as he could feel a wave of denial from her. "Hang on. That's not me being judgemental, just an observation. And you have every right to be on your guard. I would be as well, and I can tell if I'm being lied to. You don't have that advantage, so I understand. Really, I do. What does concern me, however, is his present whereabouts. You called the hospital for a reason, I assume? So you must have thought you saw him, or didn't you?" He already knew this, of course, but he was really hoping she could tell him something substantial about that blasted painting. It was driving him crazy. And he didn't like the thought of Alan pursuing Catherine. No, Tristan didn't like that at all.

"You're right, of course. I did have a reason," she said to him. "Though I haven't seen Alan. Not in real life, anyway. I dreamed about him. Without going into detail, when I visited a gallery with Leah, the dream suddenly became very real." *Great, that makes two of us.* "The girls became paranoid and bullied me into calling the hospital. Good thing they did, as it turned out, because their paranoia was justified. But really, he could very well be in the Netherlands. As far as I know, Alan has no connection to England."

Really? Was she that blind? He looked at her. "Besides you, you mean." Okay, now he'd made her uncomfortable. That was perhaps a bit much, but he did need her to be on her guard.

"Yes, well, there's that," she said. "I don't think Alan's on a killing spree or out for revenge."

She laughed, though he could hear it was tinged with nerves. "I know he has every reason to hate me, but somehow I don't think he does. This might be naïve of me, I know. Anyway, I'm sure Leah would, um…"

She'd stopped speaking abruptly, and Tristan felt her embarrassment. *Yes, that was a nice slip of the tongue.* "See him coming?" he finished for her with a grin.

She looked at him a bit sheepishly. "You knew?"

Well, they had been ninety-nine percent sure. He smiled. "No, but you just confirmed my suspicions."

She rolled her eyes. "Just peachy. What is it with you and honesty?"

He grinned at that and refilled her glass. *She felt compelled to tell him the truth? Surely that was a good sign?* "Well, I don't know, Catherine dear. Perhaps it's my stunning appearance. It might be my killer smile, which makes you spill the beans. Or perhaps you just trust me?" He gave her his most genuine smile.

She laughed. "Odd as it may be, I think you're right. I do trust you, but I've trusted the wrong people before, you know," she finished rather sadly.

"I promise I will never lie to you, Catherine." *And he wouldn't. Not anymore. He was done with the lies.* She deserved better from him. "I may hide the truth from you at times because of my work or because I think you're not ready for certain things, but I will never lie to you." *Not again, anyway.* "You have my word." She believed him. He could feel it and in response he could feel his muscles relax.

"Thank you, Tristan. That means a lot to me."

"Are you worried?" he asked, really wanting to know.

"About Alan, you mean? No, not really. I was quite upset when I found out he was out of the hospital. Okay, I was in hysterics, to be honest. The more I think about it, the more relaxed I am about it. Tristan, can I ask you something?"

"I thought you knew. You can ask me anything. If I can't, or if I don't want to answer, I'll tell you." He would. No more lies.

"Well, the past few weeks have been somewhat crazy. World wise, I mean, not just Alan. I mean, let's just say Leah and I aren't the only ones with, um…gifts. Have you, as an empath, noticed anything different lately?"

Tristan sat up straighter. *Well, the world is about to end. That might have something to do with it.* He actually considered telling her right at that moment. *No, she wasn't ready. Or maybe he wasn't. Anyway, now was not the time.*

"Look, if you can't say anything, I'll understand. Just forget I asked," she said.

He felt embarrassment from her again and couldn't suppress a laugh. "Will you, for once, be patient and let me think for a minute before you jump to any conclusions? Good grief, woman!"

"Sorry," she mumbled.

Apparently, she wasn't blessed with the virtue of patience. "I think I know to what you're referring. This has been a crazy year at the very least. Something big is just around the corner, but the outcome isn't set yet." *Yes, that would do nicely.* "Do you believe we create our own futures, Catherine?"

She looked at him in surprise. "Of course, I do. The future isn't set. It's what we make of it."

Tristan nodded. "I agree. A lot of people don't, however, and they're starting to lose hope. Maybe that's what you and your friends are picking up on. Despair is a very strong emotion. It can be felt by more people than just empaths."

"Losing hope?" she said. "I think you're right. That's what we've been picking up as well. Question remains, why? Oh, and does going to New Zealand sound familiar to you?"

What the hell? Did Leah see something? He gave Catherine a rather piercing glare. "Why do you ask?"

She shrugged. "It might be nothing. Lee saw lots of important people in New Zealand, that's all. I thought it might make more sense to you."

Of course, it made sense to him. New Zealand would have the best chance of survival, if there was any such thing. They would be moving heads of state and other selected few to an underground facility on Friday. This was something he could not share with her, though, without revealing the rest. "Does any of this make sense?" he, therefore, replied. "New Zealand is a beautiful country. It's an island. It's the farthest from England." *Take the hint, Catherine!*

She stared at him. "You know something."

It wasn't a question. He felt a flash of annoyance that he couldn't tell her more. "Yes," he confirmed her suspicions, feeling quite unhappy.

She frowned. "I'm sorry. I shouldn't push. I know you're being as open as you can. This has to do with your job, right?"

He just looked at her.

"Okay. So farthest from England. You're obviously trying to tell me something. England will be in danger? Is that why they're moving important people to the other side of the world? That's it, isn't it? Something's going to happen. And you're here to help? Or to prevent it from happening? Oh, my God, is your client the prime minister?"

He burst into a laughing fit. *The prime minister? Well, in all fairness, he could see how she would reach that conclusion, but still, she couldn't be further off.* "The prime minister? Whatever made you say that? I can honestly say my client is not the prime minister, Catherine. Though I agree with you the poor woman could do with some help. Alas, it won't be from me or my company. As for the rest, no comment." He smiled at her.

She smiled as well. "Okay, I'll take that as a yes, then. Can I do something about it, Tristan?"

I truly, truly hope so, my dearest Catherine, but what to say? He gave her another smile. "I think you should continue doing the things you already plan to do."

"Hmm…well, tomorrow we're having the cocktail party. That will go through as planned. And Samhuinn is coming up, of course, this Saturday."

Yes, he'd heard about that. She pronounced it differently than he'd expected. It sounded like sa-win. Naturally, being an elemental, Catherine would have an interest in nature religion. "Yes, I've heard some people mentioning it as well. I'm sorry. I'm not really familiar with nature religion. What exactly is Samhuinn?" He'd googled it, of course, but there were many interpretations and he was interested to hear her thoughts, although he could practically feel Eve rolling her eyes at him being seriously interested in something like this. Catherine smiled, however, and he could feel her enthusiasm.

"Samhuinn is the beginning of the new year," she began. "It was, at least, for certain people many years ago. We still treat is as such. It's also the darkest festival we celebrate because it's connected to death and rebirth. The veil between our world and the otherworld is at its thinnest, and we honour our ancestors during our ritual. We actually open a gate so they can celebrate with us. To me, Samhuinn is also about the goddess, in her form of the Cailleach, the dark one with her burning cauldron. Many fear her, but she always makes me feel safe and loved. Somehow being in the arms of death can be very comforting. We write something down on a piece of paper. Things we want to let go of, and we burn that in her cauldron. It's also a time to set in motion new things or wishes, to let it simmer, so to speak, so it can seed at Imbolc in February."

"So it's quite a powerful time, this Samhuinn?" he asked. That could work to their benefit.

"Oh yes, I'd say the most powerful. Even more so this year, as we'll be under a blue moon as well. It only occurs once every few years and almost never on Samhuinn. It's the second blue moon in a month, you see, and it's been a while since we had it on Samhuinn. So 2020 is turning out to be quite a special year for us." She smiled.

Good. The more power, the better. "And you always celebrate the festivals?" he asked.

"Yes, always. Sometimes not as extensively as we would like to, but we always celebrate. It's our way to keep connected to the turning of the seasons, I suppose. Being an elemental, it's very important to me personally. It'd feel like neglecting nature, and thereby myself, if I forego the festival celebrations."

"London must be a difficult place to celebrate nature, though," he said with a frown.

"Why? Because it's not bursting with trees or it lacks a coastline? We have plenty of parks, you know. Besides, honouring nature is inside us. A beautiful place helps, yes. I suppose it's the same for Christians. Having a beautiful church can be very helpful to put you in a certain state of mind, but you can find God everywhere. I think it's more about sharing the feeling and experience of community than a place of power or worship. That's my personal opinion, of course," she said, giving him a small smile.

He liked her reasoning and concluded he might actually be

interested in nature religion himself. Something to look into, if there would be a future for them to look into, though he had been brought up a Catholic. "I think I can relate to that feeling. So, you do celebrate outside? Don't you worry about other people seeing you?"

She laughed. "Why? Afraid we're going to be locked up?" She grinned. "Sometimes we do have people watching us. We are, however, careful in choosing a place for ritual work. And most people are just interested. We've never had any disturbances during a ritual. Afterward, though, sometimes they come up to us and ask what it was we were doing because they felt moved. That's a good thing, I think, and we always explain what it is we do. Do you know London Fields? Just beyond Shoreditch?"

He nodded.

"That's where we'll be this Saturday. Most of it is still abandoned. They opened the front side again, but the back is still closed to the public."

He raised his eyebrows. *Not so much a law-abiding citizen, then.* "And I suppose you don't consider yourself a part of the public?"

Catherine grinned. "On the advice of counsel, I decline to answer."

"Hmm…indeed. Good thing I don't represent the law then, Catherine."

She stared at him, obviously a bit spooked. After all, he hadn't given any particulars about the company he was working for. For all she knew, he could be representing the law. The spooked sense faded, though, and was replaced by something akin to cockiness.

"Good thing, indeed," she answered him rather mischievously.

Yes, definitely cocky. After their lunch, she insisted they'd do the dishes together. He objected but finally gave in and was pleased to notice they both enjoyed sharing such a domestic task together. He made them a pot of tea and then filled a plate with chocolate biscuits. He smiled to himself remembering Roy's words. *There are two kinds of women, boss. Women who like chocolate and complete bitches!* He was pretty sure Catherine liked chocolate. He noticed she'd moved to sit on the couch in the living room, her feet tucked underneath her, her boots thrown carelessly to the ground. She looked very much at ease. Tristan liked having her here. He poured her a cup and was glad to notice she immediately went for the biscuit.

"A promise is a promise, of course," Tristan said as he went to pick up his cello. "Is there anything in particular you'd like to hear, Catherine?"

"Do you compose as well?" she asked.

"As a matter of fact, yes. Would you like me to play something for you?"

"Very much. I mean, I love some of the masters, but if you compose yourself, I'm dying to hear it."

Tristan sat in front of her so she had a good view and then played. It was harder to concentrate on his playing having her this near and sensing her every emotion, so he closed his eyes and tried to focus on the emotions of the piece instead. As the music came to an end, he opened his eyes again and gave her a shy smile.

"Wow," she said. "Just wow. There's no other word for it. That was beautiful. It's like air or something, so soft and swift. What's it called?"

"L'aura è tua messaggera," he said with a smile. He was pleased she truly liked his music.

"That sounds wonderful the way you pronounce it, but I have no idea what that means."

"It means the breeze is your messenger. I wrote it when I first arrived in England. I lived in Brighton for quite a while when my father was still working here, and I just loved the smell of the ocean. The way the breeze catches your face.

That first night when I was sitting in my new room, still surrounded by unpacked boxes, I wrote this piece. It's still one of my favourites. I'm glad you like it. I had a feeling you'd understand."

She gave him a warm smile. "I love it. And I wasn't far off either with my air comment. Can you say it again?"

He laughed. *"L'aura è tua messaggera,"*

She closed her eyes for just a second. "It really is a beautiful language. I won't try to repeat it. I'm sure it'd sound even worse than your Dutch," she finished with a grin.

Little minx! He raised one eyebrow. "Really? You were laughing pretty hard as I recall, or my memory must be faulty."

She looked at him with an innocent expression. "I have no idea what you're talking about. Now shut up and play something else for me."

Oh, dear. He was putty in her hands. "Yes, ma'am!" And he played again. After she'd finished her third cup of tea—and the biscuits were almost gone—he was allowed to have some tea as well. He put the cello in its stand and then sat next to her on the couch.

"It's a beautiful instrument, Tristan. It looks very old. Not that I know much about cellos."

He took a bite of his chocolate cookie and looked at her. "Well, it is very old. Eighteenth century, to be exact. It used to belong to an Italian composer Nicolò Paganini." He was amused to see she almost choked on her tea.

"Eighteenth century! Like what, it's a Stradivari or something?"

He smiled. "Not or something. It's a Stradivari, yes. Why, Catherine, you look positively shocked?"

She looked a bit embarrassed. "Yes, well, I mean…they're supposed to be really expensive. I mean, I certainly don't own an Erard harp, and they're not anywhere near the prices Stradivari go for."

He decided to tease her a bit and looked to her with an

understanding smile. "Aahh, you think I stole it." She looked even more embarrassed. How cute!

"No! God, of course not. They're really rare, aren't they?"

Time to put her out her misery. He nodded. "Yes, they are. I believe there are only about sixty left in the world. I consider myself very lucky to own one. It's my most treasured possession. It was a gift from my parents. Obviously, I come from money. Though they always taught me to take care of myself. When they moved back to Italy a couple years ago, my mother wanted me to have something that would remind me of them, so they bought me my cello. I had one, but it had a little accident when I was thirty-eight." God, he'd felt like James Bond on that particular occasion. His first cello had actually saved his life! Little accident indeed. He'd been on a mission in Russia. Terrorists had been planning to take the life of the president, and Tristan had been undercover as part of the orchestra. They'd been told it would be a one-man job. They'd altered his cello to contain a sniper, which had actually saved the life of the president. They hadn't known about the second attacker, though. When Tristan guided both cello and president to a safer location in the building, the man came out of nowhere and Tristan had hit him with the cello with all his might. It had knocked the man out cold, but the cello had been beyond repair. "Needless to say I was quite moved when they left me with this beauty." He lovingly touched his cello.

"I can well imagine. I'm glad your parents gave you such a magnificent reason to play again. Damn, I hope my harp doesn't get a complex should they ever meet."

He laughed. She was funny. She talked about objects like they were alive. He liked that. "I'm sure my cello will be on his best behaviour."

When it was almost five, she got up. "My, look at the time. We've been chatting away, haven't we?"

He looked at the clock. He hadn't even noticed time passing

by. As far as he was concerned, she could have stayed all night. "We sure have, but if it were up to me, you'd stay here all day." *Yes, day was good. Nice and innocent. Never mind what he really wanted to do with her. Wow, best not think about that particular fantasy.* He walked to the kitchen to retrieve her picnic basket and give her time to adjust. He noticed his last remark had left her quite confused. She'd followed him to the kitchen.

"You'll see me tomorrow, though," she said.

Right, the cocktail party. No fun though. Loads of people to divide her attention. "True, but then I have to share, and I hate to share, Catherine. I just have to make sure you won't forget about me, won't I?"

Before she could respond, his mouth was on hers. As her eyes fluttered closed, he pressed his tongue against her lips, demanding access. She opened and let him explore. A small groan escaped his throat as she gave in to him. Her arms went up around his neck. In one fluid movement, he pressed her against the wall. As their kiss deepened, she softly nibbled on his lower lip, which drove him crazy and made him pull her even closer, not caring that she could feel his arousal. He could feel her elements closing in on him like molten lava when he took possession of her mouth again. Heat, passion, pure gold. It was like nothing he'd ever experienced before. Once he finally let go of her, he was pretty sure he felt the way she looked. Slightly dazed and he noticed her lips were rather swollen. She was magnificent.

"I'm pretty sure I'll remember your name tomorrow," she said, her voice a bit shaky.

"Good," he replied with a smile, but he knew his eyes would show something more serious. "See you soon then, my elemental." He handed her the picnic basket. "You'd better go now before I decide to keep you here."

She laughed a bit nervously. After a few seconds, he felt her pulling herself together. She gave him another smile before she stepped into the lift. When the doors closed, he leaned against the wall.

"Christ. Now for a really cold shower!" He went back inside and closed the door.

* * *

Tristan didn't like the look on Charles's face. He looked way too smug. They were sitting in Tristan's living area, away from the noise in his work room, where Roy's team was busy analysing Charles's info from that afternoon. Not that Catherine's family appeared to be in any immediate danger. Charles had reported nothing out of the ordinary.

"Another cup of tea, sir?" Charles asked.

Tristan gave him an annoyed look. "Yes, by all means, why not. Let's have some more tea. And do at least try to hide that grin, Charles."

Charles grinned. "Yes, sir."

"I don't understand what's so funny about this," Roy said from behind his laptop. "Sure, we need her to trust us and I'm not blind, boss. She's really gorgeous. I can see that. Just... don't get too involved, okay?"

With Roy, the job always came first. It had been that way for Tristan for many years as well. Something inside him was changing, though. He wanted more out of life. Something just for him. Sure, Roy enjoyed his one-night stands and with his looks he had no trouble finding a suitable lady to oblige him, but he'd never wanted something more permanent. It was one of the reasons why he was really good at his job. No attachments. Well, almost none. He was pretty sure Roy would take a bullet for him.

Charles was different. He'd actually been married until he'd lost his wife on the job. An assassin had gotten his wife instead of him. Tristan only knew her from photos and stories. His boss had known her, though. He'd described her as a warm-hearted woman. Very ladylike with a generous nature. Charles had been more carefree back then. After the incident, he'd become more introverted, the way Tristan now knew him. Also, his blocking powers had increased tenfold. His boss said this could happen after a traumatic experience. "Sometimes people lose their power altogether. Sometimes they increase. Why or how this happens, we still do not know. It's the one good thing that came out of this whole mess."

Charles had never looked at another woman, but he never gave up on the concept of love. Tristan knew Charles had high hopes of him finding true love. It was why it was so hard to stay annoyed with him. He knew Charles really meant well.

"Oh, do shut up, Roy," Tristan replied good-naturedly and saw him smile.

"Well, I think it's absolutely wonderful you had such a good time, sir. I really have a good feeling about Miss Catherine. Never you mind our cynic over there," Charles said, nodding in Roy's direction. He stuck out his tongue in reply.

"Just don't come crying to me when she breaks your heart," Roy said with an all-knowing expression.

"Miss Catherine would never break his heart!" Charles cried out.

"No. I might break hers, though," Tristan softly said to him.

Charles looked at him with a sad smile of his own. "Not on purpose, sir. Never on purpose. Hope is a great thing, you know. It's bigger than us. You hold on to that."

Tristan gave his shoulder a soft squeeze. "Thanks, Charles."

"Damn, those girls are persistent!" Roy cried out, a headphone dangling from one ear.

Tristan looked up. "What?"

"Deborah just called Catherine on her mobile. She's been checking up on Alan. Not that she found anything, of course, but she has Meg and Sue on it as well."

"Is she worried?" Tristan asked with a frown.

Roy shook his head and laughed. "No, not in the least.

She was eating ice cream through the entire conversation and actually sounded a bit bored. Well, it's good they're looking. They might think of something we don't, right?"

"Absolutely," Charles answered him. "Shall I make us spaghetti Bolognese?"

"Hell, yes, Charles!" Roy gave him a thumbs up before Tristan could respond, but Tristan smiled his approval to Charles just the same.

"How many are staying?" Charles called from the kitchen, indicating Roy's team.

"Just us, Gilly and Peter," Roy replied. On cue, the rest of the team quietly started packing their stuff and exited the apartment after they were done with a nod to Roy. Peter was Roy's second in command and Tristan assumed Roy had kept Gilly behind just in case they needed her abilities. Peter helped Charles set the table. Charles always made his sauce from scratch and had to shoo Roy from the kitchen three times. At length, though, they all sat down for dinner. Charles was quite a good cook and Tristan smiled as Roy was already on to his second helping. They were discussing the day and even talking about insignificant stuff, like what kind of movies they had seen. Roy was explaining to Gilly why she just had to go and see the latest Marvel movie. Tristan liked these domestic moments.

"Oh, speaking of which, I have the most excellent idea for our outfits tomorrow, boss," Roy said.

One look at his face told Tristan his friend was having way too much fun with this. He put his fork down. "Well, let's have it then."

"We're going as Holmes and Watson. You can be Holmes, boss. It's only fitting. And the best part, I can carry my gun as usual. Nobody would assume it's the real deal. Brilliant, huh!"

Roy was obviously very pleased with himself, but even Tristan had to admit, it was a good choice. Sherlock was at least a detective, so less pretending to be someone else. He was so tired of pretending. "Good choice, Roy. And how, pray tell, are we to obtain such costumes on such short notice?"

"Already got them, boss. Well, Gilly got them, to be fair. Knew just the place, didn't you, Gilly?"

Gilly looked quite shy to be spoken to directly in Tristan's presence but answered nonetheless. "Yes, a friend of mine owns a costume and party shop, so I picked them up this afternoon. Roy gave me your size as well, sir," she finished with a blush on her cheeks.

"That's very nice of you, Gilly," he said to her, giving her a warm smile. "Thank you."

"Oh, it was no trouble at all, sir. Glad to help out." She looked at him for a split second and dropped her fork. She dove under the table to retrieve it and re-emerged with a blush on her cheeks. She quickly stared at her plate again.

Tristan gave her a break by focussing his attention on the others. After they'd finished, Roy dug up some ice cream out of the fridge while Tristan made them all coffee. He was Italian, after all.

Around seven, Tristan decided to call it a night. Peter was checking up on the cameras while Roy was helping Charles to put everything in the dishwasher.

"She's leaving with Leah, sir," Peter said from behind one of the laptops.

Roy quickly came over to his side. "Pull up the conservation from a few minutes before, Peter." Tristan heard the video feed but didn't really focus on it.

Roy nodded. "They're going to catch a movie at the Odeon, boss. Nothing special."

Tristan nodded to indicate he'd heard him but was distracted by Gilly, who was looking out his window.

"Sir, isn't that Alan, the man we're looking for?" she asked, pointing to the street below.

Both he and Roy jumped to her side. "Go!" Tristan yelled. He barely noticed Roy grabbing his gun along the way, already down two flights of stairs, his heart racing. Tristan was fast, but Roy was even faster and he stormed out of the door, hitting the streets with Tristan hot on his heels.

"You take the left. I'll take the right," Tristan barked out at Roy. He looked up and down while he ran, searching for signs that Alan had climbed up or was hiding behind one of the cars. He passed the takeaway shop and scanned its customers. No Alan. Tristan didn't even bother enhancing his empathic abilities. They wouldn't work on Alan, anyway. Tristan and Roy met halfway on the other side of the block.

"Any sign of him?" Tristan asked, still frantically looking around.

Roy ran up and down their side of the building again, just to be sure. "None. Bugger! Can this guy become invisible or something?" He sighed. "Check on the Odeon?"

Tristan nodded grimly. "Let's go."

Roy informed Charles, who insisted on tagging along, of their plans as they might need his blocking capabilities, but Tristan overruled him. "No, Charles. I need you there with Peter and Gilly. Make sure they arrive home safely, okay?"

"Yes, sir," Charles replied, though Tristan knew he wouldn't be too happy about his orders.

Of course, they found nothing suspicious at the Odeon and no sign of Alan. "So much for our second wild goose chase," Roy said to him, his voice holding a touch of bitterness.

Tristan gently punched his shoulder. "Come on, Watson, time to give up the ghost. We'll catch him in the end. We always do."

Roy snorted. "All right then, Holmes. You're the boss. Well, I don't know about you, but I could really use a beer."

"Fine," Tristan said. "I'm buying. Though we'd better invite Charles over or we'll never hear the end of it."

Roy laughed but gave Tristan his phone nonetheless. It was

already connecting. They might as well enjoy the rest of their evening. Catherine obviously was, so he would try to as well.

* * *

"So, never?" Roy asked him. "Not once?"

"No, Roy, not once. Why? Do you make a habit of jumping out of airplanes?" Tristan laughed. They both were enjoying a pint of Guinness in The Wenlock Arms and were now discussing things they'd never done before but would still like to do someday.

Roy leaned back. "Oh, I don't know, boss. I would have thought with all your flying hours you would have gotten plenty of opportunity."

Tristan saw Charles shake his head in disbelief and smiled. "If I jump out of a plane, I should bloody well hope it's on my own terms, Roy, and not because my plane gave up the ghost."

They all laughed at that. "What about you, Charles? What's your guilty pleasure?"

Charles smiled and took a sip of his beer. "Guilty pleasure, no less? I don't know about that, but I've never seen the Northern Lights. I hope to before I leave this earth. Well damn, I'd better hurry up then, hadn't I?"

And they burst into another laughing fit. *Okay, we might have had one too many*, Tristan thought. He was sure they would pay for that in the morning. He tried to focus on what Roy was saying.

"That's still not something you'd like to do, though. It's something you'd like to see," he said, jabbing a finger at Charles's chest.

"True," Charles replied. "All right then, something I've never done but would like to do. Let's see…I guess I would like to play an instrument." He looked up when Roy snorted loudly. "What? I never had the opportunity to play. My parents were poor when I was growing up, and later in life I just didn't have the time." He looked at Tristan. "I always love to hear you play, sir. Yes, when we get through this, I might want to learn how to play the trumpet. I think it would suit me."

Before Roy could reply, Tristan smiled at him and said, "You should really do that, Charles. I think a trumpet would look great on you."

Roy put a hand on Charles's shoulder. "Yeah, it would, man. I'm just messing with you. You know me. Hey, I think instruments are cool."

Charles smiled. "You haven't told us yours, Roy. Or did you think we wouldn't notice? He's always trying to get away with that, isn't he, sir? Pumping us for personal information while revealing none himself. Well, no more, mister. Out with your darkest secrets."

Roy grinned. "Are you sure you want to know? I don't know if you older fellows can handle it?"

On cue, both Tristan and Charles harrumphed.

"Okay. I'd like to have a threesome someday. You know, just to experience it." There was silence. "See? I knew you putzes wouldn't be able to handle it."

Charles tucked his hand under his chin and looked at Roy. "No, that's not it. What's shocking to me is that you haven't had a threesome before. We actually took bets on that ages ago, didn't we, sir?"

Tristan just grinned. They took one look at each other and had another laughing fit. Roy took it in his stride, though. "Oh, fuck you guys. I'm buying another round." And he got up to get them another round of beers.

THURSDAY

Tristan softly closed the door to his boss's office. Well, that had gone well. Naturally, everybody was a bit on edge. Impending doom and all that would do that to people. Trevor was mostly in total control, though. Now, not so much. Their seers had picked up on something, but they couldn't tell what it was. Whatever it was, it wasn't decided yet. They could only see the future based on people's choices. As long as they didn't make them, the visions would be blurry. Like now. Tristan wasn't exactly sure what his boss had wanted from him. Everybody knew he was no expert on seers. He found the whole art of divination debatable at best.

In the office, though, Tristan had felt sure Trevor thought it was connected to Catherine and the asteroid and seemed frustrated with Tristan once he'd appeared to disagree. It wasn't so much that he had actually disagreed, as he'd tried to explain several times. He just didn't have anything substantial that would fit their suspicions. He had confirmed Leah was indeed a seer and that they were aware of them moving important people to New Zealand. Trevor had swatted those remarks away like an irritating, little fly.

"Yes, yes, they know. I heard you the first time, Tristan. Frankly, I couldn't be bothered. Is she happy? Feeling good about herself, full of confidence? We need her to be in a good place. I can't stress this enough!" His voice turned a bit hysterical at the end.

Tristan had assured him that as far as he could tell Catherine was currently quite happy with her life and developing feelings for him of a positive nature. His boss had relaxed just a bit after that.

"Good. Yes, that's good. You go now and make sure your team is all set for this party tonight. Can't believe people are out there having parties and whatnot. Oh well, better run along with you now." Trevor practically pushed him out of the door.

"Well, that was weird," Tristan said, standing in the big white hallway. He texted Eve.

Boss acting out of character. Noticed anything weird? T

He had just turned a corner when his phone buzzed.

I know. He's in freak mode! It's those blasted seers. Can't trust them for shit. Still in the building? Wanna go for coffee? I have news. E

Tristan looked at his watch. Sure, why not. He had plenty of time before the party began. And it wasn't as if they were any closer to locating Alan. Thankfully his team would not be involved with the big move tomorrow. They had assigned some less powerful empaths to keep them calm. A large group of important people was a guaranteed recipe for trouble. Too many egos. He'd seen it more than enough and was glad to escape this particular one.

Meet me at the entrance in ten. T

He didn't receive any confirmation, but he knew Eve would know which entrance he meant and would be there on time. Reaching the lobby, he noticed she'd just beat him to it. She was wearing the black leather jacket Roy had put a tracker on and a long leather skirt. At first glance he thought it was black, but getting closer he could see it was actually a very dark purple.

"Looking gorgeous, as always," he greeted her, giving her a kiss on the cheek.

She smiled. "Thank you, darling."

He looked at her boots and rolled his eyes. "Do you really insist on being just as tall as me?"

Eve hit his arm and stuck out her tongue.

"Oh yes, very ladylike. Totally goes with the outfit," he said to her with a teasing smile. "Seriously, though, you look great.

Different. Happy." And she did look happy. He knew Eve was pleased to be on speaking terms again. Not just with him but with Charles and Roy as well. This was something more, though. Or he was reading things that weren't there. If Eve picked up on his thoughts, she didn't comment on them and let him lead the way outside.

"Where would you like to go?" he asked.

"Let's go to Shoreditch Grind. I like their coffee and it's relatively close to your apartment should you be needed. Want to go by car?" Eve stopped to look at him.

Tristan shook his head. "I'd rather not, unless you want to?"

"Nope. Public transport works for me."

He smiled, and they walked on, not saying much, but enjoying each other's company nonetheless.

The Grind was not too crowded, but there were just enough people for them to have a private conversation without the risk of being overheard. They ordered at the bar and waited for their coffees. For a moment, Tristan wondered if Catherine would like this place. It was rather close by, but she seemed very fond of The Albion. He'd really liked The Albion, but this place was more to his own taste. Easy-going, a bit rough around the edges and a colourful staff. He liked that. It had been too long since he visited this place. It reflected a side of London he felt at home with.

"Yes, I know you like it here. I like it, too." Eve smiled at him. "Cheers!" she said to the woman behind the counter and left her a big tip before pointing out a table in the corner to Tristan.

He nodded, and they both sat down.

"So what's up with the seers?" he asked.

Eve rolled her eyes. "Pfff...don't get me started. The famous four had the whole company in uproar, and what for? Nothing, as it turned out. Well, at least nothing substantial. And why anybody would go against him is beyond me." She threw Tristan a meaningful look.

Rumour had it their top dog was a seer himself and quite a good one at that. Not that anybody of his team had actually met the man. "So nothing from him?"

"Nope. Not a damn thing. So like I said when I texted you, you can't trust them for shit. Sometimes I don't even know why we keep them around. They never agree on anything, and they are a lot of trouble in general. Well, that's just my not so humble opinion, anyway."

Tristan winked at her. "Oh, I don't know. You can be humble at times. When it suits you."

Eve grinned.

"You had some news, you said," he continued.

Eve's grin faded. "Yes, I have. Now, Tristan, you're going to have to trust me on this and not freak out, okay?" She looked at him to make sure she had his full attention. "I'm going to say something, and you're going to respond naturally and relaxed. Best put your coffee down for a second. We don't want to attract attention by you making a mess of yourself."

Tristan could tell she was dead serious, so he made sure to heed her advice and put the coffee cup back on the saucer. "Okay, I'm ready," he said to her.

Eve leaned back. "Alan came to see me last night."

Even with Eve putting him on his guard, it still took a lot of self-control not to let out a growl. Tristan could feel his anger rising. However, he managed to maintain a relaxed attitude and said, "Really?"

Eve nodded her approval. "Hmm, yes. Took me by surprise as well. He was at my house, you see."

Tristan narrowed his eyes. He didn't like that one bit. "You told him where you live?"

"No, I did not. Give me some credit, Tristan. There are ways of finding out where people live, though. Even people like us. And I have to say, I was quite impressed. People rarely impress me. You know that. So I invited him in."

"That could have been very dangerous, Eve," he said to her in a low voice.

She shook her head. "I don't think so. Like you, I'm normally a good judge of character, thanks to our 'enhanced abilities.' From what I could tell, he just wanted to talk. So, we talked. And I found out quite a few interesting bits of information."

Tristan thought it safe to empty his cup of coffee and did so in one gulp. "Indeed? Must have been some night," he said and leaned back.

"He was ordered to get that painting into the gallery, Tristan. The painting was already here in England, he had nothing to do with moving it from its original place. In other words, he had nothing to do with the murder. He didn't even know someone had been murdered. His job was to ensure that the gallery would truly believe it was part of the Peruvian collection and exhibit it. So that's what he did. He brainwashed the crap out of some of the staff and almost got caught. That is why some people do know it's not supposed to be part of the collection. We weren't supposed to find out. That's why he's on the run now. It was part of the deal he made. They agreed to let him go if he pulled this off, and he fucked it up. Well, part of it, anyway."

Tristan ran a hand through his hair. "What is it with people and this painting?"

Eve let out a short laugh. "Funny you should ask. It scared the hell out of him as well. Get this, he saw it before. In a dream." She gave him a meaningful look.

Tristan leaned forward, almost in thought. "I take it you believe him?"

She nodded. "Oh yes, his thoughts were sincere. I have no doubt he was telling the truth. At least, what he perceives as the truth."

"Did Catherine feature in this dream of his?" he asked, already knowing the answer, but asking just the same.

"She did," Eve confirmed. "That's what scared him, I think. In his dream, she pulled him into the painting, you see. So just the other way around. Interesting, don't you think?"

"Very," he said. "Or it would be, if we had any idea what it meant. So what does he want?"

"Well, technically, his job isn't finished. I think Alan is banking on the company leaving him alone if he completes the last part of his assignment. I think he very much hopes to have a life after Saturday. He was quite outspoken about Catherine's powers. He truly believes she can pull it off."

"And pray tell what is the last part of his assignment?" Tristan asked.

"Making sure the painting reaches Catherine and stays with her," Eve said in a calm voice.

"So…what? It contains something which will help her achieve her goal? A memory?" he asked.

"I don't know, darling. I don't think Alan knows, either. He did say he got the impression it had nothing to do with the asteroid, but he admitted he could be wrong about that."

Tristan harrumphed. "Well, he would say that, wouldn't he? So why did he come to you?"

She sighed and he could feel she was a bit annoyed with him. "I think I was the obvious choice, Tristan. What? He should have come to you? You would have handed him straight over to the company and that is assuming Roy or Charles wouldn't have beaten you to it. I did revive him, you know. The way he sees it he's in my debt. And I think he…likes me. Well, like is perhaps too strong a word, but he's intrigued by me, at the very least."

Her cheeks were slightly flushed, and it suddenly hit him. This was related to her earlier happy feeling. "No, no, no, Eve. Tell me you don't have feelings for this guy. I mean, come on!"

She had a stubborn look on her face. "And what if I do? Have feelings for him? They're none of your concern. Just like yours aren't mine, Tristan," she stressed as he was about to interrupt her. He remained silent.

"He has killed people," he whispered. "Doesn't that bother you?"

Eve looked at him. "Oh, don't be such a hypocrite, Tristan. Why would that bother me? I've killed plenty myself. As have you, or do I need to remind you?"

"Under orders, Eve. Under orders."

She swept her hair over her shoulder in an annoyed gesture. "I'm not asking for your approval here, you know. It's not like we're planning a wedding or anything. I'd say we have bigger things to worry about."

Tristan tried to be reasonable. "Look, I'm just worried that he's clouding your judgement. Okay? I don't think he'd be good for you. I do care, you know."

Her face softened. "I know, Tristan. It's like you said, though. You and me, that's never going to work again. It has taken me a long time to accept that that's a good thing. And that we can be friends if there's a future to be had for any of us. I'm quite reconciled with that. I want something more out of life, though, than just the job. I know you know what I mean. You've been feeling exactly the same and don't you deny it."

He shook his head. "I have no wish to deny it, Eve, you're absolutely right. Don't get me wrong, I think it would take a 'special' person to hold your interest. I know that's how it always worked for me. There's so much about my life I can't share. I would at least want to be able to share my gifts with my partner."

She nodded. "Exactly. And if this does lead somewhere, it might be a good thing, you know. If he does kill someone I don't approve of, I just revive them."

Eve looked rather smug, and Tristan couldn't help but roll his eyes. "That would be an interesting sight." His expression turned serious. "What if one day it backfires and he turns on you, Eve?"

She shrugged. "Then I'll guess we'll finally find out if I'm able to revive myself. The company has always wondered about that, you know. I have to say, I'm quite curious myself.

Not that I'd be volunteering to find out. Besides, first he needs to get over Catherine. He thinks he's still in love with her."

That surprised Tristan. "After what she did to him?"

"I'm sure there's another story in there. He was very careful with his thoughts on that particular event. To him, she's the epitome of goodness and that's something he envies. Purity. He covets it. I don't think he blames her. Mind you, he's glad not to be a vegetable anymore. He said it was a relief to be around me. Because I'm a mind reader, there's no need for him to pretend. I think he's quite tired of pretending."

Tristan nodded understandingly. "And so are you, aren't you?"

She sat up straight. "Yes. Yes, I am. Anyway, I thought you had a right to know. Not just as a colleague or as my friend but also as my former lover." Eve hesitated. "We kissed. It was just a kiss and very different from what we had, but it was real. I could tell. Do you know what I mean?"

He sighed and thought about the kiss he'd shared with Catherine. "I do, Eve. I do. I'm glad you got to experience that again. Please, be careful, though. Will you do that for me?"

She smiled. "Always am, darling."

He threw the sugar stick at her. "No, you're not. You're reckless and headstrong. You'd dive into a pool head first without checking to see if there's any water in it, you silly woman, but I'll hold you to that promise."

They both laughed. "Now, don't you have a party to get ready for?" she asked.

"Fuck the party. I need another coffee after you dumped this on me, a double. You're buying."

Eve laughed but got up to get them their coffees.

* * *

Tristan and Roy arrived at Catherine's party half an hour after it had started. Roy had been watching the live feed to check when there would be enough people for them to blend in easily. The penthouse had filled up pretty quickly. Apparently,

Catherine's and Deborah's party was quite popular. Tristan noticed Catherine immediately in her Fawkes the phoenix outfit. She looked stunning. He smiled at her but focussed his attention on the hostess, however. "Holmes, ma'am, Sherlock Holmes and my partner, Watson," he said, taking off his hat.

The hostess smiled at him. "Of course, sir. I assume you have an alias as well?'

"Why, yes, ma'am. That would be Visconti, Tristan Visconti."

She smiled again and crossed his name off the list. "Welcome to the party, Mr. Holmes, Dr. Watson. Enjoy your evening."

They walked towards Catherine, and Tristan took her hand to kiss it. "You look amazing. Are you a phoenix, Miss van Dyk?" he whispered into her ear and felt her shiver.

"Why, yes I am, Mr. Holmes. And may I say you two look quite dashing." She took a step back and held out a hand to Roy. "Dr. Watson, a pleasure to meet you."

And she was pleased to meet him, he could feel it. Had she been worried he'd bring a woman as his date? He heard Roy thanking her for including him in the invitation, calling her ma'am as well and giving her his first name.

"Kate," she replied. "When you say ma'am, I start to look for my mother."

Roy gave her a smile. "Kate it is, then."

Catherine showed them inside, and Tristan noticed the turning of quite a few heads. One of them was walking towards them right now. Ah, Deborah, the business partner and an empath herself.

"Kate darling, John needs you in the kitchen. Is this our new neighbour?" she asked with a warm smile, but Tristan could feel a gentle nudge against his mental walls. She was trying to get a read on him and he felt slightly amused. Obviously her powers were nothing compared to his own—very few were—but he decided to oblige her and let his defences down just enough so she could sense his genuine feelings for Catherine.

Catherine sighed. "Tristan Visconti, may I introduce you to Deborah de Vries, my friend and business partner. Deb, this is Tristan and his friend, Roy."

"It's so nice to finally meet you, Tristan," she said, shaking his hand.

"And you, Deborah. I trust you approve of what you feel and see?" he asked with a smile. No point in beating around the bush, but Deborah looked a bit like a child caught with her hand in the cookie jar.

"Well, yes, but then I would have to give you the benefit of the doubt and assume you're playing fair, Mr. Visconti," she said, and he felt a rush of desire wash over him.

Well, Deborah certainly wasn't playing fair. Tristan was being put to the test. He would play along, for now. He made sure to communicate an appreciation of her looks but nothing more than that. He only had eyes for Catherine, and he made sure she would pick up on that as well. "Well, since we're both empaths, I could make the same remark about you." He felt a rush of gratitude before she answered him.

"You're actually in the wrong, Mr. Visconti. I'm not an empath. I have empathic abilities, and I have healing ones. I guess my genes are a mixture of my mum and dad. My father is a healer and my mother was indeed an empath. I have a kid brother who has the same abilities as I do."

Really? That must be some gene pool. He could feel her powers when he'd walked in the door. "Then they must be quite powerful abilities, as I felt you searching through my thoughts. And please call me Tristan."

Deborah shook hands with Roy as well, and she promised Catherine to show them around and behave herself. He was sad to see Catherine go, but he'd realised beforehand he'd probably have little opportunity to really speak with her. It was her party, after all. They followed Deborah around the room, introducing them to people here and there and after the grand tour downstairs, she showed them up to the rooftop, which was rather magnificent.

"I seldom meet people with both a mental and physical ability," Tristan said to Deborah. "It's not unheard of, but quite rare." That obviously pleased her.

"Yes, Kate said you know a lot of people with special powers. Roy, do you have any as well?" she asked.

Tristan looked over at his friend, who showed Deborah a big smile.

"Who me? Nah. I don't need special powers; I have my killer looks." Roy always knew how to charm the ladies and Deborah was no exception.

She laughed at his little joke. "I'm sure that's true," she said, waving at a group of people who appeared to be dressed as the Fantastic Four. "Are you old friends?" she asked.

Roy looked at Tristan, who answered her question. "Depends on what you'd call old friends. We've known each other for over a decade and he's still alive, so that's saying something." Tristan looked at Roy with an evil grin, which made Deborah laugh again. Roy just rolled his eyes at him.

"Well, I certainly understand why Kate likes you," Deborah was saying. "You share the same weird sense of humour. I never quite understand her more sarcastic side."

Tristan looked at her. No, she probably wouldn't. Deborah was a serious person, despite her sensual looks, and was most likely the financial and logical half of Catherine's company, Elements. He could see how they would complement each other. Roy excused himself to Deborah and went looking for a drink.

"I understand from Catherine you used to be in the music business?" he asked her politely.

Deborah nodded fervently, giving another wave to a man dressed as Gandalf. "Yes, for quite some time, actually. I used to run my own venue back in the Netherlands."

"Don't you miss it?" he asked. Running a massage business

was not exactly the same thing, though he did remember her remark about her being a healer as well.

She shrugged. "Sure. Sometimes. I can do more good in the world this way, though. Besides, I work with a lot of artists, or I should say 'on' a lot of artists, so I'm still part of their world as well. At first, Kate thought it was better to keep a low profile, but word gets around and now at least thirty percent of our clientele is made out of musicians, I'm quite proud of that. She's actually quite good with the more…umm…high maintenance people. She doesn't tolerate any bullshit, you see. She gives it to them straight. Oddly enough, most of them really seem to appreciate that." She grinned at him and took a sip of her cocktail. "What about you? Catherine said you help people as well. Important people as I understand it."

Tristan smiled "Well, that depends on your definition of important people, I suppose. I believe every human being is important."

Deborah nodded her approval. "That's a nice thought. I agree. However, some people create a greater ripple effect if they do something good for the world. Or screw it up." She frowned.

He guessed she was thinking about Alan. "Did you know him well? Alan, I mean," Tristan asked.

Deborah shook her head. "No, not at all. I mean, I never even met him. They'd just broken up when we started to get really close. I know him from pictures, though. And I was there to witness the after-effects it had on Catherine." Her face hardened.

"She's lucky to have a friend like you," Tristan said to her.

Her face softened. "Thank you, Tristan. I'm lucky to have her as well, you know. She always believed in me. When we first met, my healing abilities were practically non-existent. Catherine has a gift of bringing out the best in people, and over the years my healing powers have grown substantially. Now they're equal to my emphatic abilities. I have her to thank for that. She's like a sister to me. Not just in a spiritual sense but just on a day-to-day basis."

He smiled. "That's something to cherish. I'm an only child, you see. You ever thought about going back?"

"To the Netherlands, you mean?" she asked. He nodded. "No, never. My whole life is here now. My friends, my social network, even my kid brother is thinking about moving here. My parents still live there, but England isn't all that far. They like to visit, and I fly out every two months or so to visit them. Have you ever been to the Netherlands?"

"A couple of times, yes. Mostly the larger cities, though. Amsterdam, obviously. I like the down-to-earth attitude."

"Yes, we're known for that," she said with a smile. "Oh, look! Roy has found a drink. He's over there talking to Kate."

Tristan followed her gaze, smiling at Deborah's effort to refocus his attention on someone else. Indeed, Roy was talking to Catherine. Wondering what they were talking about, he encouraged Deborah to lead the way.

"Honey, this is one hell of a party! And you have my permission to like our new neighbour. He's cool," Deborah said as soon as they reached Catherine and Roy.

Tristan laughed at Deborah's remark and smiled at Catherine. "See, I'm cool," he said.

Catherine looked frustrated about something, however, but one glance at Roy left him quite clueless as to why. He cast her a slightly worried look. She caught him looking, immediately relaxed and gave him a kiss on the cheek. "Of course, you're cool. You're Sherlock Holmes, for God's sake!" They all grinned.

Catherine excused herself to go check the party downstairs, and Deborah decided to join her, leaving Tristan and Roy up on the rooftop terrace. "What was up with Catherine? She looked annoyed when we interrupted you guys," Tristan said to Roy.

Roy raised his eyebrows. "I'm not sure. Was she annoyed?

I told her you think very highly of her and that she must be very special. She pretty much said the same thing about you. Hmm, come to think of it, I did warn her we're not exactly long-term relationship material. Was that a no-no?"

Tristan sighed. "Well, it might not have been the smartest thing to say to her, but I can't imagine her being annoyed about that. She must have reservations herself. Catherine's a smart woman."

"Yeah, that's what I figured. How much did you tell her anyway? About the company, I mean. She seemed pretty well-informed."

Tristan frowned. "What do you mean? I haven't told her anything. Well, she knows the company I work for helps people, and she thinks Charles is my personal driver, but she doesn't even know you and I work together. She introduced you to Deborah as a friend of mine, remember?"

"Let me think here. I want to get the phrasing right. Yes, she said something about me being worried of her blowing your cover to kingdom come. Yes, that was just before you guys interrupted."

Tristan stared at him. "Really, Roy? She was pumping you for information, man. Damn, that little minx! She's more cunning than I realized."

Roy ran a hand through his hair. "Bugger. I almost answered her as well. Wow! That has never happened to me before, boss. You know that."

"Well, no harm done this time. I guess it's safe to assume she wasn't playing fair, Roy. I wouldn't put it past her to make good use of her powers."

"Won't happen again, boss. I'll be on my guard from now on."

They'd just finished another drink—non-alcoholic to keep their wits about them—when Tristan felt his phone buzzing. He saw Roy take out his as well.

Call me ASAP.

"It's the boss," Roy said. "Don't bother. I'll find out what's going on." Roy swiftly moved through the crowd to find a quiet place. Five minutes later he came back with a murderous look on his face. He motioned for Tristan to move over to a quieter side of the rooftop.

"Prime minister has gone bonkers. She's going to announce the asteroid in less than ten minutes on national television. There's a team en route, but they won't make it to the studios on time. Not before the damage is done. This is what the seers have been picking up on. Fuck!" he said in a whisper. "In a few minutes, we're going to have a full-blown panic here. You understand that, right?"

Tristan nodded grimly. "Where's Catherine?" he asked.

"Downstairs just a few seconds ago. What do you want to do, boss? Your call."

"Have the entire team on standby. For now, we'd better stay here. If the beans are really spilled, I'll have to fill her in tonight. Shit, this is not how it's supposed to go." He sighed in frustration. *Stupid woman! Great timing to develop a conscience.* "Let's go downstairs, Roy."

His friend nodded while texting the entire team. "Done. They're all on red alert. Well, let's brace for impact, shall we?"

Once they reached the bottom of the stairs, Tristan spotted two Dalmatian-looking fellows who seemed to be in charge of the catering and headed straight over. "Excuse me, gentlemen, have either of you seen Catherine?"

The taller of the two replied. "Oh yes, dear Kittycat. She's over there, you see. With Deb and the others." He pointed to the fireplace in the middle where Catherine was indeed standing next to Leah. He noticed she was looking for him as well. As their eyes locked across the room, he tried to send her his most reassuring smile.

The TV screen flickered and the BBC news tune filled the room. "This is a special broadcast. We have a live connection with Downing Street where our prime minister will address the nation."

The screen showed the prime minister sitting behind her desk. She took a deep breath and rearranged the papers before her.

"Good evening, ladies and gentlemen. I sit before you with a troubled heart. I should state up front that after giving this speech, I will lay down my position as prime minister, as my declaration will mean a breach of security protocol. However, I feel very strongly that the people of Britain have a right to know what's going on. That they have a right to be with the people they love."

Everybody went deadly quiet.

"Some people at the news network have agreed to arrange this live feed at great personal expense, for which I'm very grateful. They will make sure I'm able to finish my speech before anyone can interfere." She took another deep breath and looked straight into the camera. "It's with great regret that I have to inform you all that an asteroid is on a collision course with Earth. The point of impact will be England, near London, to be exact. Unfortunately, this is of little consequence, as the asteroid will eventually damage the entire planet. It's too big.

"Everything that is humanly possible has already been done, to no avail. The asteroid remains. We don't have the means to destroy it or change its course. Trust me in saying that we did all we can, globally. The common opinion was to avoid mass hysteria, and I'd agreed to that as long as there was hope, even a little. Hope has run out, however, and if I'm getting the opportunity to spend my last moments with the people I love the most, so should you.

"The asteroid will hit Earth this Saturday at precisely two minutes after eight p.m. Greenwich Mean Time. It's now Thursday night, which leaves us less than forty-eight hours to enjoy each other, to enjoy life. I appeal to you all to focus your efforts on contacting or being with your loved ones. I know I will. Turning against any form of authority will be completely pointless. Only the highest-ranking people have known about this. Your local police officer will be just as shocked hearing this news as you are. Please help each other in reaching your loved ones in any way you can. I also appeal to hospitals in the hope they will try everything in their power to leave the patients in good care. I understand hospital personnel will want to go home as well, and they should get that chance. I'm hoping, however, hospitals will either make room for their own family members to join, or leave their patients in the care of their loved ones. Please be careful going out into the streets, as people will be scared. There is no point in getting yourself killed in a car accident, trying to reach your loved ones. Take care of yourself and each other. I wish you all Godspeed and a peaceful ending."

The screen went black. It took a few moments before the room came back to life. People were just staring at each other, not believing what they'd just heard. Tristan, however, only had eyes for Catherine. How was she handling this? She was currently hugging Leah, whispering something to her. Looking around, she seemed to be pulling herself together and reached for a kitchen chair near her.

"Could I have everybody's attention, please? I notice some people are already leaving, which I perfectly understand, of course. I'm so sorry. This was obviously not how this was supposed to end, but a party seems very trivial now, doesn't it?"

People were coming down from the rooftop terrace, and most of them stopped to listen to Catherine.

"I know we've all had a very nasty shock. Well, that's the understatement of the century probably. I don't want to keep you any longer, but I do want to wish you well, and most of all, wish you hope. I know it seems hopeless now, but our Earth has survived many things, so all may not be lost. In the meantime, take our prime minister's advice, spend as much time with your loved ones as you possibly can, and please, return home safely. You're all very dear to me, and I'd hate to see anything bad happen to anyone before all hope is lost. So please be careful out there. We don't have any idea how people are going to respond to this. It might not be very safe outside. So again, please be careful. Thank you."

As she stepped down from the chair, people applauded.

"Well, I have to say, she sounds like you, boss. That was a pretty amazing speech," Roy said. "I'd better go and meet the team. I assume you're going to stay here?"

Tristan nodded. "Yes. Keep me posted, though," he answered automatically, his eyes on Catherine. He noticed people were shaking her hand and he thought he heard someone saying "if anyone can do it, you can." Apparently, some of her customers had an inkling of what she was able to do. Not that any one of them would probably get close to the truth. He refocused his attention to Roy.

"Always do, boss. Come, I'll say goodbye to her, and we can get this show on the road."

They joined Catherine and her friends. "I'm very sorry we had to meet like this," Roy said to her.

"As am I, Roy, as am I. You're welcome to stay."

Tristan felt humbled as he realized Catherine had simply assumed he would stick around and was now extending that invitation to his friend.

Roy smiled at her. "Thank you. That's very kind of you, but I have things to attend to. It's probably weird to say I hope to see you again, but I do mean it."

She gave him a warm smile. "Take care, Watson. Get home safely." He saluted her and then left with a last meaningful look at Tristan.

Romy crashed onto the couch. "So, what's the plan? How are we going to save this bloody planet?" They stared at her. Tristan stared at Romy as well. So they had a plan? He should go about this very carefully. The power of Catherine's friends could be beneficial to their success, but it could also backfire.

A man who Tristan guessed to be Meg's husband walked around in an irritated fashion. Tristan looked around and tried to remember everything in Catherine's file. Thankfully he had a good memory for names and faces. Besides Deborah and Leah, he spotted Meg and Romy, who were both working for Elements part-time. Meg had a shop of her own and was to be carefully watched as a possible master of death, and Romy did something with sports, if he remembered correctly. Sue, the red-haired woman was the healer they had on file. Two women, looking identical, had to be Rezna and Gezna, also part of their circle. That left Joni, who could have elemental powers as well and Sheila, who he couldn't locate. Maybe she wasn't here. He refocussed his attention on Meg's husband. "Please, Romy, don't be dramatic. I know you and your whole little group think you're special, and I'm not denying you people can do things, my wife included, but this is the fucking planet were talking about! Meg and I will go home and be with each other as much as we can, right, Meg?" He looked over at his wife, who'd come to stand next to Catherine.

She looked sad. "Harry, you know I want to be with you more than anything. If there's any chance, any chance at all, we can do something to save the planet, I have to give it a go. I wouldn't be able to live with myself otherwise."

Romy's husband stood as well. "Oh, come on, Meg, that won't be a problem, will it, since we'll all be dead in two days, anyway. That's pretty much bullshit!"

Catherine raised her hands. "People, please, let's keep it civil. No one's forcing anybody to stay. I certainly won't. Harry, Martin, I understand your feelings. Really, I do. Of course, you want to be with your wives. We're all in shock now. This is probably not the time to be planning anything. I think you should all go home, have a good night's sleep and rethink this tomorrow."

"We're going to plan something though, right? Right?" Deborah asked, looking around the room.

"I can't speak for anybody else, but I will, yes," Catherine replied.

Leah re-entered the room. Tristan only now noticed she had been absent for a while, and he immediately enhanced his abilities not to slip up again. He needed to know where people were.

"I just talked to Ryan on the phone," Leah said.

Ah, Ryan, the New York boyfriend. Of course, Leah would have called him straightaway, Tristan thought.

"The prime minister's news has spread like wildfire," Leah continued. "I think half the world knows by now. Ryan says people are going crazy in New York already. There's a run on supermarkets to get people enough food to last them these two days." She shook her head.

"Well, at least that won't be a problem here," Catherine said, looking around. "I could feed an army with what's left over from the party."

"You've got that right," John said from the kitchen, still dressed in his Dalmatian suit.

Tristan took a seat on the couch and let his calm spread through the room. "Look, if I may suggest something? There are people on the streets everywhere by now. It won't be the best time to return home. Also, I'm not sure how long the public transport lines will be open to the public. Who came by car?"

Meg, Romy, Sue, the twins, and John raised their hands.

"Good. Now it's probably best to wait a few more hours until after midnight. Then the streets will be less crowded, making if safer to travel. Anyone with a car can drop the others off. In the meantime, Catherine, if you're planning something, it couldn't hurt to discuss it. It'll give us something to do, and we'll spend our time together in a useful manner."

Everybody seemed to relax a bit. "Well, that makes sense," Martin said. "I suppose it'd be better to wait a bit. I hadn't thought about the madness outside."

They all agreed, and John and Chris selected a few plates with finger food, so they could nibble on something. They also brought back a couple bottles of sparkling water.

"Best to keep our heads clear, don't you think?" Chris asked. There was a mumble of agreement.

"Though getting completely pissed sounds like a pretty good idea as well right about now," Harry said with a sigh.

Meg smiled at him and patted his shoulder. "We'll get through this, sweetie, we always do." Harry squeezed her hand.

Tristan noticed Catherine was looking at him, her eyes full of questions. Yes, he was sure she would have a lot of questions for him. At least, now he would be able to give her some answers. If she'd be willing to hear them. He would find a way to get her alone later this evening. The time had come to lay all his cards on the table. He focussed his attention on her when she started to speak.

"Okay. We had a Samhuinn ritual planned this Saturday. I was going to use my elements to try to restore as much balance to the world as possible, using them full force. The original plan was to combine all our powers and use me as a vessel. It would multiply mine. I'm not sure this will work, though. It's something we never tried before. I was actually going to suggest a trial run for tomorrow, but all things considered, we'll have more important things to do. Everybody will want to be with family or say goodbye. Speaking for myself, I'll definitely want to see my mother and uncle if I can."

"Right," Leah said. "Let's look at this thing logically." A few of the girls looked at her with a smile. "Yes, well, as logically as possible," she said in a huff. "We have an asteroid. If it's going to destroy Earth, it must be pretty big. I'm sure some idiot pressed a red button to try to nuke the damn thing, but even if they were able to blast a piece off, it still remains large enough to annihilate our planet, but it's still an asteroid. It's made up out of the elements, right?"

Clever girl, Tristan thought.

"I guess," Sue replied before anybody could respond. "Yes, I think you should be able to connect to it, Kate."

"Okay, that's good," Deborah said, "but connecting to it won't destroy it, right? How do we go about that?"

They all looked at Catherine, but she looked at Meg, who shook her head. "Oh, sweetie, I wish I could, but I'm no master of death. You know that. I can only see death. I can't control it," Meg said.

Well, that ruled out another master of death. Even with all the impending doom hanging over their heads, Tristan was still relieved to hear Meg say those words.

The twins looked at each other and frowned. "No. Not control it. How about summoning it?" one of them asked.

They all stared at the twins. "What do you mean?" Meg asked the question that had to be on everybody's minds.

"Well, it's Samhuinn, which is ruled by the Cailleach, the goddess of life, death and rebirth," one of the twins said to the group. "She's not exactly cuddly, but could you summon her, Meg? Maybe if we're able to use Kate as a vessel, the Cailleach can take her over, which will enable Kate to not only connect to the asteroid but also destroy it. She'll have the power of death, so to speak," The other woman smiled at her twin sister.

"Oh, boy, I don't know, Gezna. That's an awful lot of ifs," Catherine said. "As you said, the Cailleach is perhaps the most unpredictable of the goddesses I know. If I let her take over, there's no knowing what she'll decide is the right thing to do. She might think it's a great idea to destroy Earth."

"Maybe Deborah could gauge her intentions? And, Leah, you could try focussing on the Cailleach to see an outcome," Tristan suggested. Their seers would have to work on that as well. He would make sure to get Roy that message.

He noticed Leah looking at him with a speculative gaze. "That's actually not bad. I could do that. Deb?"

"I could try meditating and focus on her, sure. Get a feel for her vibe. It changes every year."

"Joni, what about your powers? Do you think you can tap into the earth and make it stronger?" Catherine asked.

Joni looked up at her with a serious expression. "Of course, Kate. Anything I can do to help. Consider it done."

John and Chris looked around the group. "Is there anything we can do to help?" Chris asked. "I mean, really, if there's anything we can do, just let us know."

John put an arm around him. "Well said, my love." He gave him a kiss.

"That's sweet of you guys, and I'm not saying no to that offer, but right now I can't think of anything. I mean, you're both special to me, you know that, but you don't have any special powers that could be of use right now. No offence," Catherine said with a warm smile.

"None taken, sweetheart, but the offer stands. If you guys need extra locations or food or anything, let us know," John said.

Harry, Martin, and the twins' spouses looked at John and Chris. Judging by their feelings, Tristan guessed they didn't have any special powers and probably felt as if they should say something, too.

Catherine had obviously noticed the look on their faces as well and stepped in. "Thanks again, guys. Look, I'm sure there are lots of things we're not seeing right now. It's fair to say we don't have any idea what we're going to wake up to tomorrow. It's going to be another world. We might need all sorts of things, and when it comes down to plain muscle power, it's always nice to have a few men around. Anyone who's willing to help out would be more than welcome."

All the men in the room made noises of agreement. "Sure,

Kate." "Anything you need." "You just give us a shout." "Of course, we'll help."

Tristan saw her smile, and quite a few of her circle sisters did as well.

"Thank you, gentlemen," she said. "It's good to know we have some male backup power on hand."

Sheila came back from the hallway. "The whole entrance is full with presents, Kate. Do you need any help getting them in here? Some of them look quite big or heavy."

"Oh, that's right," Meg cut in. "I completely forgot with all the commotion. It probably seems silly now, anyway, but your friend left a painting for you, Kate. I thought it was rather impressive."

"Which friend?" Catherine asked.

"Um, I don't know actually. He introduced himself as Saruman. Did you catch his name, honey?" She looked at her husband, who shook his head.

"No, I think none of us mentioned any names," Harry answered. "We were pretty much into the whole role playing game."

Meg went to retrieve the painting from the hallway and then set it down gently in front of Catherine, who unwrapped the other half of it. The second the whole thing was revealed, she and Leah both jumped up as if something had bit them.

"Fuck!" Catherine cried out. Leah forcefully swung her away from the painting. Aside from Tristan, the rest looked shocked. Apparently, Alan had found a way to sneak the painting inside. *Well, good for him.*

"It's the painting from the museum, isn't it?" Deborah asked with a frightened look on her face. "It's Alan's painting."

Tristan examined the painting, removed something from the back and then looked at Catherine. "Is it, Catherine? Is this the painting you were talking about?" Obviously, he knew it was the same blasted painting, but he needed her confirmation.

She just nodded. "I can't believe he was in here, in my apartment. Just like that. Why didn't he talk to me? I didn't even see him."

"Yes, you did," Meg said. "I saw you looking at us. You know, when we were all standing together. He was right there next to Harry. God, I can't believe I'd just been standing there, talking to him. He was really nice to us and very nice about you, Kate."

"Yes, he was," Harry cut in. "He said more than once how enchanting you'd become."

"What else did he say?" Tristan asked quietly. He handed Catherine a little white note. It read, *Soon you will see.* He looked at her. "It was stuck on the back of the painting. It's the original, by the way."

Harry and Meg glanced at each other. "Um…what else did we talk about?" asked Harry. "Nothing much really. We talked about *Lord of the Rings*, obviously, and about the Halloween party. He said this was the first one he could attend. That you were old friends and that he'd been otherwise engaged before this party. Well, he wasn't lying about that, now was he?" he finished sarcastically.

"No, he certainly wasn't," Catherine replied quietly. "Soon you will see. What do I have to see? The world coming to an end? He'll die with it. Why would that make him happy? No, that can't be it. What then?" She continued to mumble options under her breath.

"And you're still not seeing the big picture," Romy said, pulling Kate back to the conversation at hand.

"What?" she asked.

"From the dream. That's what he said, right?"

Catherine looked confused for a moment. "Yes. Yes, you're right. That's what he said to me. You think they're related?"

"I should think so, yes," Romy replied.

Her group agreed, and there was even a mumble of

agreement from some of the men.

"Yes, that's all very nice, but if we don't know what it means, it's not going to do us any good," Leah cut in, always the practical one.

"Leah, can you see something beyond Saturday?" Tristan asked. They all looked at her.

Leah sighed. "I'm not sure, Tristan. I think I can, but it's hard to distinguish between real visions and wishful thinking right now."

He nodded. "I understand. You'll let us know when you do get something, anything you're convinced of that is real?" As far as he could tell, she was a pretty powerful seer. Maybe even more powerful than their own and he needed all the help he could get.

"Of course, you have my word," she promised.

They talked over several possibilities and scenarios for another hour until people were starting to get really tired.

"Okay, enough is enough, people," Catherine said. "It's way past midnight, and we've done as much as we can for tonight. Anybody who doesn't want to go home is more than welcome to crash here."

Tristan cut in. "That goes for me as well, if anyone needs a place to stay for tonight."

She smiled at him. "Thank you, Tristan. Everybody who does go home, will you please, please text me the minute you arrive? Otherwise I'll be up the rest of the night worrying myself sick."

Tristan stood. "Listen, everyone, just one more thing. Tomorrow's going to be another world. Try to keep that in mind when you wake up and don't panic. The electricity might be down. The phone lines may be down, including the mobile network. I highly doubt public transportation will still be functioning, and you probably won't be able to get groceries. These are just some of the things we're going to have to deal with, just to give you a heads-up, so to speak."

Everybody got up. "Thanks, Tristan." Harry said. "You seem to know a lot about these sort of situations. And of course, Kate," he turned to her with a warm smile, "we'll text you."

Tristan nodded. "Unfortunately, I do. Not on this scale, of course, but I have a pretty good inclination what we're going to face the next two days."

Meg and Sue divided everyone else into two groups, which left the twins, and John and Chris free to use their own cars, as they lived in different parts of London. Meg and Sue said they both had big vehicles. Deborah and Leah decided to stay at Catherine's, for which Tristan was sure she was secretly grateful. Of course, like he had expected, she wanted to talk to him. So when he walked down with the others to see they at least left safely, she went down with him, leaving Deborah and Leah upstairs.

"So," Tristan began when the cars were out of sight and they walked back into the hallway, "you probably have a question or two." This was going to be a lovely conversation. Catherine smiled at him, but he could still feel her determination. He wasn't going to weasel his way out of this one. Not that he wanted to. He just dreaded her response. He needed her on board, after all. Their whole world depended on it.

"As a matter of fact, I do. For starters, how come you weren't surprised about a minor little thing like the world coming to an end?" Her voice dripped with sarcasm.

They slowly walked upstairs, and Tristan stopped on the third floor. "My place for a moment?" he asked.

"That would probably be best for now, yes," she agreed.

Tristan opened his door and then they sat on the couch next to each other. "To answer your first question, I was very much surprised, but not for the reason you just mentioned. Unfortunately, I've known that our world is coming to an end for quite some time, and as you've probably guessed by now, yes, that's the reason I'm here. The broadcast wasn't supposed to happen, however. Obviously, somebody at our company screwed up big time because usually we keep tabs on what certain people are going to do. Our prime minister did an excellent job of hiding this until it was too late. She had a point, of course, but I know what this will do to our society, and it isn't going to be pretty. It's going to make your attempt a lot harder." He looked a bit sad.

"So, you lied to me?" she said. *Well yes, obviously, but you mean something else.* He looked at her quizzically. "About the prime minister, I mean. You said she wasn't your client. Has Roy gone to check on her? Shouldn't you be with your client?" Catherine let out a sigh and continued. "Look, I'm not mad. I figured your job involves a certain amount of secrecy, and I understand you can't tell me everything."

He laid his hand over hers. "Catherine, I never lied to you. One of many things my boss isn't too happy about. You're right about one thing. I should be with my client." She nodded and was about to stand again to let him leave when he softly said, "Which is why I'm still here. I thought you'd have figured it out by now." She just looked at him. "You're my client, Catherine. I was assigned to encourage and help you save the planet. I have to admit that I wasn't really looking forward to this assignment. As I said, we knew about the asteroid long before anyone else. To be frank, I had little hope we could do anything to make a difference. I thought this whole mission was a bit pointless and a waste of time." He looked at her. "Then I met you. And from the first moment I shook your hand, I was intrigued. I couldn't get a grip on your emotions, which was a first for me. I've met other elementals before, but it never was a problem. In hindsight, I think that's probably because I've never met someone who's a true elemental, so to speak. Meaning someone who has the ability to summon earth, air, fire and water at will, all at the same time. As I've told you before, there isn't anyone on our planet, as far as we know, who can do that. And we know quite a lot."

He smiled. She was still sitting next to him, which gave him the courage to continue. "When I found out what you could do, my hope returned. It was frustrating, you see. I'd been assigned to a hopeless mission, in my eyes at least, and from the moment we'd met, I really liked you. Which made it even more hopeless, because I wanted to get to know you better, and I felt as if that wouldn't be possible. By then I'd met Leah, and I have to admit to having Roy check out some of your other friends. I knew you weren't alone with your powers. That night in the restaurant, which I enjoyed very much, by the way, you changed my life. From that moment on I knew what you could do, in theory, at least. I started to believe you could do this and that I could help you believe in yourself." Catherine stared at her hands. Tristan shifted on the couch. "Well, say something. How mad are you?"

She shook her head. "I'm not mad, Tristan. Confused, yes, and maybe a bit disappointed, but that's probably also directed at myself for not knowing the truth. I hate looking like a fool." She pushed a strand of hair away in an irritated manner, making some feathers fly. "Actually, yeah, I am mad. Because you didn't trust me enough to tell me the truth. We could have made plans much sooner if you'd confided in me instead of leaving it to the last moment. Come to think of it, that's only because everyone knows now. When the hell were you going to tell me we had to stop an oncoming asteroid?"

Tristan sighed. "I was going to tell you." She looked at him sceptically. "Really, Catherine, I was going to tell you. Tomorrow, in fact. I wanted to talk to you first, so we could come up with a plan to involve the rest of your group. They're very strong women, by the way. You have some amazing friends. There would have been no mass panic, only within your circle, and I could have helped to make you all focus, see clearly. Well, that's gone to the dogs now."

She sighed. Tristan felt her struggle with several emotions. Disappointment, anger, disappointment again and finally, resignation. His heart went out to her. She sighed again.

"I can't believe I'm going to let you off the hook here, but my anger isn't going to help any of us. Just for the record, Mr. Visconti, you're not forgiven. Once I kick this piece of shit to kingdom come, you're going to have to do a lot better. A whole lot better. Do I make myself clear?" Catherine took a deep breath. "Okay," she said. "On a practical note, how much help are we getting from your company?"

Okay, out of all the questions, I didn't see that one coming. "Don't you want to talk about this?" he asked. "I mean, I completely understand that it's a lot to take in."

She shook her head. "I'd rather not. For one thing, it's counterproductive because it'll only fuel my anger again. In my mind, I know you were probably right to act as you did, but my heart still feels betrayed and disappointed. Unlike my elements, I can't shut that out on command."

That left him terribly sad. He'd hurt her, but he nodded. "Of course, anything you need."

He felt a rush of sympathy from her, quickly followed by another wave of anger.

"Look, it hurts because I care, okay? It's not very often a man comes along for whom I have feelings. Let's leave it at that for now."

He gave her hand a soft squeeze. "Okay, but for the record, that goes for me as well. The having feelings part, I mean."

She smiled, a bit too ironically to his liking. "I bet they're pleased with that at your company."

He felt the emotion drain out of his face. "No, they're not, but that's not your concern." He got up from the couch. "You asked what kind of help you could expect from my company. I'll be here as long as you need me. So will Roy and Charles, who belong to the same division. Furthermore, location-wise we'll make sure nobody gets in your way. We've already cleared London Fields. It'd be good to know the exact location, however, and your approach route." Catherine actually laughed. Tristan looked up. "What?" he asked.

"Nothing. It's just I feel as if I'm suddenly in *Mission: Impossible* or James Bond."

He smiled a bit sheepishly. "Sorry, occupational hazard, I guess."

"Tristan? How bad is it going to be? On the streets, I mean. You sounded pretty worried about that."

He nodded. "I am. I've been in this situation before. As I said earlier, not on this scale, much smaller, but people don't respond very well to mass destruction. There are exceptions to the rule, of course, as with everything. On a whole, though, expect the worst. People won't be going to work anywhere. The prime minister may have addressed caretakers in her speech, but I doubt very much if they'll heed her advice. Traffic will be absolute madness. People will be trying to get away from England as far as possible, only to realise that airplanes aren't flying, either. Well, maybe tomorrow they still will, to some degree, but it'll be quite costly. Most people won't be able to afford a ticket out of here. Boats, same story. People on the mainland will have a better chance of getting farther away from England. And they will try, believe me. You'd be amazed what people are capable of doing when faced with mortal danger."

Catherine nodded. "Where would you go, if you could, I mean?"

"I wouldn't go anywhere because there's no need to. You'll stop it. I know you will."

She smiled. "Well, thanks for the vote of confidence. I think you have to work a bit harder to get me to feel the same, but that's not what I meant. If you were just another, um, civilian?"

He smiled at that. *Civilian. How cute.*

"Where would you go?" she finished.

He thought about it. Besides her and his own team, which

included Eve, there were only his parents. "I'm not sure. I'd like to see my parents, I guess."

Catherine gave him a sad smile. "Of course. Italy is a bit hard to reach. I mean, what you just said, you probably wouldn't even make it to the mainland."

"That wouldn't be a problem. I do have some other skills, you know. The company didn't just hire me because I'm an empath. Well, actually, that was the main reason they hired me, but they expect a lot more than that from their employees. I can fly as well, for example. I even loved it so much, I bought my own plane. Just a Cessna, nothing fancy, but I could, in theory, fly to see my parents."

She looked at him with one raised eyebrow. "Nothing fancy. You do realise you're talking about a plane, right?" She shook her head. "Look who I'm talking to. You own a Stradivari, for God's sake. A Cessna must be like buying a bicycle to you."

"In all fairness, I didn't buy the Stradivari, remember? My parents did. However, my job does have a nice 'high-risk' payment, so I make a pretty decent living."

She stood as well. "I think I should try to get some sleep. It's been a long night."

Tristan walked her to the door. He could feel her anger and underneath that, disappointment. It was killing him. He should have trusted her sooner. It was all about choices. And with this choice, he might have closed a door he didn't want closed.

"Catherine? Are we good? I mean…"

She gave him a soft kiss. "Shh. I know why you did what you did, and I understand. It doesn't mean I have to like it, though. So are we good? Not exactly, not right now, at least, but we will be. Someday we will be. I promise."

He smiled and kissed her. "Thank you. That's important to me. You're important to me. I hope you know that."

She nodded. "I do."

"Listen. I heard you say you wanted to visit your mother

and uncle tomorrow. If you have any trouble reaching them or getting there, let me know. Charles will be happy to drive you anywhere, and we have means to get gas as well should that become a problem."

"Thanks." She turned around. "Is Charles really your personal driver?"

Tristan smiled. "Yes, he is, but as you've probably guessed by now, he's much more than that."

"Hmm...yes," she said. "I like him."

"He'll be delighted to hear that. He encouraged me to listen to my heart. He knew I liked you before I did."

Catherine held the door to the lift. "So, I'll see you tomorrow?" She looked at him, and he could feel she was a bit worried.

"I'll be here, Catherine. Should you need me in the middle of the night, just call me. I mean that. Whenever, wherever. Just call."

She smiled. "I'll do that. Goodnight, Tristan. I hope we'll be able to get some sleep."

Tristan frowned. "Do you need help with that? I could calm you."

She shook her head. "No, thanks. I'm good. Really, I'm doing remarkably well, considering what I've heard tonight. Hmm...I think Jane would be quite proud of me, actually."

He looked confused. "Jane?" *Was there a Jane among her friends? He'd seen plenty of Miss Bennet's and Mr. Bingley's and Mr. Darcy's at the party and he knew Catherine was a huge Jane Austen fan, but he certainly didn't know the books by heart.* He felt like he was constantly screwing things up but was quickly put out of his misery when she continued.

"Sorry, *Pride and Prejudice* reference. Never mind, not important. Sleep well, Tristan. I'll see you tomorrow." She blew him a kiss from the lift, and he caught it.

When the doors closed, he went back inside. Well, all

things considered, he thought that had gone rather well. She had not bitten his head off, and she still trusted him. She was just disappointed he hadn't trusted her sooner, and that was only to be expected. No, that could have gone a lot worse. Savouring his last few moments of peace, he leaned against the cool glass of one of the windows.

He fished his phone out of his pocket and hit the connect button.

"Roy? I'm coming over. Make sure the team is ready. Yes, it went okay. Well, as okay as was to be expected. Yes. See you soon." He disconnected. As he grabbed his keys, he let out a big sigh. "Oh well, who needs sleep, anyway?" he said, before closing the door behind him and locking up.

FRIDAY

Are you going over to the girls?" Roy asked, hanging on the couch in Tristan's office.

Tristan looked up from his laptop. They hadn't slept at all last night, but that certainly wasn't a first. One night without sleep wouldn't kill them.

"Yes, in a minute," he said, closing his laptop. He had Roy prepare a video for Catherine and her friends, so she'd understand everything she needed to know about the asteroid. He'd gone over it three times to judge if it contained enough information and whether it was understandable or not. He thought he could explain it to her now should she have any questions. He was sure she would have a lot of them. If anything, Catherine was very thorough.

Charles would drive her to her mother's. He would just have to confirm a time with Catherine. Roy had gone over the entire grounds of London Fields again to have it completely sealed off from the general public, just to be on the safe side. He'd also connected the girls' mobile phones to their own grid, so they'd be able to reach each other.

"Turbines are still up and running, boss. Don't know how long they will last after MI5's confirmation later this morning, though. Power could go down by twilight," Roy said to him. "I took precautions for your apartment, of course."

Tristan nodded. "Thanks, Roy. I'll be at Catherine's most of the day. I really need Leah to focus on the future, and I want to drill Deborah on this Cailleach goddess."

It was the one factor Tristan wasn't too thrilled of. Too much of a variable. Whatever Catherine had said about the Cailleach being her favourite goddess, a search on the Internet had left him with a pretty dark vibe. This wasn't your average love and healing goddess. Destruction and decay were practically what she was known for. Though Catherine had warned Tristan the Cailleach was often misunderstood, he still didn't like the idea of Catherine possessed by a goddess of destruction and death. They'd decided to ask Alan as a contingency plan. Eve would know how to reach him, a fact Tristan didn't like very much. Last night, he shared the information Eve had given him with Roy and Charles. Just them. He owed them that much.

"And you trust Eve's judgement?" Charles had asked. "I don't mean to imply that I don't trust her, sir," he'd continued. "You know I didn't, but after all that's happened this week I think I can again. It's more. Do you think it was her own opinion?"

Tristan had looked at him understandingly. "I know what you're thinking, Charles. You think Alan might have planted this trust in her head. However, I don't think so. I still don't want him anywhere near Catherine, but if by tomorrow we still don't have a good feeling about this whole goddess thing, we're going to have to involve him. For now, though, I would prefer not to tell Catherine. She has enough on her plate as it is."

"Your call, boss," Roy had said, and Charles had nodded his agreement. They started packing stuff they would need for the next two days.

Tristan had also filled in his boss on what Catherine and her friends were planning to do, but not about the Alan part, though.

"Shouldn't she be focussing on her own powers, though? I don't like this whole involving goddesses plan, Tristan. You'd better talk her out of that. She really should be able to do this herself," his boss had said. That had struck him as an odd assumption.

"Why do you say that? Is there something you know? Something I don't? I have to say, boss, you've been acting strange the last twenty-four hours. If it's something that can help save our planet, I think it's pretty damn important to be in the loop." He'd looked at Trevor to gauge his responses and his emotions. There was definitely hesitation there.

"I'm sorry, Tristan. I can't tell you any more than that. I wish I could. I really do."

"This comes from him, doesn't it? From the Serpent himself?" Tristan had asked. People around the company had started to refer to their big boss as the Serpent a long time ago, as their company logo had two entwined serpents.

Trevor had nodded. "Yes. He says it's vital that all should be revealed at precisely the right moment. As he is the strongest seer the world has ever seen, I have to believe he knows what he's doing, Tristan. It's all I have."

Tristan had understood, but he'd still been surprised. "You've actually met him? I thought nobody ever did?"

His boss had shrugged. "Some people do. I've met him twice now. Once when I felt like leaving the company. I was called up to his office. He persuaded me to stay. I saw him again this morning."

"And you're absolutely sure we're working to stop this thing? Right?" Tristan had asked. He had to ask. If only to interpret his boss's reaction. He'd only felt genuine shock and anger. Whatever the Serpent had planned, his boss had truly believed they were doing everything they could to stop this thing.

"Of course! What are you implying, Tristan?"

Before Trevor could have worked himself up into a state, Tristan had raised his hands in surrender. "Nothing, boss. Just tired, forgive me." His boss had let it go.

"Yes. Well, we're all tired. I know we're putting a lot of strain on you and your team, Tristan. I truly believe you are the right man for the job, though." He'd looked tired himself.

Tristan had thanked him for the vote of confidence and had said his goodbyes. After all, he wasn't sure they would see each other again and he'd always had a good understanding with Trevor. "It's been a pleasure working with you, boss."

Trevor had smiled grimly at him, but had shaken his hand

with a firm grip. "Likewise, Tristan. Now get yourself out of here, and go save this bloody planet. You make sure our girl delivers." And Tristan had left his office.

Now he looked around to see if he had everything he would need. He looked at his friends. "Look, I'll be at Catherine's for quite some time. Charles, I know you have to drive Catherine to her mother's, but if you and Roy want the opportunity to say your goodbyes..." He didn't quite know how to say this. He'd never been good with saying goodbyes himself. He knew Roy had a kid sister who believed he worked for the government and his mother was still alive. Charles had lost his parents quite a while ago. The only person he cared about besides himself and Roy, was his stepdaughter, Cherise. After his wife had been killed, he'd always looked after her, even though she wasn't his own child.

Charles looked at him. "Thank you, sir, but I already talked to my stepdaughter. She has a husband now, as you know. I know he really loves her. She'll be okay."

Roy shrugged. Tristan knew he sucked even more than him when it came to saying goodbye. "Yeah, I guess I should drop by my mum's. I'll give her a ring, boss. Promise. What about you, though? Don't you want to see your parents?"

Tristan shook his head. "It would be a very tight fit, flying back and forth. I know I could make it, but I don't want to leave Catherine here. Of course, I'd like to see them, but I'll manage somehow. Maybe I'll give them a call."

"You really should, sir. We could work around it, you know, if you do want to fly out. Roy and I can hold the ford for a while."

Again he shook his head. "No, my focus should be with Catherine now. Besides, I don't want to leave her alone. Thanks for the offer, though. Okay, I think I have everything. Keep me posted, guys." He gave them his warmest smile and closed the door to his office.

* * *

"Good morning, Catherine. Can I come in?" Tristan said to her after she'd opened the door. She looked a bit disgruntled. He figured she was probably still mad as a snake.

"Don't you look chipper. Sure." She held the door for him. *Note to self, not a morning person,* he thought with a smile.

"Morning, ladies," he greeted Leah and Deborah, who offered him a croissant, which he took. "Thanks, Deborah. Did you girls get any sleep?"

Leah shrugged. "A bit. We were up rather late with phone calls and such. After all, we don't know how long we'll still have a connection."

Tristan nodded. "That's one of the reasons I came over. I took the liberty of adding all your numbers to ours. You'll have no problem reaching each other. Unfortunately, I can't do that for all your loved ones. That would be a bit hard to explain. As far as recharging goes, plug everything in as long as we still have power and turn off your 5G. It'll save batteries."

Leah looked surprised. "Wow, thanks, Tristan. Your company really has some pull. And, of course, we understand. It'll be very convenient to be able to reach each other."

Tristan gave her a small smile. "You're more than welcome, Leah. I also wanted to remind you that as of today you can't go in any lifts anymore. We don't know when the power will shut down, and you don't want to get stuck inside. Take the stairs, ladies. Everywhere."

They all nodded. "Good thinking," Catherine said. "Anything else that might come in handy?"

"Be careful when using a car. Not everyone in London has one, and I've had a lot of reports coming in about stolen vehicles. People are desperate to reach their families and will do things they normally wouldn't. When you drive, try to never to do so alone, and maybe bring something to defend yourself, like a baseball bat."

Deborah stared at him. "And you're not even kidding. I can tell by the look on your face. Wow, I never thought I'd have to worry about things like that."

"Nor should you, Deborah, in a normal situation. These are extreme circumstances. And I have to say, it's going rather well, so far. Lots of people think it's some bad joke, and there are still others who haven't heard the news. Because of this, some companies are still up and running. Mind you, tomorrow will be worse because it's the weekend and news has a funny way of spreading like wildfire. Eventually people will realise this isn't a joke and react differently, most likely panic. We saw the first wave of that last night, just after the news. Leah, I also put a tail on Ryan. I'll give you updates on him whenever I can. New York is in a bad state. Roy told him the best thing he could do is stay put and go outside as little as possible. He said he wanted his kid sister to stay with him, and he'd try to get to her today, but he'd remain inside after that."

Leah's eyes watered. "Thank you, Tristan, I don't know what to say. That means a lot to me. Ryan told me yesterday on the phone he'd try to get to Cindy. She's handicapped, you see. They're twins. Ryan is the eldest by a couple minutes. There were complications at Cindy's birth, and he grew up feeling responsible for that. He loves her very much. I hope he can get to her."

Tristan looked at her. He hadn't known about that. This was obviously important to her, and he couldn't have her stressing over this. "Give me a minute." He took out his phone and walked into the hallway.

"Roy? Remember Ryan, Leah's partner? Yes, his twin sister is handicapped. She won't be able to get to him by herself, and I don't know if it's wise to have him go to her unprotected. Can we spare an escort? Thanks, Roy. I'll let them know."

He walked back into the room. "I can't make any promises, but they will try to give Ryan an escort to her home and make sure they arrive back safely. As long as there aren't any big disasters happening, they might be able to spare someone for a few minutes. It's the middle of the night now in New York, and it'll be easier to move around. They'll contact him and give it a go."

Leah nodded. "Again, thank you. I know you don't have to do this." Obviously, Catherine had filled them all in last night.

He shook his head. "No, I do, actually. It's my job to see to it you have everything you need to succeed. That doesn't stop at supplies and safety. Your chances of succeeding will improve if you're in a positive state of mind. Worrying about loved ones would be considered counterproductive, which is pretty much what I just told my boss, seeing as my cover's blown, anyway," he finished with a slightly arrogant smile. "He hates being lectured, but he did see my point. A lot is riding on this."

Catherine sighed. "Don't remind us."

"I also came by to check when you wanted to visit your mother, Catherine. I'd feel a lot happier if I knew Charles drove you, if you don't mind."

She smiled at him and shook her head. "Not at all. To be honest, that would probably make my visit a lot easier. I was planning to go just after lunch, if that would be convenient for Charles."

Tristan nodded. "Not a problem. Let's say one thirty?"

"That would be perfect, yes," she confirmed. "On a more practical note, should we start defrosting our freezers and such?"

Tristan shook his head. "No, don't do that. Not yet, anyway. As I said, some companies are still up and running. People don't want to risk pissing off their bosses and losing their jobs over some sick joke, which is working in our favour at the moment. As long as the turbines are being checked, we'll have power. I did hear, however, that MI5 will confirm the prime minister's announcement later this morning. From then on, things will escalate. People will leave work, of this I'm sure, but we'll still have a few hours before safety protocol automatically shuts down the plants. Your fridge can go a good six hours without causing a minor flood. So if you possibly can, try to postpone it until morning or late this night."

Deborah looked at Tristan. "Will travelling be safer tonight or early tomorrow morning?"

"Probably early in the morning, but if either you or Leah want to check your homes, I'll make sure you get there. Just give me a call."

"Thanks," she said. "Now if you'll excuse me, I have to get a feel for a certain goddess, and I need some peace and quiet for that. Kate, can I keep using your guest bedroom?"

"Of course, sweetie. Be careful," she added.

"Always," Deborah replied with a smile.

"Well, I'll go into the other room and try to do my homework as well then. See if I can get anything useful for a change," Leah said with a wink at Catherine.

"Good luck, hon. I'll drill Tristan on the asteroid."

Leah smiled. "You do that, and make sure Joni receives all the information she needs as well."

Catherine nodded. "Absolutely."

After Leah and Deborah had closed the doors behind them, Tristan came over to give her a kiss. "I didn't say good morning properly when I came in," he said with a boyish grin. "Good morning, Catherine."

She slowly let go of him. "Good morning, Tristan," she replied. "I could get used to such a greeting."

He smiled. "I'm glad to hear it. So could I. I wasn't sure how you'd feel about me after all the things that happened last night. I believe I heard you say something about drilling me?" He pretended to look scared.

Catherine laughed. "Yes, company man. For your sake, I hope you've come prepared, and you're not getting rid of me that easily."

Tristan opened the suitcase he'd brought. It even had a DVD screen inside. "I'm glad to hear it. And I have everything here you might want to know. We've made a little film about the asteroid's course. You can see what to expect. I'll make sure Joni sees it as well. Anyone else?"

"Meg," Catherine immediately replied. "She may not be a master of death, but she knows more about it than anyone I know." She hesitated. "Well, that's not exactly true, of course, but Alan isn't really an option, now is he?"

Tristan sat next to her, putting the suitcase on the side table in front of them. "He would be, if we could find him." That was true, after all. He could not find him. Eve could, of course, but it wasn't exactly lying. At least that's what he told himself.

She looked at him. "You're trying to find him?"

"Of course, we are. I'm certainly not a fan, but even I have to admit his powers could come in handy. So far, we have nothing." Still true, he didn't know where Alan was staying. For all he knew, he was with Eve right now. Wouldn't that make for an interesting conversation. *I think there's a good chance your ex is hooking up with my ex.* Not such a good idea.

She looked at him, smiling sadly. "You're forgetting he's also an empath, which doesn't make him a seer, but his powers are very strong. Whenever he feels anxious, he'll move. I don't think you'll find him unless he wants to be found. He was able to walk around here for more than two hours without being discovered. And that's with a bunch of specially gifted people present. I think that says enough."

"Any more insights on the 'soon you will see' card?" He tried to direct her thoughts to where he wanted them and away from Alan.

"None." Catherine sighed. "Alan always liked riddles and puzzles. I never had the patience. Funny thing is, I thought I'd be more scared, knowing he's out there fully restored, but I'm not. I don't know why exactly. Maybe I'm just being naïve, but

I'm actually kind of glad I didn't destroy his soul after all. It always bothered me that my powers could do something like that." She gave Tristan a soft smile.

Well, that was good. She shouldn't be afraid of Alan. If what he told Eve was true, Alan wasn't holding a grudge against Catherine. Still, Tristan wouldn't put money on that. "I understand the sentiment, and I'm glad you're not worried. I hope you'll forgive me if I worry for you, though."

Catherine smiled. "Hmm, I think I can live with that. Now, show me what you have, and we'll see what we can do about this thing."

"Yes, ma'am," he said before hitting the play button.

They kept at it till it was almost one thirty and Tristan reminded Catherine that Charles would be waiting downstairs for her. He closed the laptop as Catherine went to say goodbye to both Leah and Deborah, who were still in their respective rooms. He also suspected that they were trying to give them as much time together as possible. He appreciated that. When Catherine came into the living room, he walked with her, taking two steps at once on the staircases, until he became aware she couldn't keep up and slowed down.

Charles had the car running and was about to get out when Catherine resolutely opened the front passenger door. Tristan smiled and gave her a quick kiss goodbye. "Good luck," he said to her. She smiled at him and he went back into the hall, taking the stairwell back up three at a time.

"Ah, Leah. Excellent," he said when he re-entered Catherine's apartment. "Just the person I was looking for. How is the seeing coming along?"

Leah looked at him. "Still not sure, Tristan. I can't really control it, you know? It just comes and goes as it pleases. It always has."

"There are ways to enhance your powers, you know. Our seers often deprive themselves of other input. They submerge into water to get a clearer reading, for example." He could feel she was surprised by that.

"Well, that actually sounds fascinating, Tristan. My visions are always quite clear, though, once I have them. It's just hard for me to steer them into a certain direction. And I often see just a few moments ahead. A couple of days at most."

"That would be enough, though. A couple of days is good. Listen, Leah, I really think you're quite powerful. I say this because our seers seldom get clear visions. We have one who can really look into the future, but that's the exception. Could you try? For me?"

She looked a bit sceptical but nodded. "Sure, Tristan. Deborah and Kate actually have a sort of lagoon at Elements. I could try over there, if you like."

He smiled. "Thank you, Leah. That would really make me happy, yes. Just give it your best shot. Before you go, though, could you ask Deborah to come out if she's ready? I'd really need to know more about this Cailleach."

"I need her, anyway. I don't know the access code to go through the moss wall. Hang on, I'll go get her."

She walked to the room Deborah had gone into. A few seconds later they both emerged from the room and Deborah looked at Tristan. "You wanted to know more about the Cailleach, I understand? What is it you want to know, exactly?" she said as she entered her code to allow Leah entrance. "You go right through, hon. You know where the lights are and such, right?"

Leah nodded. "Yes, I can help myself. I'll let you know when I'm done. Don't let him drill you," she said with a wink at Tristan. He smiled at her.

Tristan motioned for Deborah to move to Catherine's living room area. "Shall we sit over here?" He sat down on the couch and Deborah sat down across from him. "Did you get anything at all so far?" he asked her gently.

She nodded. "Yes, I did. It's quite strange, actually. I would never associate the Cailleach with anything soft, though I'm sure Kate would disagree with me, but she almost feels gentle to me. She has never felt gentle to me. That must work in our favour, right?"

Tristan thought for a moment. "I don't know. Maybe. She is a goddess of death and rebirth. Catherine is obviously very fond of her. If those sentiments are shared by her, she might feel gentle because she knows what's coming and wants to soften the blow. Or something like that. Honestly, Deborah, I don't know. I have to be honest here. I'm out of my depths on this part. So I'm going to go with your judgement here."

He felt her uneasiness and could sense she dreaded the responsibility of getting it wrong. He understood that all too well. "I'm not asking you to be right, Deborah. I'm asking you to be sure. As sure as you can." Now she felt frustrated.

"I know, Tristan, but that's a rather tall order. I wish you hadn't said that. About her trying to soften the blow. I hadn't even thought of that. Christ, what a mess! How am I supposed to figure out what she wants?"

"I could work with you if you like. I know very little about gods and goddesses, but I could enhance your empathic abilities. You know, lend you my powers. Transferral. If you let me." He looked at her, his eyes and mind open. He felt her surprise and a slight sense of awe.

"You'd do that? I'm flattered that you'd trust me with your powers, Tristan, but that could be quite dangerous as well."

He shrugged. "Only if one of us is hesitant to either receive or give back our respective powers. I'm not. So how about it, Deborah? Willing to give it a go?" He gave her a warm smile, which she returned.

"You really care about her, don't you?" she asked. It was obvious she meant Catherine.

He nodded. "Yes. Yes, I do."

Deborah sat up straighter. "Okay. I trust you. And I thank you for your trust, Tristan. It means a lot to me." She held out her hands, palms up and he placed his hands over hers. The second their hands touched, he could feel the connection as his empathic powers recognized hers. He gently guided his powers her way and could feel her mind whirling, reaching out to the Cailleach. After that, his senses were cut off as his powers had gone over to Deborah. He focussed on his breathing and went into a meditative state.

"Tristan…Tristan? Come back to the here and now. Focus on your breathing. Become aware of your surroundings," he heard Deborah's voice say to him. "Now wiggle your fingers and your toes. When you're ready, open your eyes." He did as she instructed and felt his mind and body return to the here and now.

"How long was I out?" he asked. She looked exhausted. He felt fine. More than fine, actually.

"Almost two hours. I'm starving. Are your powers intact?" she asked a bit nervously.

He reached out to his empathic abilities. "Yes, still there." She'd done an excellent job. Power transferral was a tricky thing. Or, at least, it could be. If the other person didn't have your best interest at heart, you could get seriously damaged. He'd seen people at the company wind up in their mental hospital wing and never get out. Of course, Deborah was one of Catherine's most trusted friends, so he'd decided to trust her as well. It all came down to intent. If you had the other person's well-being at heart, the energy would guide itself back to the one it belonged to. If you didn't, the energy could overload or backfire. Either one with catastrophic results. It could have left him or Deborah powerless. He nodded to her. "You did great, Deborah. Did it work?"

She smiled. "I'll tell you all about it over lunch. Leah just came back as well, and it is way past lunch time. Come on, company man."

He hesitated. "But did it work?"

"Food, Tristan! Food!" Deborah wacked him over the head. "Yes, Tristan, food."

Leah joined them, hair still wet and looking at him with a murderous glare.

Tristan thought it was probably best to give in. They looked quite dangerous. Maybe he'd worked them too hard. "Okay, okay. Lunchtime it is."

* * *

After lunch, Tristan took Leah aside. Deborah had said she was absolutely sure the Cailleach's intentions were soft and gentle and that she would mean no harm to Catherine. Tristan, however, didn't like this part of the plan at all. It was much too vague and he kept asking Deborah questions if she was absolutely certain Catherine would not be harmed by this so-called goddess. Deborah had said so several times until she cried out, "What more do you want, Tristan? A sacred vow! Good grief! Let it go already." He'd mumbled an apology and passed her another croissant as a peace offering. The only thing Leah had shared over lunch was that she had seen something beyond Saturday. Deborah had been pleased by that news, but Tristan picked up on Leah emotions. They were mixed with fear. As Deborah left through the moss wall to clean up in Elements, Tristan and Leah went to sit in Catherine's living room.

"You're not happy with what you saw," he said.

Leah looked at him. "No, I'm not. Though I do owe you a thank you. That was the clearest vision I ever had. Full colour. A real 'the hills are alive with the sound of music' kind of vision. Look, considering what we're about to face, anything that I see beyond Saturday is a good thing, right?"

He nodded. "Yes, I would say so. Unless it's another asteroid you saw, and please don't say that." He tried to lighten the mood and it worked. She actually smiled.

"Ha! Wouldn't that be something? Thankfully, the answer is no. No more asteroids. I did see another ball, though. Are you familiar with the ball drop in Times Square?"

"New York? Yes, of course. Who isn't? It's quite famous."

She nodded. "Well, that's what I saw. The ball drop on New Year's Eve. We were all there. And I do mean all of us. You and Roy were there as well. And I saw Alan with a dark-haired woman."

Eve! Tristan thought but said nothing. "There must be more, though. A ball drop wouldn't have scared you like this."

"No, you're right, of course. It dropped way too fast. There was an explosion. I saw a lot of people lying on the ground. I'd rather keep that last part between us, if you don't mind. Catherine has enough on her plate as it is. Besides, the future isn't set. It is what we make of it. My vision can change. There's no need to worry her about something that might never happen."

He looked at her. "Okay. She won't hear anything from me. You don't want to tell her about the ball drop, either?"

She shook her head. "No, I will tell her about that. It will give her confidence. I'll even say it moved too fast. Catherine knows me way too well. She'll feel my anxiety, and this will explain it."

Tristan looked at her. She and Deborah reminded him of Charles and Roy. They too would do anything to protect him and keep him safe from harm. "You're a good friend, Leah. I can see why Catherine is so fond of you and Deborah. It's a blessing to have such good friends in your life."

"Sounds like someone who's had that experience as well?" she said with a smile.

"Thankfully, yes. How do you think she'll react?"

"Good. If anything, Catherine's an optimist. Way more than me. She'll skip over the whole dropping too fast part. Trust me. Catherine's a 'we'll cross that bridge when we get there' kind of woman. Deborah is the more worrying type. Always planning ahead. It's what makes them a good team."

He smiled at her. "Yes, I sort of figured that out myself. Leah? If we get through this, would you do me a favour?"

She looked at him. "Depends on the favour."

"Fair enough. If you get any other visions, would you be so kind to let the company I work for know? We could really use your insight."

She looked surprised. "Oh! Umm, sure, Tristan. How do I reach them?"

He handed her a business card. It was just a PO box and their general number, but it would be enough. If she asked for him, they'd know what to do. Leah took the card and tucked it in her wallet.

"You wouldn't be interested in a change of career, would you?" he said with a teasing smile, meanwhile gently making sure the business card went to a place in the back of her mind. In time, she would remember she had it.

Leah laughed. "Hell no! I have enough problems as it is, making my deadlines. And now with the film coming out next year, it will be total mayhem, I imagine."

"Film?" Tristan asked, and Leah went on to explain that her first book was in the process of becoming a movie.

* * *

"Hey, sweetheart, how did it go with your family?" Tristan asked Catherine as soon as she walked through the door. He gave her a kiss. He noticed Leah and Deborah exchange smiles.

"It went fine. A bit emotional, of course, but I'm glad I saw them. Not that I won't see them again, but...well, you know what I mean."

"I do," he said. "I just got off the phone with Meg. Leah said you might need a place to practise or come together, and Meg's store seems the most suitable location. You can gather there tomorrow afternoon as well before the ritual. Roy will make sure you have a clear route from her house to London Fields."

"Oh, excellent. Thanks. Meg was fine with it?" she asked.

Leah and Tristan nodded. "Yes, she was happy to help out. The Cailleach feels 'soft' to her, if that means anything to you? And, Deborah, you said you got the same vibe, right?"

Deborah nodded. "Yes, she does feel soft, almost gentle, so I think we won't have any trouble on that account, Kate."

He was glad she felt relieved by that bit of information.

"Well, that's one less thing to worry about. Lee, anything?" Catherine asked.

Leah looked at her. "Yes, actually. It's good news for now, though maybe not in general. I saw the ball drop. In New York, I mean."

Catherine looked excited. "That's good, right? That's like way after tomorrow!"

Leah frowned. "Yes, darling, but if you let me finish. It dropped rather fast. I'm not sure if that is something to be happy about."

"Oh," she said, and Tristan felt her excitement ebb away. "No, that's not good. I mean, it's good for now, right?"

"For now, we'll go with good," Tristan said, looking at Leah with a slightly accusing glare. He didn't want Catherine to worry. They had agreed on that. She did that more than enough. He saw Leah roll her eyes, but she let it go.

"Deborah, could we go over the information one more time?" he asked, walking over to her.

Deborah sighed but motioned to the living room nonetheless. "Sure, Tristan. Let's go over it again."

Tristan did his best to hide his smile but forced himself not to take pity on her. This was important, after all. It was still their greatest variable in this whole ritual and he needed to be sure Catherine would be as safe as possible. He didn't like the sound of "letting her take over." It sounded way too much like being possessed. He explained as much to Deborah.

"Well, basically that is exactly what it is. It just has a very negative sound. Look, I won't make light of it. There's always a risk. It's the whole 'in perfect love and perfect trust' thing, I guess."

"Wait. You'll have to explain that to me," he said.

"It's what we say to each other, Tristan. One of the things, anyway. If you don't trust each other within a circle, that can affect the outcome and the people inside it. We're creating a sacred space, and in doing so, we're trusting each other with our lives. Even with our souls. Catherine will go one step further and trust her body and soul to the goddess."

Tristan mulled over that while Deborah looked at him. "What if she doesn't want to give Catherine her body back? A god or goddess is not corporeal. What if she sticks around, so to speak, does that ever happen?"

Deborah looked at him with a sad smile. "Of course, it happens. Where do you think exorcisms come from? Theoretically speaking, though, those usually involve entities with bad intentions. We have to assume the Cailleach has good intentions. Catherine trusts her. She always has. And even I have to admit, they do have a special connection. She always represents her at Samhuinn, you see. This won't be the first time. Each year is different. I've cried in her arms and crumbled before her in fear. None of that is Catherine. That is pure Cailleach. And she always gives her back to us. Sometimes Catherine can be a bit…off, afterwards. Chocolate helps. It grounds you to the earth. The Harry Potter books got quite a lot of those little things right," she said with a smile.

"And you're really sure she feels soft, Deborah? I know, I sound like a broken record. I just don't like the whole idea of something else inside her."

Deborah smiled, a knowing look on her face. "I understand, Tristan. You care about her. Just don't forget, we do too, and we've known her a lot longer. You have to trust us that we know what we're doing."

"In perfect love and in perfect trust?" he asked her with a smile.

She laughed. "See? We'll turn you into one of us one day. Come, I see dinner is ready."

Having learned from his earlier mistake by denying the ladies food, he quickly got up and followed her to the kitchen. "After you, milady."

* * *

Tristan had been somewhat surprised when Catherine had asked him to go down to his apartment after dinner, but he had complied nonetheless.

"Why are you trying to ground and centre me?" he asked, handing her a glass of wine.

Catherine looked up. "Excuse me?" she asked.

"I can feel earth all over the place. You're obviously trying to ground or calm me for something."

Now she felt annoyed. After she explained to him what she wanted, he understood why, because he was pretty annoyed himself. Catherine thought it was a good idea for Tristan to visit his parents. She had deliberately been trying to keep him calm and relaxed, using her earth element, which corresponded with those feelings, so he wouldn't freak out. And people thought he could be manipulative! It didn't do her much good, though because he could already feel himself starting to freak out.

"No. Absolutely not. Out of the question!" He stood again after having just sat down. "Is that why you wanted to talk down here?" What the hell? Didn't she want him here? What was going on?

She just looked at him. "Will you let me explain?"

He felt all her emotions surface. She was deliberately giving him her feelings. The pain of losing her father, the worry about her mother and the rest of her family and her friends.

"I wasn't there when my dad died. I still have nightmares about that, you know. Sometimes I wake up screaming in the middle of the night and he'll look at me with disappointed eyes. I know it's my imagination. My father would never be disappointed in me. He's just reflecting my feelings in the dream and my guilt, but I wish I could have been there. Done more. Most of all, though, I wish I had the chance to say goodbye."

Catherine had tears in her eyes, and Tristan felt his own throat tighten. Not just for her, but he knew his mother would be worried sick. He could just picture his father comforting her, always trying to be her rock, but he would be scared for Tristan's safety as well. They were both very religious people, and Tristan knew they did not fear death themselves. They would only fear for the life of their son, even if they did believe he would join them in a better place afterwards. Tristan was not so sure about that himself. Catherine was not finished, however.

"If there's anything I could wish for is to have that chance, should we not prevail, to say goodbye. Shh...I know what you're going to say. That we are going to prevail and I do think we have a chance, but let's be realistic here, Tristan. It's no more than a chance. I won't deny you this. This window of opportunity if you like. You have to say goodbye to your parents. You'll never forgive yourself if you don't. I believe in an afterlife and I believe in reincarnation, but I also believe in lost souls. What if you'd feel so guilty for not saying goodbye that your soul doesn't know where to go? I won't have that on my conscience. Besides, Roy and Charles will be here every step of the way. We could still stay in touch, right? If you can honestly say I won't be safe here without you, I'll leave it alone."

He felt like a caged animal. "Ah, Catherine, that's just not fair. Don't get me wrong, of course, I'd like to see my parents, but I'd be worried sick about you." He would be worried sick, but he also understood what she was saying and in his head he was already doing the math. It couldn't be his own little plane. It wouldn't be fast enough. One of the company's Syberjets would be and he was sure he could get his hands on one if he pulled some serious strings. Then it would only be a two-hour flight. He could say goodbye to his parents and be back on time for Catherine to face the asteroid. In theory, it could work. He was actually considering it but snapped out of it when she spoke again.

"That's nonsense. You said yourself we'll be able to reach each other by phone, or do you honestly think Roy and the rest of your division can't handle this?"

"What? No, of course not. I trust them with my life."

"Well, apparently not with my life. Tristan, look, this would really make me happy."

He sighed and ran his hands through his hair. God, she really wasn't playing fair. "Emotional blackmail. Just great. An empath beaten by means of emotional blackmail by an elemental. That will go down well on my file."

She smiled. "So you'll go?"

He came over to her and cupped her face. "It's as if you want me to leave, Catherine."

She looked at him, and he felt a rush of desire, warmth and love wash over him. It left him breathless. "I don't want you to leave. Or perhaps I should say that I don't want to leave. I want to stay, Tristan." She looked straight into his eyes, leaving him no room to mistake her meaning.

Tristan pulled her even closer. "Then stay." He knew this was not a good idea. It would only make their attachment stronger. If they did pull this off, he'd eventually have to leave her. The company didn't allow relationships for people like him. He didn't want to think about leaving her, though. He wanted her in his life, dammit. He would find a way, he promised himself as he took possession of her mouth. He felt her fire surrounding him, and he welcomed it and embraced it. She moved with him, anticipating his every move, and he felt his own powers going over to her. It wasn't anything like the exercise he'd worked on with Deborah that afternoon. It was like he was sharing his gifts with her, like she was sharing hers with him. It took him a second to realize that he knew how her elements worked and he was actually a part of them.

She tried to pull his T-shirt over his head, and his hands went up to assist her. He threw it on the ground and made quick work of her T-shirt and bra as well, leaving him a clear view to admire her magnificent breasts. When her hands touched his naked skin, he let out a soft hiss and reached for her earth element to ground himself. It embraced him, which enabled him to pull her up. He felt her legs twist themselves around his waist. Kicking off his shoes, he slowly moved towards the bedroom. If they could make it to the bedroom.

Catherine started to nibble on his ear, and Tristan felt the fire take over. Laying her down gently on the bed, he reached for the button on her jeans and pulled them off. Her nails dug into his shoulder blades and he arched his back. In one fluid movement, she rolled him on his back and he let her take control. Making quick work of his own jeans and shorts, Tristan leaned back to admire Catherine. Her hair cascaded all the way down to her lower back, and he thought he'd never seen anything more beautiful. Her eyes were like emeralds. He'd never seen them so bright. He sat up to caress her breasts. When his mouth closed around one of her nipples, she let out a soft moan. He was quickly losing control and felt her control slipping as well.

As she sat down on his lap, he thought his head would explode. Somewhere in the middle they must have switched places and Catherine somehow had removed her knickers, for he was lying on top now and moving faster. He could feel her mind and the fire engulfed him, taking him over and pushing him over the edge. He breathed out her name and could actually feel her climax. Another second and Tristan was sure the world had just ended.

SATURDAY

Tristan loved to watch Catherine. She looked so peaceful asleep. He gently pulled a lock of hair out of her face. He sighed. Last night had been one for the books, and he wasn't sure how he could ever go on without being able to have this. Sex with Eve had always been good and he certainly never had any complaints, but this had been, magic. He didn't have another word for it. Ah, she was awakening. Making love to her had left a lingering connection somehow. He could sense her elements more clearly. He wondered if it would be the same for her.

"Good morning, beautiful," he said, gently kissing the top of her head.

"Good morning," she said, a bit self-conscious. "Do you mind if I take a shower here?"

"Not at all, though I wouldn't say no to sharing one, either."

She smiled. "I have little confidence in your powers of self-control, Mr. Visconti, and you do have a plane to catch, so to speak."

Tristan looked at her with puppy dog eyes. "I promise to be good."

"Well, that wasn't really my concern," she said, a faint blush on her cheek.

Tristan kept looking at her as she was trying to locate her clothes. He'd already established they were all over the place like his own and thought it was rather cute to see her slightly embarrassed. He could almost feel her thoughts now. Not that he could pick up actual words, but he'd now experienced first-hand her elements were tied to her emotions. She was quite a vocal person when it came to her emotions. It was almost like being able to read her mind. For example, she was now reminiscing about last night, and he was pleased to sense what she was feeling. He felt a sheer amount of awe and wonder coming from her, mixed with a feeling of content and pure pleasure. Like seeing a rainbow for the first time and not being able to quite explain the magic of something so beautiful. He felt the same way. Tristan decided to give her some time alone, though. "Oh, go on then. I'll fix us breakfast in the meantime and see if there's any news we should be aware of."

She gave him a grateful smile and then went into the shower. She didn't take long and came out of the bathroom with a towel wrapped around her head and wearing one of his T-shirts.

"Hmm, that looks much better on you than on me," he said while getting some croissants and two *pains au chocolat* out of the oven.

"Ooh, that smells nice. And thanks, I guess. Any news?" she asked as she sat and then buttered a croissant.

"Power is down, as expected," he said. "A few more cars were stolen, some supermarkets have been robbed, and there was an incident at the docks. People were trying to get out by boat, and there was a shooting. One man was fatally injured, and two were wounded. Try to avoid public transport today. Don't go near the Underground. Nor the docks or any shopping malls. People will become more violent during the day. Maybe I should just stay here?" He'd already received confirmation from the company that the SJ30 had been fully fuelled and was ready for take-off, but he could cancel that any given moment.

Catherine sighed. "Tristan, we've been over this. I'm not a child, and Roy and Charles will still be here if I need anything. London Fields is set up, and I wasn't exactly planning on anything else." She paused. "Hang on. If the power's out, how the hell did you make these?" She pointed at her croissant.

"I have my own generator. It's not rocket science, you know."

Catherine rolled her eyes. "Oh, bla! Anyway, you're going. You'll be doing your parents a huge favour, and if the shit really hits the fan, you could even get back in time. Though I really think you shouldn't. You're the one saying I have nothing to worry about, so stop worrying. Not wanting to leave me here alone isn't exactly a vote of confidence."

That annoyed him. "That's slightly unfair, don't you think?"

"Yes, but if it's working, I won't be taking it back." She gave him a kiss. "I thought we agreed on this."

He sighed. "We did. Okay, I'll leave instructions with Roy. If there's anything, and I do mean anything, that you need, you give him a call. He'll notify me if he thinks I'm needed."

"I promise," Catherine said.

Somehow, he didn't trust her for a second. She was probably crossing her fingers behind her back. He wouldn't put it past her. He'd told her it was a four-hour flight, which was true. It was four hours there and back again. She had jumped to another conclusion, and he hadn't corrected her. They'd agreed he would leave after breakfast, so he'd be in Italy well before dusk. He'd check in with her as soon as he arrived.

After breakfast, Catherine went into the bedroom to get dressed as well. She returned, her hair still wet, hanging over one shoulder in one big braid.

"Do you want me to go upstairs with you?" he asked when she joined him the living room.

"No, I'll explain to the girls. Don't you worry about that. As long as you don't forget to text me once you're there because this whole you flying a plane thing doesn't sit very well with me." She smiled.

Of all the things to be worried about. "Yes, ma'am," he said as he gently pulled her braid. He guessed Catherine didn't like things that were out of her control, though this trip had been her idea. Not unlike him. He didn't like things out of his control either. He was becoming more and more attuned to her mind. He sighed. How long would he have to enjoy those privileges? "You do realise I've flown that thing like a thousand times, right?"

"Even so, I hate things that are out of my control."

See, I'm getting better at this. He looked at her. "That makes two of us."

Catherine looked sympathetic. "I know." She stood on tiptoe to give him a kiss. He leaned forward and immediately deepened it. She sighed into his mouth.

"You should go now," she mumbled, "before I decide to keep you here."

He smiled under her lips. He'd said something similar to her on one of their dates. "I'll see you soon. Remember, don't try to control your powers. Let them out full force. Connect to the Cailleach, and it'll work. You can do this. I know you can."

She laughed. "Yes, sir. Thanks for the pep talk. Now get out of here." She gently pushed him toward the stairs in the hallway. He closed his front door and then gave her one last kiss.

"You're not getting rid of me. I'm in love with you."

She sighed, pretending to be annoyed. "Now he tells me." She smiled. "I love you too, Tristan."

He let go of her hand and then walked down the stairs. Next stop, the company.

* * *

"You so totally had sex with her!" Roy pointed an accusing finger at Tristan, hanging on the sofa in Tristan's office like a slouch.

Tristan sighed. What was the point of denying? "And what if I did?" There. That took the wind out of his wings.

"Oh. Well, nothing, I guess. It's just you got this whole glowing look going on. It's freaking me out. You're not turning 'the hills are alive with the sound of music' on me, right?"

Tristan almost choked on his coffee. "The hills...what? God no! I'm still a badass."

Roy smirked. "Sure, boss. Whatever you say. So, that good, huh?" He winked at Tristan.

"I'm not discussing the details of my love life with you, so don't even bother trying. Now, walk me through the London Fields set-up one more time."

Roy punched his shoulder. "Nice distraction tactic. Okay, I'll give you a break. Come over here," he said, opening his laptop. Tristan moved to stand next to him, so he could look at the screen. Roy pointed to a spot somewhere on the far end. "This is where the circle will be. I figure the park is most solid over here. Considering the power they'll be raising, we need that ground intact for as long as possible. The trees over here and here," he pointed them out to Tristan, "are a liability. So are the Lido and the cricket buildings on the other side. Let's face it. We have no idea what the blast radius of their circle will be, so we made sure to be as far away from the buildings as possible."

Tristan looked at the screen. "That's completely on the other side, though. Surely they won't raise that much energy?"

Roy raised his eyebrows. "Really? Have you met these women? You were there last night, right. I think we'll be lucky if there's still a park left once they're done. Perhaps I'm wrong. Let's hope so. It was you who warned us to give the circle a wide berth, remember?"

He smiled. "Point taken. And better safe than sorry. Okay, so where is the team going to be?"

"At the perimeters." Roy pointed to several dots on the screen. "Charles and I will be as close to the circle as I deem safe. Though Charles is quite confident he can shield Catherine and all three of us, at least for a few seconds, should we need that. You can join us from this side," Roy said, pointing at another spot.

"Now, I want to know every move she makes while I'm off to Italy. I'm serious about this, Roy."

Charles had been awfully pleased Tristan was flying out to see his parents. "Oh, I knew she'd be a good influence on you, sir. I think that's a great idea. You'll be back in plenty of time, and I promise to take good care of her." Charles had suggested he could offer his services at Meg's place so

Catherine would have someone to practice her powers on. He and Roy had both agreed this was a good idea and probably the least dangerous. Charles was a really powerful blocker, after all. With Catherine trying out her powers full force, he would stand the best chance to make sure Meg still had both her house and shop intact. Charles would also give it his all during the ritual itself, trying to give Catherine as much of a protective shield as he could. It might give her a few extra seconds to destroy the asteroid. Catherine had protested when she heard what Charles was planning to do for her, but he'd persuaded her by telling her she would do the same for him. Catherine had looked at him and had given him a hug. Tristan smiled at the memory. Charles had been so embarrassed.

"Don't worry about it," Roy said. "I'll keep track of her every single minute. Besides, you really think Charles is going to let her out of his sight?"

Tristan smiled. "No, probably not. I know how persuasive Catherine can be, however, don't let her trick you into something. Despite appearances, she has a devious streak. Make no mistake."

Roy grinned. "You sure know how to pick them, boss. I'll be on my guard. Promise," he added quickly, seeing Tristan's rather grim face.

"Good," he replied. "I don't want to have to worry about either one of you as well. I have enough to worry about as it is."

Now Roy looked at him with a serious face. "Aww, that's nonsense, boss. We can hold our own. Don't worry about us. We'll be fine." His tone turned lighter. "We have been known to deal with similar situations, you know. And let's face it. If you've seen one asteroid, you've seen them all."

Tristan couldn't help but smile. "All too true. Okay. You should be heading over to Meg's. I'll be back in five hours, give or take. I'll keep you posted. Stay clear of that circle of hers, Roy. I think there will be one hell of a blast radius if you get too close. I'm going to see if Eve's still here, say goodbye, and then head to the hangar."

Roy smiled at him. "We can do this manly hugging thing, right?"

Tristan grinned back. "Hell, yes, we can! Come here." He gave his friend a big bear hug.

Once Roy had left to pick up Charles, Tristan made sure he got everything he needed and locked up his office. He walked over to the other side of the building and walked through the glass hallways. Soon he reached the Oak Room and knocked. No answer. Tristan tried the door, and it opened at his touch. Maybe she had stepped out for just a second. Eve would never leave her office unprotected. Tristan looked around but saw so sign of her inside.

"Eve? Are you here?" he called out. No response. That was weird. All her favourite books were gone. He stepped inside and closed the door behind him. All her personal items were gone as well. He went over to her desk. It was unlocked. Tristan soon found out why. There's was nothing in there. All her files were gone. *What the hell?* He took out his phone and dialled her number. Straight to voicemail. This was getting weirder and weirder. He dialled another number.

"Roy? Could you locate Eve for me? She isn't here."

"Sure thing, boss. Is something up?" he asked.

Tristan decided not to worry him. "No, it's probably nothing. I just need to know where she is." He waited a few seconds. He could hear Roy's fingers drumming over the keyboard.

"She's at home, boss. Well, the jacket is. Do you want me to check up on her?"

He hesitated. Eve had promised to wear it whenever she went out. So far she had done just that. "No, that's a negative. Thanks, Roy. That's all I needed to know."

"Okay. We're almost at Meg's. I sent escorts to pick up the other ladies. We'll wait for them and get started. Take care, boss."

"You too, Roy." He disconnected. Eve must have had her reasons for clearing out her personal belongings. Taking one more look around her office, he closed the door behind him, leaving it unlocked, like she had left it.

* * *

"She's ready for you, sir. I assume you want to check her yourself?" a man in a blue overalls asked him. "Here are the weather conditions in print, sir. And you need to sign these for the boss."

He nodded. "Yes, thank you." Tristan signed the paperwork and proceeded to do a walk-around. He checked the condition of the tires and walked to the front of the plane and made sure it was as bird-roof as possible. He also checked the wear on the brakes to see whether they were within tolerance limits. Tristan also looked over the fan blades for any nicks and let his eyes move over the entire plane for any signs of fuel, oil or hydraulic leaks. She looked good.

When he stepped into the cockpit, he programmed his flight plan into the computer, checked the speed bugs on the primary flight display, set the initial altitude to climb to 5000 feet, checked the status of the oxygen bottles, and tested his oxygen mask. After he'd established all the electrical circuit breakers were in place, he also checked ACARS for departure clearance. The system essentially allowed him to text message the company to receive weather reports and his flight plan, and it automatically sent some of the information back to the company. He was barely finished when he received clearance to taxi out to the active runway. All in all, it was an hour later that Tristan was up in the air.

While keeping his focus, he let his mind wander. His parents would certainly be surprised to see him. It had been over a good six months since the last time he visited them. They had all been so busy lately. First his assignment in Colombia, then Prague. It was good to be back in England, even if London wasn't his favourite city. Catherine loved London, and his liking of it had increased seeing it through her eyes. He certainly approved of Shoreditch. It was a nice neighbourhood. He still owned a house in Brighton. If all this was over and he could find a way to see her without the company breathing down his neck, he might take her there. He thought she might like Brighton. One just had to know where to go and avoid the tourist traps. Yes, he would do that. He might even take Catherine to Italy. His mother would probably die of happiness if he ever brought a woman back home. They'd had never met Eve, though they had known of her existence.

Eve. He was glad they were on friendly terms again. He'd missed her. He wondered why she had packed all her personal belongings. Then again, her file cabinet had also been empty, so maybe someone cleaned it out for her. Maybe they were moving her office? *No, that's ridiculous. Like the company would arrange such a thing at a time like this.* He couldn't help but shake the feeling she'd left the company. Eve had been restless the entire week. She had never been the epitome of calm, but Eve was good at acting. They all were. They had to be. Perhaps he was reading into things that weren't there. It was he who was restless. Perhaps he picked up on hers because he was the one having second thoughts. About his life, about the company, about Catherine.

Tristan had always been proud to work for the company, making a difference and making the world a better place. A safer place. Those were things that mattered to him. Yes, it came at a great personal cost, but it was worth it. Or at least, it always had been. Ever since Catherine came into his life, things had changed. He knew someone like her would be of great value to the company, but he would never allow that to happen. Funny. Why was that? Didn't he trust them anymore? This last week trust had been kind of a theme. The longer he thought about it, the more he realized he didn't trust them anymore. Not implicitly, at least. Like the murder of his contact. He was pretty sure that had been an inside job. At first, he'd been sure Alan was behind the kill, but he trusted Eve's judgement. Alan wasn't behind that kill. Someone had been helping him behind the scenes to make sure Alan could get the painting inside the gallery. It had the company written all over it. Tristan wasn't as naïve to think they never killed anyone because it was convenient. Collateral damage, they called it. This had been planned to the second, though. He was almost halfway, still reminiscing when he received a phone call from his boss.

"Tristan here."

"How far out are you? We need you back here asap. Alan's here, and he only wants to talk to you. Says he has vital information. We put him under a lot of pressure, but he won't budge."

"Shit! It will take me at least one hour, boss. I'll turn around right now and get there as fast as I can. Whatever you do, though, don't let him out of your sight."

"Trust me. We won't." His voice sounded dangerously low. "Get back here safely, you hear me? That's an order."

"Yes, sir. Tristan out."

He diverted back to London and asked for clearance from air traffic control. After he'd received his clearance, he programmed his new flight plan and sighed. "This had better be good, Alan." Exactly one hour later, Tristan exited the hangar he'd just left a couple of hours earlier. One of the company's cars was already waiting for him, motor running. Tristan got in the back.

"Sir," the driver nodded to him. "He'll meet you at Aldwych tube station." And with one more nod to Tristan, he drove off.

Convenient, Tristan thought. Aldwych was an abandoned tube station. It had been for many years. No spectators. Not that the streets were very busy to begin with. Looking outside, they were almost completely deserted. So they had let him out of their sight. Again. He felt sure his boss wouldn't be too pleased about that. Alan had apparently set his own conditions. Either his information was very valuable or someone inside the company was protecting his back. His thoughts shifted to Eve. No. She wouldn't betray him. Not on purpose, anyway. He was sure of that.

When they arrived, Tristan exited the car, thanking the driver. Checking to see if anybody was watching, he made quick work of one of the locks to the entrance and granted himself access. As it was still locked, Alan must have entered from a different side. Tristan pulled out his gun and took the safety off. Just in case. When he reached the platform, Alan was already waiting for him. Tristan slowly walked towards him, all his defences up. Alan looked at him with a slightly amused expression.

"So sorry to interrupt the reunion with dear old Mum and Dad," Alan said with a strong Dutch accent. "But I think you'll find my information rather valuable. Wouldn't want the world to end, now would we?"

His eyes were almost black, Tristan noticed. He could barely see where the iris began and the pupil ended. It made him harder to read. Not that he could. Alan had all his defences up as well.

"I have to say, Kate left me quite disappointed," Alan continued. "She used to be much smarter when she was still with me. Must be the company she's keeping now. I left her several clues and she still hasn't figured it out. They assured me she would, you know." His eyes glittered, and Tristan suppressed a shudder. "Your precious company. Guess they were wrong. Wouldn't be the first time, right? But then again, you know more about that than I do."

Tristan tried very hard to keep his cool. For the life of him, he couldn't understand what Catherine had seen in this guy. Or Eve, for that matter. Both strong, intelligent women. "Okay, I'll bite. What hasn't she figured out?"

Alan smirked at him. "You want to know what really happened all those years ago, company man? I have to say, it's quite the story! I knew she would come to stop me, you know. Kate was always very easy to read. Well, at least to me." He glared at Tristan. "The irony is, I wanted her to stop me. Oh, I couldn't care less about that monster's life, but I did care that she thought I was evil. I know you think you're way better than me. The fact of the matter is, you and me, we're exactly alike."

Tristan tried very hard to supress his anger. They were nothing alike! He kept his mouth shut and just looked at Alan.

He narrowed his eyes. "You disagree. I knew you would. You'll think about our conversation, though. Later. And then you'll realize I'm right. Anyway, it's of little importance now." He shrugged. "I thought my plan was brilliant, you see. I would give up the only thing she thought I could never do without. I gave her my powers of death. I never thought she'd actually believe I would try to kill her. That actually hurt. I underestimated the power of fear. I will never do that again. Well, you know how it ended. She destroyed me."

Tristan couldn't hide his shock. "So what are you saying? She has your power? She's the master of death?"

Alan nodded. "Of course. She has been all these years." He reached for his inner pocket, and Tristan pulled out his gun.

"Wow, man, relax!" Alan laughed. "Do you mind?" he asked, pulling out a box of small cigars. "I'd offer you one, but somehow you don't strike me as the type." He lit one of the cigars, which was as small as a cigarette, just a bit longer, all the while keeping his eyes on Tristan. He sighed in content. "Aahh, that's better. Now, I suggest you get this valuable information to her. This whole Cailleach plan is completely ridiculous. Must have been the idea of one of her idiot friends."

"Why didn't you tell her yourself?" Tristan asked rather bitingly. He thought the remark about her friends was uncalled for. Catherine had approved of that plan as much as her friends. Clearly, Alan wasn't a fan. Shocker.

Alan laughed. "Oh, please, as if she'd believe me. She'll believe you, the righteous empath." His black eyes were cold like stone. "So run, little empath. Go save our world. I didn't wake up for nothing, you know. Oh, and, Tristan, just so you know, I haven't given up on her."

"I know. Eve said as much," Tristan calmly replied.

For the first time, he saw something flicker in Alan's eyes. A moment of insecurity. When he focussed, it was gone. Replaced by the dark, black tunnels. "How did you manage to recover so quickly, Alan?"

Alan looked at him with a speculative gaze. "You of all people should know that. Or maybe you don't have the proper clearance for that information?" He smirked.

It was a façade, though, Tristan could feel it. So he did have feelings for Eve. Not that he would ever admit that to him.

"Where will you go?" he asked, not expecting a truthful answer, but asking nonetheless.

"Oh, I won't be far away. Don't you worry. I expect we'll see each other sooner than you'd like." And he turned his back on Tristan. Calmly walking towards the other end of the platform, smoke coming from his cigar.

Tristan hesitated for one second, then checked his watch. Dammit! He was running out of time. Would they still be at Meg's or on their way to London Fields?

Roy, where is she? he texted. Two seconds later his phone rang.

"How did you know? I'm so sorry, boss. I wouldn't have let her go, but she insisted. It's like you said, she can be very persuasive. I know I screwed up man. Do you want me to go after her? I'm sure she's going to be fine." Roy was talking at high speed.

"Roy, calm down. What the hell are you talking about? I just want to know where she is. Has she gone somewhere by herself?" He heard Roy take a deep breath.

"Right. Yeah. She went to your apartment to retrieve her necklace. It's precious to her and she said she wanted to change clothes as well, so she'll be up at her apartment after she finds it. I gave her the keys. Again, I'm sorry. She was out of the door before I even knew she was planning to go alone, I swear."

Tristan had to grin. "Relax, Roy. I'm not mad. I do know a thing or two about Catherine. Once her mind was made up, you didn't stand a chance. We're good, man. Gotta go, though. I really need to catch her before she enters the circle. Make sure to give it a wide berth. Hopefully, I'll see you in a bit."

"Yeah. Good luck, man. Not that we need it, but you know what I mean."

"Yes, I do. See you soon, Roy." He checked the time. Sending for a company car would take too long, and it was only a two-mile run. He was in good shape. It would take him fifteen minutes tops. He exited the tube station and started to run.

* * *

"Catherine! Wait!" he yelled from across the street. She was about to get into a car when she heard his voice and looked around. Tristan kept running towards her.

"Goddammit, Tristan, you should be in Italy by now. I thought we agreed you'd go to your parents. What the fuck!" She looked really angry.

Trying to catch his breath, he spoke to her. "No, wait. Catherine. Look at me. Something happened. I don't have time to explain. I think I found the key to destroying this thing. Now we have precious little time, so just listen and hear me out, okay?"

She gave him an almost imperceptible nod.

Tristan took a deep breath and tried to ignore the stitch

on his left side. "Okay. We've been going over this for the last thirty-six hours, and you still feel as if you're missing something, right? What if you *are* missing something? I need you to go back for me. To when you were facing Alan across the industrial building."

Catherine looked confused but remained silent.

"What if Alan wasn't trying to kill you that night? You said you felt death coming toward you. And it suddenly hit me. What happened to it? Where did it go? You unleashed your elemental power on Alan and that hit him full force, but where did his power go? The power of death?"

"What?" She shook her head. "It backfired, I guess. Why is that so important? Tristan, I haven't got time for riddles, and this isn't helping!"

"Hang on. I don't think it backfired at all. I think it went into you. I think Alan transferred his power of death to you, which would make you a master of death. Combined with the elements to connect to the asteroid, you'd have the power to destroy it. You won't have to rely on the Cailleach. You had it all along." She really needed to believe him.

She started to point out that was just ridiculous when Tristan continued.

"Just think about it, Catherine. The dream. 'You're still not seeing the big picture,' he said. Then the painting with his message, 'Soon you will see.' What if those things weren't to scare you? What if Alan tried to make you understand you have his power? You said yourself you weren't even frightened of him anymore. I think that is why Meg sees a dark grey mist around you and just a bit on everybody else. Because you can control death. I really think that is the key." He had no intention of sharing the actual conversation with her. That would only leave her very worried. And whatever his opinion of Alan, he had to admit that even Alan hadn't meant her any harm. He felt her hesitation. She wanted to believe him, and he grabbed hold of her hands. Immediately he felt their connection re-establish.

"Think, Catherine, think. How did it feel? Our lives may depend on it."

She closed her eyes and while holding her hands, Tristan could see through her eyes. In a flash, she was back in Amsterdam facing Alan. As Catherine watched herself release the elements to charge him, she turned her focus away from her elements and focussed on the grey mist coming toward her instead. It swirled through the elements and came straight at her. Her eyes widened. That wasn't possible. She would have died. As she relived the moment, the mist had almost reached her. For a moment, it clung to her, as if getting to know her identity, and then it went inside her. Her eyes flew open. No, no, no. That was unbearable because it'd mean she'd made a terrible mistake, and the responsibilities of that came crashing down on her full force. Tristan's heart broke, but he was afraid to break their connection.

"But...but then he never meant to kill me," she said. "Oh God. Oh God, I almost destroyed his soul, and he never meant to kill me! Why, Tristan? Why did he do that?" Her eyes were overflowing with tears, and he could feel grief and guilt washing through her like a rat gnawing his way out from the inside.

Tristan sent love, peace and quiet over Catherine. "Breathe, darling, breathe. It's going to be okay. Alan's obviously fine, remember. And he's here for a reason. So you can destroy this thing. If anything, he'd want you to focus on that. That's why he gave you all those cryptic messages, I think. He must have thought you'd figure it out." No point in repeating his actual words. Asshole! "Now, look at me." He softly lifted her chin, and she looked him in the eyes. "You can do this. Give it all you've got and it'll be enough. I promise."

Catherine gave him a feeble smile. "I know. I felt it inside me. I think maybe I knew all along. That's probably why I've been feeling so restless for the last couple months. With impending doom hanging over our heads, it must have activated death inside me. I just didn't recognise it and didn't accept it. That's probably why Meg couldn't get a grip on it either." She let out a long sigh. "Will you be here when I get back?" she asked.

Tristan smiled and laid his hand over her heart. "I'll always be here, my elemental." He leaned over and gave her a soft kiss on her forehead. "Now go."

He watched as she got in the car and waited till she was completely out of sight. Then he stormed into their garage and retrieved his bike. He'd noticed she took off at full speed, but his bike could easily overtake any car made by men. It was one of the fastest. And it needed to be fast. One look at the time told him he'd kept her way too long. Stupid! Would she make it in time?

Tristan raced through the streets of London, running several red lights. He was actually amazed some were still working. Not that he encountered any obstacles along the way. Reaching London Fields in what would surely prove to be a new world record, he ditched the bike on the ground, motor still running. He passed several team members alongside the edges of the park, signalling to them to stay put and that everything was okay. Catherine had shown him the exact spot where their circle would be, and he jumped over a park bench, taking a short cut. He couldn't see a damn thing as all the park lighting was completely dark and he almost collided with a swan, who angrily hissed at him. Finally, he could see the circle of women. His eyes scanned the perimeters, searching for Roy and Charles, who he knew would be out there somewhere in the dark. He thought he saw some movement way across the field, but he couldn't be sure. As his eyes adjusted to the dark, he could see Catherine wasn't there. He hadn't expected her to be. She would probably have reached the park by now, though. She would make it; he was sure of it. He felt the ground vibrate beneath his feet. Jesus, what were they doing? He moved his wrist and his watch lit up, showing him the time. Five more minutes. Where was she? This was cutting it pretty close.

Across the field, he could see the earth move, a cloud of dirt and grass that was quickly moving closer. It was Catherine! She was running, her feet barely touching the ground. The earth was twisting around her now and for a moment Tristan feared it would swallow her whole. When he focussed, he could see it weaving around her, though, giving her wings. She'd almost reached the circle now and he saw red-haired Sue opening her arms to give her access. The other woman had to be Sheila, but he couldn't be sure from this distance. Tristan tried to move a little bit closer, ignoring his own advice to Roy and Charles, but the wind was too strong. It kept throwing him back. The moment Catherine entered the circle and the women closed it behind her, there was a deafening bang and Tristan was thrown backwards by the power of the circle. Scrambling to his feet, he shook the dirt out of his hair and looked up. He would never be able to describe what he saw at that moment.

He couldn't even see the women anymore. There was one big circle of the most brilliant light he'd ever seen. It hurt his eyes just to look at it. Trying to focus, he could see whirlwinds weaving in and out of the circle and he could barely make out Catherine at its centre. This had to be her element of air. The word twister came to mind, but he quickly dismissed it. This was so much more powerful. Terrifying, yet beautiful. The next moment he couldn't see her anymore, as the circle raised a man-high wall, surrounding the women inside the circle. He couldn't tell whether it was made out of fire or water. Maybe both. He'd never seen anything like it. The wall appeared to be running both upstream and downstream, never clashing in the middle, but twisting in and out. Fire taking over water. Water taking over fire. The ground was shaking more violently beneath his feet and he noticed big cracks showing up a few feet from where he was standing. Earth. The final element she would be calling upon. It wouldn't be much longer now. It couldn't be much longer, for the earth beneath him was losing. "Just a few more seconds, dear earth. Hold on, hold on," he was whispering, almost like a mantra.

There was a flash in the sky above him, and he could see it. The asteroid. It was actually a rather amazing sight. Suddenly time seemed to slow down. He could feel Catherine within the circle. She wasn't scared or angry, she was the epitome of calm. And then he could hear her voice inside his head as clear as though she was standing right next to him. *You don't belong here.* A second later time sped back up and the sky burst open. Tristan squeezed his eyes shut to protect them from the blinding light and threw himself flat to the ground. Bits of dirt and grass hit his head and he protected it with his hands. Only a couple of seconds had passed when Tristan carefully looked up. He could see stars. They were still here. She did it! She freakin' did it! But where was she? He stood up fully now, frantically looking around him. He started to run towards the circle. Reaching the women, they were all knocked out cold. He checked Leah and Deborah for a pulse. They each had one. He had to assume the others were alive as well. Catherine wasn't among them, though. Searching he could see two people over on the other side by a tree. That must be Roy and Charles. He ran towards them and came to an abrupt stop when he could see their faces. It was Eve. Beside her stood Alan.

"Quickly. Help me move Catherine on her back," Eve whispered to him. "Gently!" she added, as Alan turned her over too fast and they could hear one of her ribs crack. They all cringed. Tristan shrugged out of his jacket and gave it to Alan who carefully put it under her head. "I can't feel her, Eve," Tristan heard him say.

"What do you mean, you can't feel her?" Tristan asked a bit hysterically while looking at Catherine. No. He shook his head, tears filling up his eyes. No, it wasn't true. She wasn't dead.

"Tristan. Tristan! I need you to stay calm, okay? This was supposed to happen. Why do you think I'm here? Now stay out of my way or be of use watching for signs of the others. Nobody can know about this. This is vital! Tristan, do you hear me?" Eve slapped him across the face and looked at him with an almost frantic glare. He just nodded, absently rubbing his cheek, fearing he would throw up otherwise.

Eve moved her hands over Catherine's heart and closed her eyes. Tristan could see a flash of golden light as it entered her body and Catherine arched her back from the ground and let out a huge gasp. Then, she fell back to the ground.

"Yeah, that hurts like hell. I remember," Alan whispered. "Did it work?"

Eve looked at them both. "Of course, it did. Don't be ridiculous. She's breathing, isn't she? I'd say that qualifies as alive. Now we need to get the hell out of here before Roy and Charles come to. The less they know, the better." It was only now that Tristan noticed they were lying on the ground, just a few feet away, unconscious.

Alan looked at him. "Sorry, man, couldn't have any spectators. They're just unconscious, no harm done."

Tristan looked at Eve. "You're asking me to keep this from them?" He pointed his finger to where Roy and Charles were lying on the ground.

Eve gave him a sad smile. "Plausible deniability, darling. It will make it easier. At least for them, I think."

"Wait! Eve, what does this mean? The company knew she was going to die?" Tristan grabbed hold of her hand as she was trying to move away from him.

"There's no time, Tristan. Yes, they knew. Of course, they knew. And they will expect a full report from me. They won't get it. I'm done. I'm leaving, Tristan. They'll never give him a fair chance." She looked over at Alan.

Her office. She had cleared it out herself. "Eve. You know I can't let you go. They'll hunt you. They'll make me hunt you. For God's sake, you know that. They don't have anyone like you! Let alone him!"

She smiled at him. It was a sad kind of smile. "But you'll give us a head start, won't you, darling?"

He looked at her. She'd saved his life. And now she'd saved Catherine's as well. He lifted his eyes and looked straight at her. "As much as I can give you. Be safe, Eve." As he let go of her hand, she and Alan ran off into the darkness.

EPILOGUE

Still no word from Eve?" Roy asked.

Tristan looked up from his phone. His personal phone. She'd texted him twice so far. Once to let him know they were safe and once to confirm her orders had come directly from the Serpent himself. Both times the texts came from a burner. Clever girl.

"No, nothing," he replied. He didn't like lying to his friend, but he owed her. A lot. And he definitely owed her this much. And Roy didn't need any more trouble.

He'd been put through the ringer the last couple of days. Of course, the company was glad to still be there, but as far as they were concerned Tristan had disobeyed orders big time. His clearance level had been degraded to five again. Not that he cared about that. His team has suffered with him, though, and he did care about them.

Using the satellite for personal use had been a big mistake, of course. He knew that. The company wasn't stupid and someone was always watching. He'd learned that from both Charles and Eve. So they'd been stuck inside for the last forty-eight hours, after his boss had yelled at him for using the satellite to check up on Catherine. He'd felt bad for Roy. Roy hated office duty but had held his ground while the boss interrogated them separately. At least their stories matched. He knew the real reason his boss was mad at him, though. By sending her his cello, they knew he had feelings for Catherine and that was a liability. He was becoming a liability. They probably would have fired him if he wasn't their strongest empath. They still could. After all, he had lost them their only reviver as well.

"I understand why you let Eve go, boss," Roy said. "I would have, too."

Tristan smiled. "Thanks, Roy. That means a lot." He realized it was also his way of saying "I forgive you" for all the stupid paperwork. The company knew he'd been in close contact with Eve, but they could hardly blame him for her disappearance. Not that they hadn't tried to blame it on him.

Tristan thought about Catherine. Thankfully Eve had done one hell of a job and Sue and Deborah had been able to heal her afterwards with no more broken ribs. He was sure Romy had glamoured some poor doctor to sign her release papers as Catherine had been let out of the hospital a couple of days later. Of course, that had given them plenty of time to clear out his apartment with the girls staying at the hospital almost full-time.

He dreaded to think about her reaction to the empty apartment. It was why he'd left her his cello. She would understand his meaning. It had been worth it. Somehow, he'd find a way to get it back. It wasn't like he had time to play it anyway. She would take precious care of it. He was sure of that. He also counted on Leah to remember his business card in due course. Now was not the time, though. He had told his boss about the ball drop, and he was sure that information would spread like wildfire through the company. Their top seers would have definitely been assigned to this event. The company took its seers very seriously. Too seriously, in Tristan's opinion. Or Eve's, he remembered. So far, they had not been assigned to that particular vision. He guessed losing both Eve and Alan had cost him a lot of goodwill. He shrugged. Whatever was going to happen in New York, it wasn't his concern right now. There were plenty of dangerous people in the world who needed to be stopped or persuaded to change their course. The company was very good at making people believe they had a change of heart all by themselves. It was what made them almost unnoticeable.

A knock on the door made both men look up from their desks. "It's open," Tristan said and his boss walked in, looking rather grim. *Oh great, now what?*

"I'm sorry, Tristan. I tried, but this is out of my hands. They want to see you upstairs."

"Oh!" was all he could say. Upstairs meant the Serpent's office. There was nothing else there, though nobody knew this for sure. Nobody ever went upstairs. Unless they were needed by the man himself. "It's okay, boss. I know you did the best you could."

"Come, I'll walk you there." He motioned for Tristan to follow him. Tristan looked at Roy and mouthed at him to stay put. Roy nodded. Tristan followed his boss to the far end of the hallway until they stood before a very large painting. It was nothing like the corn field, but it was also a landscape painting. For a moment, Tristan's thoughts flew back to the Peruvian painting that had given them so much trouble. Would she still have it? His boss moved closer to the painting, and it revealed an iris scan. There was a click, and the painting swiftly moved aside, revealing the doors to a lift.

"After you," his boss said to him. Tristan got in and watched his boss press the top floor.

"You can only access it from this level?" he asked.

His boss looked at him. "Don't be ridiculous. There are several access points throughout the building. I suggest you forget you ever saw this one."

"Yes, sir," he replied. The doors opened after just a few seconds.

His boss held the door for him. "You can't miss it. It's at the end of the hallway. There's just one room. This is as far as I go. Good luck, Tristan. Try and be…well, yourself."

Odd bit of advice. Being himself had gotten him into this mess in the first place, but he said thank you nonetheless. The doors closed again and Tristan was left alone. It was very quiet. Almost like the quiet downstairs where Eve's laboratories were. He moved through the hallway and stopped in front of the double doors. The handles were made out of the company logo. Two serpents entwined. Their body's twisting all the way down, representing the seven chakras of the body. Their heads touched each other, like they were glued together, and they had red eyes. Ruby eyes. It gave Tristan the creeps. He knocked before he lost his nerve.

"Enter!" a man's voice said and Tristan pulled open one of the doors. It was heavy. The room itself was ovular. One part was just plain white walls, one bookcase on either side. The other half was completely made of glass, except for the floor. Even the ceiling was made out of glass. In the middle was a grand partner desk. A tall man stood in front of it.

"Tristan Visconti. We meet at last. Sit." He pointed at the chair in front of the partner desk and Tristan obediently sat down.

"Sir," Tristan said. Strange. He couldn't get any reading on the man. No emotions. None.

"No, you wouldn't. I'm a blocker, you see." He smirked. "And obviously a mind reader. I find it convenient for a man in my position."

Shit! Tristan couldn't help but think. The Serpent smiled at him. Tristan thought it looked a bit twisted. Upon closer look, he could see several scars on the man's face.

"Up until recently you had an impeccable track record, Visconti. What happened to you? Or should I ask, who happened to you? Is she really that special?"

Yes, she bloody well was. So far, he'd loved three women in his life. His mother, Eve and he told Catherine he loved her as well. It sure felt the same. Or something close to it, at least. Love was a treasured thing to him. He didn't even care the Serpent could pick up on his thoughts. His chin went up. "You tell me, sir. Last time I checked, she did save the planet. How many people can say that?"

The Serpent banged his hands on the desk and leaned over.

"Plenty! Plenty of people have saved this planet over and over, agent, and don't you forget it!"

"With all due respect, sir, not from an asteroid." Tristan refused to be stared down and boldly looked back into the Serpent's face.

The man stood up from behind his desk and walked towards the window. "If she's that special, it might be better to recruit her." His tone of voice had changed. It now sounded speculative instead of angered.

Over my dead body! Ever since his clearance level had been upgraded, Tristan had seen more of the company than in all those years before. He wasn't sure he liked what he saw. He'd always made fun of Charles's more cautious approach to the company, though he was one of their most loyal employees, still, Charles kept some things to himself. Tristan understood that now. Maybe the company wasn't to be trusted with everything. And Catherine definitely fell into the category of keeping some things to himself. "She would never agree to that, sir."

He was still looking out the window. "You might be able to persuade her to come to our way of thinking."

"I might, but I won't do that, sir."

He turned. It was strange to see the anger but not be able to feel it. "You would dare to go against company orders? Do I need to remind you that thousands of lives depend on us every day? And you would throw that all away for one silly girl?"

He could feel his own anger rising. "She has a name, sir. And please refrain from calling her silly. It's disrespectful and she deserves better. Certainly from us. You don't understand the first thing about her if you think she'd come willingly. Even if I could persuade her, which I won't, she would never approve of this place and, you know what, I'm starting to question my own reasons for staying."

"You go too far, Visconti! I could have you fired with one stroke of my pen!"

Tristan reached inside his jacket, pulled out his own pen and threw it on the partner desk. "By all means, be my guest!" They were staring daggers at each other when a voice from above interrupted.

"Enough!"

From behind one of the bookcases, a woman entered the room. She had long red hair like Sue's, but she was smaller. "Thank you, William, that will be all," she said to the man.

"Madam…," he started to say when he was silenced by her look.

"I said, that will be all."

The man left the same way she had come in. The moment he left the room, Tristan could feel his powers again. Damn. Charles was one hell of a blocker, but he had nothing on this guy. He looked at her and was thrown off-balance. This woman felt warm, loving even.

"You're the Serpent," he said.

She smiled. "Of course. In my line of work, anonymity is a true blessing. I'm sure you understand that, Tristan" She spoke his name like a caress. "Forgive the charade, but I had to be sure you really cared for her. Even I have been known to be wrong, you see."

No, he didn't see at all. What was it to her if he really cared for Catherine? "I'm sorry, ma'am, but I don't see how that would be relevant to you?"

"Well, I have great hopes for her. For all of you, actually. I'm glad Eve decided to keep in touch with you. Oh, don't look so shocked. I wouldn't be much of a seer if I didn't catch that bit of information. It was rather vital to my plans. Trust is a wonderful thing, isn't it, Tristan? In time, I'm sure you'll learn to trust Alan as well and he you."

He seriously doubted that. "I don't understand. Why is Catherine so important to you? Is something else going to happen?"

"Catherine isn't important to me, Tristan. She's everything

to me," she said. The Serpent slowly walked towards him, her long red hair waving behind her like fire. When she got close enough, he could see her eyes. Green eyes. Eyes he had seen before. Impossible! But he realized the truth before she spoke the actual words.

"You see, Catherine van Dyk is my granddaughter."

ABOUT THE AUTHOR

Lisa is the author of the poetry collections *Nothing is Forgotten* and *When Words Start to Sing,* and *The Elemental,* part I of The Fire Trilogy. She also wrote a short story for teenagers, *The Bridge Between Yesterday and Tomorrow,* which will be released late 2015. She has a background in social services and music, but writing has always been a part of her daily life. One night she dreamed the outlines of *The Elemental* and took it as a sign from the Universe to pursue a career in writing.

She grew up in a small town in the Netherlands where her parents always taught her to think outside the box. She has a degree in social studies and joined the Order of Bards, Ovates & Druids as an adult.

Lisa loves London—according to her, "the city where magic dwells"—and can often be found there. She still resides in the Netherlands, however, with her partner and their dog, Miss Ginger Rogers, and if you're lucky, you may find her in her favourite coffeehouse, Barista cafe.

Lisa is also an editor for Folk Harp Folks, a magazine published by The Dutch Folk Harp society.

www.the-elemental.co.uk